Old Sins, Long Shadows

by

Gail MacMillan

Riverhaven Rogues

Old Sins, Long Shadows

Cover Art by *The Wild Rose Press, Inc.*

The Wild Rose Press, Inc.
PO Box 708
Adams Basin, NY 14410-0708
Visit us at www.thewildrosepress.com

Publishing History
First Tea Rose Edition, 2020
Print ISBN 978-1-5092-3067-9
Digital ISBN 978-1-5092-3068-6

Riverhaven Rogues
Published in the United States of America

Chapter One

"Ya young bugger! Steal from me, will ya! I'll see ya rot in hell, I will!"

Wielding a cudgel, Dos MacLintock charged across the dingy, lantern-lighted cellar toward the younger man. "After all I've done fer ya! Yer no better 'n any of the other street scruff lyin' about in the gutters! I should ha' known not to take ya on!"

Douglas ducked the blow but stood his ground.

"With the paltry wages you pay, I've scarce been able to keep body and soul together. So what if I've nicked the odd keg of brandy or a few bottles of wine? It's all smuggled goods...goods that could see you hanged if I spoke to the authorities, you miserly old pillock!"

"Ya've got a filthy mouth, ya have!" Dos aimed another blow. "And ya'd best keep those threats to yerself...if ya want to live to see another dawnin'!"

Douglas dodged again, but this time he took to his heels. Bursting up the stone steps and out of the cellar, he fled. Slipping and sliding, he raced to the front of the building and into the midnight, rain-slick streets of Edinburgh.

What to do, what to do? The question raced around in his brain. Bad enough MacLintock had discovered his thieving. Douglas had been foolish enough to utter a threat. Now he had no doubt Dos would send a nasty bunch of villains to shut his mouth, men who would do anything for the reward Dos would likely offer in return for Douglas's being silenced. His body would be left to rot in a refuse heap or thrown off a wharf.

He had to get away, but to where? As he paused, panting, in an alleyway, his back against the wet stones of a quayside building, he could conjure only two possibilities. Either he could head back to the Highlands and hope to find sanctuary among the clansmen he'd deserted years before, clansmen who might or might not welcome his return, or…here his thoughts hit upon a second solution. He had a brother, a man he hadn't seen since he was a lad, a brother who'd become the notorious Jacobite outlaw known as Brazen Brodie. All but run to ground by redcoats, Brodie had vanished from Scotland several years previous. Rumors had it he'd fled to America. Possibly Douglas could do likewise, perhaps even find his brother.

But would Brodie want any part of him? Their parting, years before, had been far from filled with brotherly love. Douglas had been a lad of fourteen, while Brodie, considering himself a man, behaved as more than his eighteen years.

Douglas flinched at the memory of the raging anger he'd experienced toward his brother that stormy afternoon on a Highland hillside. They'd come to blows, and he, Douglas, had suffered a humiliating physical defeat. Nevertheless, the pain caused by that beating had been minor to that caused by the name Brodie had yelled after him as he ran away, stumbling through the heather, tears coursing down his battered face. The memory of that moniker still hurt like a knife wound in his chest each time he remembered.

He drew a deep breath. Years had passed. Mature men now, perhaps both he and Brodie could get over the past. He could but hope.

So it was off to America. The next question was how to find his brother. The New World was a big place.

The image of an old drunkard named Artie Parsons bragging in a tavern that his life had once been saved by Brazen Brodie gushed into his mind. The wastrel, when deep in his cups, declared his own brother, Jonah Parsons, had followed Brazen Brodie to America and, in gratitude for saving the life of his sibling, become Brodie's boon companion and protector.

Until now Douglas had thought the elderly vagrant simply spouted fictions in the hope of eliciting free drinks. No one believed him. The authorities didn't waste time arresting him for the past crimes that had supposedly led to his rescue by Brazen Brodie. Too ancient to be of any value to the army or a work gang if they took him into custody, Artie Parsons was viewed as only another mouth to feed in a prison and another grave to dig when he died.

Hoping he remembered the name of the tavern the old sot frequented, Douglas drew a deep breath, ran a hand through his drenched curls, and headed out into the night. Although miserably cold and wet, Douglas knew he couldn't immediately return to his home, a room on the upper floor of a bordello where he lived and sometimes acted as a guard to throw unruly patrons out into the street. Even if Dos MacLintock had had no interest in knowing of his place of shelter, most of the smuggler's hirelings knew where he stayed. They'd taunted him about it.

He made a decision. He'd spend what was left of the night seeking out that old reprobate. In the morning, when Dos and most of his henchmen would be abed in preparation for the next night's adventures, he'd make his way cautiously back to his living quarters.

****

"I'm looking for Artie Parsons." Douglas consulted the barkeep.

"Over there." The big man waved a beefy arm toward a corner table. The tavern stank of stale ale, human sweat, and other odors Douglas preferred not to identify. A dwindling fire on the hearth sent out a smoky cloud that cast a sinister atmosphere over the filthy, low-ceilinged place.

Douglas followed the man's indication and saw a ragged, bearded old fellow, scraggly gray hair sticking from beneath a dirty cap, hunched over a table. His gnarled hand clutched a tankard.

"I'd be obliged if you'd get him out of here," the barkeep continued. "He gives my place a bad note."

"I'll see what I can do." Wondering how in the world anyone or anything could make this miserable place worse, Douglas turned toward the old beggar.

"Artie Parsons?" Stopping at the table, he addressed its occupant. Water dripped into a puddle about his feet.

"Who'd be wantin' ta know?" The man raised a wrinkled, dirty face to squint up at him.

"I'm brother to the man who once saved your life." He lowered his voice. "I'm reckoning you remember Brazen Brodie?"

"Brazen Brodie!" The words exploded out into the foul air. He made an attempt to jump to his feet, but only succeeded in falling back into his chair.

"Hold your tongue, man!" Douglas admonished him in a harsh whisper. "Show some sense."

"Aye, aye." The drunkard nodded, lowering his tone.

Douglas pulled out a chair opposite Artie Parsons and sat down. Placing his forearms on the table, he leaned toward the old man. "Tell me where I can find my brother."

"Whit makes ya think I'd know?" He narrowed bloodshot eyes suspiciously. "Mayhap yer no' his kin at all. Mayhap yer just someone out to collect the reward that's probably still on his head."

"Look at me, man!" Douglas glared at him. "Do you not see a resemblance?"

Here he knew he was taking a chance. He hadn't seen his brother for years. He had no way of knowing if, in maturity, they carried any family resemblance.

Artie Parsons squinted over him.

"Aye, ya've got the eyes. Ya could be brother to Brodie."

"Well, then." Douglas dug into a pocket in his drenched vest and found a couple of coins. "If you know his whereabouts, tell me. You've been bragging that he and your brother have become fast friends. Prove your words." He dropped the gleaming pair onto the table, but with a lightning fast move, caught the old man's hand as he reached for them. "Not so fast, my friend. First, the information…if you have it."

"Oh, I have it, sure and certain." Artie Parsons' eyes stayed focused on the coins for a moment before raising his gaze to meet Douglas's. "I got a letter from him only a fortnight ago."

"You can read?"

"I'm no' an ignoramus!" the old man spat at him. "I'll have ya know my father was a learned man, a man of letters…"

"Oh, aye?" Douglas had always been good at catching a lie. He raised an eyebrow as he faced Artie Parsons.

"Ah, verrae well. I have a friend…a friend who was once a professor at Oxford but developed too great a taste for the drink. He often frequents this place and takes the time to read Jonah's letters and even to write replies. Jonah gets the lady wife of the village minister to decipher them. This good woman then pens notes back to me."

"And your brother? He knows where my brother is residing?"

"I shouldna ha' said such a thing." The old man lowered his head, shaking it. "I was deep into the drink when I made such foolish remarks. I could have sent God only knows what kind of bastards after Brodie, the man who saved my life only seconds before I was to be hanged for poaching."

"I doubt anyone would pay passage to America and back simply to collect the paltry reward on a former Highland outlaw's head."

"Aye, aye, I can only hope and pray. The drink is a terrible thing, lad. It loosens a man's tongue, it…"

"Never mind all that." Douglas rolled the coins around the table beneath the old man's covetous gaze. "Chust tell me where to find my brother."

"It's a place in the colony of New Brunswick… called Riverhaven."

****

"Good God, what happened to you?" Lottie Danvers looked up from rearranging satin pillows on a divan to stare at Douglas. "You look like something a cat might drag in."

Douglas grinned as he crossed the luxuriant sitting room of the bordello. With its brocade furnishings, polished oak tables, thick carpets, and elegant lamps, it was far from the dirty, stinking whorehouses that existed down near the docks. Frequented by many of Edinburgh's elite, who trusted to the discretion of Lottie Danvers and her staff to keep their visits there secret, this was a gentleman's club.

"I can hardly say the same for you, Mistress Danvers." He cast his look over her red satin gown. "Might I say you're looking especially lovely, even at this hour of the morning with nary a customer about to enjoy the view."

"The gown is from last evening." With a weary sigh, she sank into a chair. "Sir Henry Billings just left. After he finished his visit with Lily, he decided he wanted to gossip with me over brandy. What an incredibly boring old coot! If you'd have shown up for work, I would have had you gently ease him outside and into a carriage."

"Sorry, Lottie."

"Just exactly where were you, and what have you been up to?" She looked up at him sharply, accusingly. "Do you know I had a gaggle of toughs show up here last night looking for you? They were about to tear the place apart in their quest when Captain Gallagher of the King's Own Guard came down from visiting Justine. He threatened to hunt them down and have them transported if they didn't leave at once. Furthermore, if they ever mentioned his presence in this establishment, he'd see them all in Dartmoor for the rest of their miserable lives. That sent them scampering like so many terrified rabbits. Now, again, where were you last night?"

"Running for my life." He started to take a seat opposite her, but she stopped him.

"Don't plant your wet arse there, Douglas MacMillan!" she snapped. "You'll leave a great stain, you foolish bugger. That brocade cost me more than a few pennies."

He suppressed a grin at her instant loss of the posh tone and language she affected with her aristocratic customers. He liked and admired her.

"Verrae well. I'll chust be helping myself to some of your finest brandy if I'm to be forced to stand while I tell my tale." He went to the bar and poured himself a drink. "And what kind of language is that coming from a woman who spreads the fiction that she's a lady fallen from grace, a woman who sounds every bit of it with her customers...not like a street girl who brought herself up in the world by catering to the right class of gentlemen?"

"The kind of language from a woman who you know better than to get on the wrong side of. Now on with the tale of your night's adventures."

He told her, ending with the fact that he planned to find a ship that would take him to join a brother in a place called Riverhaven, far beyond the reach of Dos MacLintock and his motley crew.

"If they come calling, looking for me, tell them I've jumped a ship headed for the Caribbean," he concluded. "They'll not bother to attempt to follow me there."

She didn't comment when he stopped speaking. Instead she stood and rustled into the room that served as her office at the rear of the establishment. When she returned, she carried a small pouch. It jingled when she thrust it into Douglas's hand.

"Whit?" He stared down at it. The sound and heft told him it contained coins…a lot of them.

"Go upstairs, clean yourself, pack, and get the hell out of here before Dos MacLintock's toughs come seeking you again." She looked up at him, her expression brooking no refusal. "I might not be so fortunate as to have a captain of the King's guard on their next visit."

"Lottie…"

"Go!"

He wet his lips, looked down at her for a moment, then lurched forward to plant a kiss on her cheek before rushing up the stairs, two steps at a time, on the first leg of his escape.

In the dingy, slope-roofed, raw-beamed room at the top of the house, he began to stuff his clothing and the few personal items he possessed into one of the jute bags he'd used to purloin bottles of wine. A fine suit of clothing he'd purchased months earlier hung on a peg by the door. On the floor below sat a pair of gleaming boots. He paused to look at the outfit. It represented a dream…a dream of one day being respectable and worthy of such finery…a time when no one would ever dare to call him by the despicable name his brother had shouted after him all those long years ago in the Highlands. In a rush, he pulled it down and stuffed it, together with the boots, into the sack. He was going where no old sins could cast dark shadows over him.

****

"Douglas, don't go." She caught at his arm as he emerged from his room, the bag slung over his shoulder.

He looked down at the thin young woman, blue eyes wide with fear.

"I have to, Daize. Doc MacLintock is out to get me."

"I can't stay here without you, Douglas." Her grip tightened on his arm, her expression frantic. "Take me with you. I'll behave. I won't cause you any trouble."

"Lottie will take good care of you, not to worry. Now, isn't it high time you were putting the bread to set?"

"Douglas…!"

He shrugged free and galloped down the stairs and out of the building.

Chapter Two

Wind whipping back his hair, Douglas stood on the star-lighted deck of the ship headed for America. The taste of salt spray on his lips invigorated him, refreshed him after too many nights spent skulking about in the shadows of fog-draped rocky shores awaiting the arrival of stolen shipments or in the confines of the brothel at the ready to evict troublesome customers.

Those days and nights were behind him. Drawing in a deep breath, he gloried in the freedom of the moment and the likelihood of more in his future. In America, he'd become a respectable man, a man with no blemish on his life. Nothing, he vowed, would keep him from achieving that ambition.

Rubbing his coat, he reassured himself of the lump of gold coins in his vest beneath. Lottie had been generous. The collection against his chest also contained the monies he'd been able to garner by selling merchandise he'd purloined from Dos MacLintock's stock. The combination of wealth gave him a feeling of security. It would allow him time to get the lay of the land, to learn if his brother would welcome or shun him, maybe buy himself a place to live. Any road, no matter what Brodie's feelings, Douglas was confident he could maintain himself until he found honest work.

He reviewed his list of skills. A smirk curled his

lips. They weren't many. Aside from evading redcoats, smuggling liquor, and throwing unruly customers from a brothel, he had few past accomplishments to recommend him.

On reflection, he decided that wasn't entirely true. At times he'd served food and beverages in the brothel and had developed the least offensive way of dealing with troublesome clientele. Generally he managed to finesse any of Lottie's difficult if distinguished customers out to a cab before things got nasty. Only infrequently had he been forced to throw anyone out on his arse. Lottie had said he had a way about him that kept her gentlemen under control with the least physical force. Perhaps there was a tavern or ale house in Riverhaven where he could find employment. It would be a start.

Most of all, he'd be free to start afresh. In Riverhaven he would be an honest citizen, maybe even become a land holder. Again, he touched his coat at the place beneath which the gold lay. Was it enough to make it possible? Looking up at the stars, he allowed himself to dream. A house and a tidy bit of land, and maybe someday a wife…a pretty wife…and children, his legitimate children.

He brought himself up short. What was that familiar saying, "Old sins cast long shadows"? He hoped none were long enough to reach all the way to America. His thoughts went back to that day years ago on a hillside near their father's farm.

Stumbling away, through wind and rain, blood spewing from his nose, face and body aching, his soul lacerated as if whipped, he vowed he'd never return to the Highlands. Not even news of his father's death had drawn him back. The man was responsible for the despicable curse Brodie had yelled after him.

Brodie, his brother. They'd been boon companions as young lads, before Annie Burns had come between them. Annie Burns with her glossy black curls and sky blue eyes, Annie Burns whose heart Brodie had won. Later, when Douglas had learned Annie, by then Brodie's wife, had died in a fire set by redcoats, a fire that had also consumed their family mill, he'd considered returning to their home. The need to kneel beside her grave and shed tears of grief and remorse had all but consumed him. Only the return of the memory of what Brodie had yelled after him as he'd fled that cold, dark day had stayed the inclination.

Shoving dark curls back from his forehead, he sucked in a great breath. To hell with past memories and nefarious deeds. Putting an ocean between himself and them—and Dos MacLintock—was the wisest thing he'd ever done.

"Headed for America, too." A man he'd noticed when both were boarding the vessel as passengers interrupted his meanderings as he came to stand beside him. A good-looking fellow with a tad of gray showing at his temples, he stood tall and straight, with a bearing that insinuated a military background. His broad shoulders suggested a muscular build beneath his fine coat, shirt, and vest.

"Yes." Catching the man's English accent, Douglas was instantly on his guard. He and others of his heritage had few friends among those sporting such an inflection.

"Do you have family you'll be joining?"

"No one is expecting me," he sidestepped the

query.

"Do you have a trade?"

"I've worked at my fair share of jobs." Douglas was becoming increasingly suspicious of the inquisitive stranger. "I reckon as how I'll find something to fill my days and belly." He turned to face him full on. "I'm Douglas Smith. And you would be?"

"Jones, Clive Jones."

"What takes you to America, Mr. Jones?" Deciding to reverse the inquisition, he continued, "What's your reason for leaving hearth and home?"

The man's shadowed countenance hardened into a mask of pure hatred as he turned on Douglas.

"Revenge," he hissed. He turned and walked away.

The word sent a quiver coursing through Douglas's gut. Was the man with the cold, dark eyes and confident manner someone Dos MacLintock had sent after him?

Almost as soon as the thought occurred, Douglas banished it. The old skinflint wouldn't waste coin hiring anyone to chase after him, certainly not one who could afford to dress as well as Clive Jones. Furthermore, he doubted MacLintock would have bothered to trace him beyond the brothel…gentlemen's club, he corrected his thoughts with a wry grin, recalling Lotti's preference for the title. He knew Lottie and her ladies would swear that Douglas had left on a merchant ship bound for the Caribbean Islands.

Dos, knowing only too well of Lottie Danvers' connections with some of the city's most powerful, would not press her further. Forced to take her word that Douglas had gone where he couldn't cause him any more trouble, Dos MacLintock would cease to concern himself with his former worker and go back to overseeing his smuggling business.

No, this man was on a more important mission than eliminating a petty thief. Douglas furrowed his forehead in thought. This man was after someone of importance at the ship's destination. Someone in the village of Riverhaven.

Nevertheless, the man's threat had soiled the evening. As if in harmony, a fog began to roll in, immersing the ship in its ghostly grip.

"Bloody fog!" The man's voice made Douglas turn toward the rear of the ship. Scowling, Captain James MacTavish had emerged from below deck and stood, hands on his hips, surveying the thickening mist.

"Good evening, Captain," Douglas addressed him.

"Good evening to you, laddie." The tall, broad-shouldered man drew a deep breath and let a smile replace his former expression. "How are you enjoying the voyage?"

"Right fine, thank you, sir. Your ship sets a fine pace."

"That she does. You'll be in Riverhaven within the month. Are you planning to stay in the community?"

"If I can find work." Douglas remained carefully evasive about his future.

"Well, it's a fine little village, that's for sure, populated in the main by folks of our ilk." The captain winked at him. "You're a Highlander…or once was, I'm guessing?"

"Long ago."

"If you plan to remain there for any length of time, let me give you a few words of advice. There's a lad there, a fine lad by most standards, but an outlaw to the bone at times. You'd best give him a wide berth if you want to keep your nose out of trouble."

"Oh, and who might this dangerous lad be?"

"His name is Brodie MacMillan, a former Jacobite, the Highland rebel known as Brazen Brodie."

Douglas's gut sucked inward.

"What has he done?"

"Mainly a few scrapes, from which he's managed to extricate himself…most of which were the result of his trying to help out friends." The captain paused before continuing, "The reason I warn you away from Brodie is because he becomes a law unto himself when he thinks someone needs his assistance and he can see no other way of obliging. A brave laddie and one of the most affable you'll ever meet, but with a wild streak that I dare say he'll carry to his grave." James MacTavish shrugged. "I thought when he married Louisa he'd settle down. That hasn't happened, not in the least."

"This man…this Brodie MacMillan…is married?" Douglas stifled the final word of "again."

"Aye, to a right beautiful woman, the only woman I know who would dare cast her lot with such as him. Of course, some of the locals still insist on calling her a witch…"

"A witch?" *Guid God!*

"Well, of course, she's not," the captain scoffed, "but she is a healer of amazing ability. Just because she's incorporated native cures into her workings, some of the old biddies have branded her as such. Let me tell you, when one of the men joked the question in the tavern, that if Louisa MacMillan is a witch, then her son must be a warlock, well, Brodie made short work of him." The captain chuckled. "Threw him clean across the room and out the door."

"He has a son?"

"Aye, and a right clever little laddie, I've heard. Maybe that's why that fool made the remark about the bairn being a warlock. Let me assure you, no one has made such a suggestion since. Brodie MacMillan is not a man to be trifled with."

Shaken by the captain's information, Douglas gripped the rail. His brother hadn't changed. He was still one of a kind, a free spirit who forever would throw caution to the wind. And married to a woman some had branded a witch, who had borne him a son.

"How is it he's not been brought before the law…for his escapades?"

"Ah, now there he has a bit of a hold over the community. You see, he is the millwright for the only grist mill within a hundred miles. If he were to be thrown into prison, folks would suffer the huge inconvenience of having to cart their grains one very long way to the next facility. Therefore, the local law enforcement has become willing to turn a blind eye to most of Brodie's…adventures.

"Well, enough jaw wagging. I must be off." The captain touched his cap. "My helmsman will be needing my assistance in this miserable mess. I hope you continue to enjoy your voyage, Mr. Smith. And"—he turned back briefly—"mind what I've said about Brodie MacMillan."

"Aye, sir. Thank you, sir."

As if one could enjoy anything after being warned away from his own brother, after learning his sister-in-law had been branded a witch.

Chapter Three

Picking wild strawberries along the side of the dusty trail that led to Riverhaven, Morag brushed a damp curl from her forehead. Although the day was too warm for her to enjoy her present occupation, she preferred the activity to listening to her mother's arguing with her father about Morag's future. Hazel Green had decided that Morag was to be sent off to Fredericton, the provincial capital, that she might meet a suitable husband.

It's not as if I couldn't find a spouse here. I don't believe I'm entirely uncomely. If only Mother would stop chasing away any young man who appears interested in me, perhaps one of them might have expressed a serious intent.

There had only been two who'd seriously dared to face the wrath of Hazel Green. Fletcher Atkin, partner to local lumber baron Culloden MacPherson, had come to visit, only to be driven off by her broom-waving mother. Hazel Green had heard rumors that Fletcher had been a gambler, a drunkard, and a womanizer back in the Old Country. It little mattered that he had proven himself a diligent, responsible individual since his arrival in Riverhaven. His past had ruined his chances with her precious daughter.

A small smile curved Morag's lips as she remembered how difficult it had been for her mother to hide her chagrin when the entire village later learned Fletcher Atkin could have been Sir Fletcher Atkin, a lord with a considerable estate in England, had he chosen to accept the position on his father's death.

"Who would have guessed?" Hazel had repeated over and over again to her husband. "That man working in Culloden MacPherson's mill, covered with sweat and sawdust, was a member of the aristocracy."

"If you'd given him half a chance with our daughter, Mrs. Green, you might have discovered the truth a whole lot earlier," Duncan Green muttered meekly.

"Oh, as I might have given that roué Brodie MacMillan an opportunity to compromise our girl?" she snapped back.

Brodie MacMillan. The name brought a soft blush spreading up Morag's cheeks. Brodie had made his interest in her clear shortly after he'd arrived in the valley. A suspected Highland outlaw, he'd nevertheless proceeded correctly in declaring his intentions by first asking her father's permission to invite her to a church supper.

Duncan Green had refused. He later told his daughter he'd been surprised by Brodie's request, but had not hesitated to turn him down. Brodie MacMillan was a devil-may-care rogue, and while Duncan personally liked the man, even secretly admired his freewheeling ways, he told Morag he'd not be comfortable with such a man courting his only child. Furthermore, he told her, her mother would never consent.

As she knelt to pick a clump of red berries, Morag thought about Brodie. Tall and handsome, with broad shoulders, narrow hips, sandy curls, and a devilish grin that always set her heart racing, he was a man who would attract any woman's attention. And he had.

Shortly after Duncan Green's rebuff, Brodie had taken up with another woman…the beautiful young widow and healer Louisa Abbot, who local residents had for a time branded a witch. In fact, some of the older, more superstitious ones, her mother included, still did. Brodie and Louisa had married some time ago and now had a son.

Still, though she was ashamed to admit it, Morag sometimes daydreamed about the handsome swashbuckler. She'd read stories of the knights of old and imagined that, given a suit of armor and a white charger, Brodie MacMillan could well be one of those heroes.

The sound of a horse galloping up the dusty trail toward her made her rise from her berry picking. Shielding her eyes against the sun, she looked in the direction of the oncoming animal.

Think of the devil! It was the man himself, riding a fractious red filly.

"Good morning to you, Miss Morag." He reined his mount to a dust-rising halt, touched his cap, and favored her with that wonderful grin that made her heartbeat quicken.

"Good day to you, sir." She bobbed a bit of curtsy, embarrassed by his sudden presence. *Wasn't it fortunate he couldn't read thoughts?*

"Berry pickin', were you?" He indicated the basket on her arm. "There appears to be a right fine crop this year. Louisa has already made up enough jam to last most of the winter."

"Mrs. MacMillan…and your son…are well?" She wished he'd move along. Marriage had in no way lessened his blatant appeal.

"Aye, right bonny. You must ride over and visit with them sometime. Louisa would be pleased to see you."

"I will," she lied. She knew her mother would never allow her to visit the home of a witch and a ne'er-do-well…never mind that Louisa MacMillan was now generally accepted as a gifted healer and Brodie a successful mill manager.

"I'd offer you to climb aboard with me, and I'd take you home out of this heat, but as you can see, this lass"—he indicated the prancing filly—"is bare green broke. Twice today she's near pitched me on my ar…backside."

"I'll be fine, thank you. I'm not yet ready to go home. I've more berries to pick."

"Ah, well, then, I'll wish you a good day." He touched his cap again and broadened that beguiling grin.

With a dashing skill that left Morag breathless, he swung the cavorting mare about, put his heels to her sides, and set her off down the trail at a full run.

Why, oh, why, Father, did you deny me the opportunity to get to know Brodie MacMillan? It may have come to nothing…he may well have proven too much for me, but I would dearly have loved to find out.

She returned to her berry picking, but her thoughts remained with Brodie MacMillan and her missed opportunity to be courted by him. *What would it be like to have him take me into his arms, to feel him stroke my hair…to kiss me?* A blush stole up her neck and heated her face beyond the warmth of the day.

What bold thoughts! And of a married man. Morag Green, you should be ashamed. You'll never know more about Brodie MacMillan than you do at this moment. Such ideas are downright sinful.

In an effort to banish the handsome rogue from her mind, she tried to concentrate on her berry picking. It didn't prove sufficiently absorbing to keep other thoughts at bay.

Will I ever find a man that Mama will accept? Will I ever marry? If only I were strong and bold like Louisa MacMillan. She heaved a sigh. *But I'm not like her. Nor will I ever be. I'll most likely end up being an old lady who does good works for the church, who wears black dresses and mittens and sits in a rocking chair by a window.*

Thinking of church brought the minister Reverend Edward Morgan and his wife Mary to mind. Morag had heard it whispered that Mary Morgan had once ridden as an outlaw by her husband's side in the Highlands. Surely such a woman would be able to understand the yearnings of a young heart for life and adventure, surely she would keep such a confession confidential. Mrs. Morgan always smiled kindly at Morag when she was leaving Sunday service with her parents. Yes, she would talk to Mary Morgan. She stood and smoothed down her skirts. There was no way her mother could object to her visiting the minister's wife.

****

"Mother, I should like to visit Mrs. Morgan this afternoon." Morag put her basket of berries on the kitchen table and looked down into them. Facing her mother with any request was too difficult.

"In heaven's name, why?" Hazel Green didn't pause in cutting up vegetables. Her gaunt, narrow face hardened. "You have chores here. The bedrooms need sweeping, there is linen to be washed…enough to keep you occupied until the supper hour."

"I thought Mrs. Morgan might need some help with plans for the upcoming ceilidh on the church grounds." The lie came so easily Morag's heartbeat quickened.

"Ceilidh indeed! Another of those despicable Scotch words! Cannot even our minister and his wife abandon such terms?" She chopped the stem from a carrot.

"It simply means a celebration of music and dance with friends."

"And food. I imagine they'll be expecting me to bring food. Lord knows, I have enough to do around here without providing sustenance for such frivolity."

"Each family will only have to bring enough for their own supper. Mother, may I go?" Struggling to hide her impatience, Morag asked permission again.

"Oh, very well, but mind you wear your sunbonnet. The sun is blazing down, and it's a goodly walk to the manse."

"Thank you, Mother." Morag hurried to the door and snatched up her bonnet she'd hung on a peg after bringing in the berries. "I won't tarry. I'll be home well in time to help you with supper and to milk Bess."

****

Headed for the manse, Morag walked down the dusty trail, the heat of the summer's day making her damp and uncomfortable. A considerable distance from her home, the manse and church were on a small island in the river. Morag had always found the location beautiful and peaceful, the two buildings nestled among tall pines and lofty maples. On fine Sundays, when Reverend Morgan preached with the windows open, Morag loved the background sounds of twittering birds and soft breezes soughing through the trees.

She paused to take a handkerchief from the bodice of her dress and wipe her face beneath the straw bonnet. Her mother declared ladies did not sweat, but something was definitely dampening her forehead and trickling down between her breasts. Possibly she should have waited for a cooler day, but the need to talk to someone who might at least try to understand her thoughts, who might be sympathetic to them, had overwhelmed her. Furthermore, her mother had agreed. She must not waste the opportunity.

Hoofbeats. From beyond a curve in the trail, a galloping horse was approaching. Turning in the direction of the sound, she hoped its rider wasn't Brodie MacMillan. Even though he was no longer a possible suitor, she did not want him to see her damp and dusty. Something about him made her acutely aware of her femininity…and of his virility.

The rider who emerged from around the bend was a woman on a white horse. Dressed unconventionally in what Morag knew to be her customary traveling garb of breeches, shirt, and vest, a wide-brimmed hat on her head, Louisa MacMillan brought the horse to a smooth stop and smiled down at the young woman.

"Miss Green…Morag. A warm day for walking, is it not? Might I offer you a ride?" She indicated a place behind her.

"I thank you, but"—she looked up at the tall white mare—"I'm not going far…only to the manse."

"My dear, you've still got nearly a mile to go." Brodie MacMillan's wife kicked her foot free of the stirrup on the horse's left side. "Climb aboard. I assure you Snow is gentle as a lamb."

Am I never to do the unconventional thing, never make a single brave move?

"I thank you, Mrs. MacMillan." Morag wet her lips as she moved close to the mare.

"Give me your hand," Louisa said extending hers. "Put your foot in the stirrup."

Morag obeyed, jumped, and landed with a bump behind the woman. Once astride the animal, her skirt caught to mid calf on both sides.

How scandalous, how brazen!

"Put your arms around me," Louisa instructed. "Hang on as tightly as will make you feel comfortable."

The next instant they were moving forward, the mare walking sedately.

"There, you see"—her benefactor said—"nothing to worry about. Snow and I will deliver you to the manse safe and sound."

Morag couldn't believe it. Here she was riding, actually riding, with Brodie MacMillan's wife, the woman her mother and a few others branded as a witch. It was certainly the boldest adventure on which Morag Green had ever embarked. But then she was on her way to consult the minister's wife on a most unconventional subject.

"Your son is well?" As they rode along, the woman keeping the mare at a walk, Morag found her apprehensions lessening to the point where she could attempt conversation.

"Very well, thank you. He's with my sister today.

I've been informed that a vessel has arrived in Riverhaven bringing medical supplies I ordered. The shipment will include a new drug called morphine. It's reputed to do wonders in relieving pain. My husband is engaged at the mill, so I decided to ride in to collect my purchases." She paused before continuing, "He said he encountered you on the trail picking berries earlier today."

"Yes." Embarrassment flooded through Morag as she recalled her romantic thought regarding Louisa's husband.

"He said he refrained from offering you a ride home." Beneath her arms, Morag felt Louisa chuckle. "For once, he showed caution…and wisdom. That mare of his, Vixen—she's appropriately named—is as wild as my husband once was…and still is on occasion."

"Do you not worry about him…" Morag started the inquiry, then stumbled for words until she finally said, "riding such an animal?"

"My dear girl, if I were to expend time and energy concerning myself about my husband and his antics, I'd die of exhaustion. When a woman marries a man, she has to know him well…as well as one individual can know another…and then be prepared to live with his good points as well as…others. I love Brodie and he loves me. Therefore we've come to grips with what both our characters have to offer. While he has a bit of an adventurous spirit, I'm not sure there are many men who would accept my practice of medicine…and other pastimes."

They rode in silence. Louisa MacMillan had definitely given Morag much to ponder.

When they arrived at the lane that led to the bridge

that provided access to the manse and church on the island, Louisa turned the mare in that direction.

"Oh, no, please, Mrs. MacMillan." Morag protested. "I'll walk from here. I mustn't take you off your path. I thank you for the ride. It was most kind of you."

"If you're sure." Louisa halted the mare and waited while Morag swung her leg over the horse's rump and slid awkwardly to the ground. Once on her feet, she hastened to pull her skirts back into position.

"I wish you good day." She bobbed a curtsy and turned to hasten down the lane to the manse. It had been wonderful, riding high up on that lovely, gentle mare. How much more exciting would it be to ride alone in the saddle itself?

****

"Morag, my dear." Mary Morgan smiled as she opened the manse door to admit the shy girl. "How nice of you to visit. Come into the parlor. We can have a chat."

Once they were seated, Morag rushed straight to the purpose of her visit, afraid if she hesitated, she'd lose her courage.

"Mrs. Morgan, I told my mother I was coming to offer my assistance with the upcoming ceilidh"—she paused to catch her breath—"but that was not the truth. Well, of course, I am quite willing to help with the ceilidh, but that is not the principal reason." Again she paused. "I wish to speak with you about a personal matter…a confidential matter."

"Of course. We're quite alone. Our daughter is off to the village with her father." She continued looking at the young woman. "Perhaps it is something you'd rather talk to Mr. Morgan about?"

"No!" The word came out louder than she'd planned, instantly embarrassing her. "No," she said more softly. "It…it's a woman's concern."

"Oh, very well." Mary Morgan settled herself comfortably to listen. "I'll be only too glad to help, if I can, but perhaps Louisa MacMillan would be of more assistance."

"No, it's not…a physical matter." Morag felt a hot blush rushing up her cheeks. "It's…about…men."

"Oh, yes?" The minister's wife sounded slightly apprehensive.

"I'm putting this badly." Morag looked down at her hands clasped in her lap. "Only I didn't know who else to consult. Mother is…"

"Your mother can be difficult at times, Morag. Everyone knows it. Please, talk to me and rest assured that anything you say won't go beyond this room."

"Mrs. Morgan, I'm past twenty and I've never had a gentleman caller. Oh, that's not entirely true," she hastened on, remembering. "Mr. Fletcher Atkin once came visiting, but Mother chased him off with a broom. She said he was a roué, not fit for a decent girl."

"She must have been disconcerted when she learned he could have been Lord Docane if he'd chosen to return to England and accept the ancestral lands and title." A smirk curled her lips, though Morag saw she tried to stifle it.

"She never admitted it, but yes, I believe she was."

"Rumor has it Brodie MacMillan was at one time also interested," the minister's wife continued.

"Yes, but Father refused him the right to court me."

"So you're concerned that you may never be

allowed the company of a suitable young man?" The minister's wife grasped the reason for Morag's visit.

"Yes." Morag swallowed and looked up to meet her companion's gaze. "Mrs. Morgan, is it wrong for me to want to meet a man, to be courted by a man…to marry a man and share his life…to"—she stumbled over the last—"to have his children?"

"Of course not, my dear." Mary reached out to take Morag's hand between hers. "It's the most natural thing in the world."

"But I fear I shall never have the opportunity. I fear I shall end up an old maid doing good works for the ch…" Appalled at what she'd been about to say, she stopped.

"That need not be the case." Apparently undeterred by what Morag had nearly said, Mary Morgan continued, "But finding love with the right man often takes courage. Sometimes a woman has to stand up to all objections to obtain what she most desires in life."

"Did you?" The words were out before Morag realized the possible inappropriateness of them.

"I did." She leaned back in her chair, her eyes taking on the dreaming look of remembrance. "Although Edward was an ordained minister, he held Jacobite sympathies. My father saw him as nothing but trouble. The day the redcoats invaded the church where Edward was preaching, Edward drew a sword from beneath his surplice and fought his way out to his horse. I ran after him, mounted another animal, and rode away with him. On that day, I knew I loved him more than life itself, that my place was beside him no matter how much my father objected."

"Oh, my!" Astonished by Mary's romantic tale,

Morag sat bolt upright in her chair. "That must have taken great audacity."

"Yes, and love."

"Have you ever regretted what you did? Have you ever been sorry you acted so reflexively?"

"Not for a minute. Morag, sharing your life with the man you love is wonderful. When you find the right man, don't hesitate. You'll never be sorry."

"I've read *Ivanhoe*. It's…it's quite daring and…romantic." Morag stumbled out the confession.

"Ah, yes, I've also read it, but"—Mary Morgan reached onto a shelf for a book—"if it's realistic romance you're seeking, you must read something more contemporary. This was written by Louisa MacMillan. I found it a lovely read. Here." She held it out to her. "Take it and enjoy."

"Louisa MacMillan is a writer? I thought she was a healer…a wife and mother."

"Louisa MacMillan is extremely accomplished, clever, and brave. She'd be a fine example to the young women of this community…if their mothers would only allow such."

"Will she mind your passing it along to me?" Morag paused in reaching for the thin volume.

"Of course not. It's only recently been published and is making quite a sensation in England, I believe."

"Thank you." Morag took the book and read its title. "*My Heart to a Highlander*."

"I believe it was inspired by her meeting her husband and falling in love with him."

"Is it really?" Morag stared down at the volume. "How courageous of her to write of such an…intimate part of her life."

"Louisa MacMillan is an amazing woman. You should visit her. I know she'd be an inspiration."

"I have…in a way. I encountered her on my way here. She offered me a ride…on her mare…and I accepted."

"Then I can only assume you were impressed. Most people are, upon meeting her—the majority in a most positive way, but a few negatively. In my opinion, the latter group is entirely wrong."

"She spoke of her relationship with Mr. MacMillan…about how they came to terms with their characters…about how they loved each other."

"I'm not surprised. Louisa is a blatantly honest woman. As I've said, you should visit her at her home. You could learn a great deal."

"I'd never dare." Morag stood and bowed her head slightly. "Mother would never allow it."

"Ah, yes, your mother." Mary Morgan's words held mild exasperation. "She's a good woman, I've no doubt, but sadly limited in her view of the world. Someday, Morag my child, you will have to face up to her…if you ever wish to have a fulfilling life of your own."

"I really must be going. Thank you, Mrs. Morgan." Clutching the book, she stood and headed for the door, no appropriate response to Mary Morgan's challenging words coming to mind.

"Call anytime, my dear. I have good ears and tight lips. Don't be discouraged. If you allow yourself to be open to it, love will come your way…sometimes in the most unexpected manner."

Chapter Four

The bag containing all his worldly possessions slung over his shoulder, Douglas stepped down onto the Riverhaven wharf and paused to take in his surroundings. The village spread out along the waterfront consisted of a few modest log and shingled buildings. Farther down shore, the skeletons of a pair of what would be ocean-going vessels stood in slipways, crews of men working over them. Beyond the settlement, forest and fields sported the bright green coverage of summer beneath a sky of flawless blue. Fresh and unsullied by fog or grime, this bright, new country made his spirits rise. A gentle breeze that ruffled his hair and warmed his body furnished a kindly welcome.

"Where might I find the MacPherson Mill?" Clive Jones's voice broke in on his musings as the man paused beside Douglas and queried a sailor who'd disembarked with them. The memory of the man's intimidating word on shipboard cast the first shadow over the pleasure of Douglas's arrival.

"A few miles upriver." The mariner jerked his thumb in the direction. "You got folks there you know?"

Instead of replying the man hoisted his baggage over his shoulder and set off in the direction indicated.

"Ya were askin' about the tavern just afore we

docked." The sailor to whom Clive Jones had made the inquiry tapped Douglas on an arm. "It's right over there. Got a powerful thirst, have ya?"

"I could do with an ale, but what I'm seeking is work."

"Ah, so ya've had experience in such an establishment, have ya?" The man squinted up at him curiously. On the voyage Douglas had proven a man of mystery, revealing nothing of his past or plans for the future.

"In a way. Many thanks." Douglas touched his cap in farewell salute, adjusted the sack, and turned in the direction the sailor had indicated. He'd continue to keep his own council and to use the surname Smith until he got the lay of the land. And until he got a gander at Brodie MacMillan and decided what kind of relationship might happen between them.

Focused on the tavern, he started forward without looking to his left and bumped squarely into a woman.

"Beg pardon, mistress." His free hand shot out to steady her on her feet and found himself looking down into a sunbonnet that protected a pair of eyes as blue as the skies and a face that would have done an angel proud. Glossy black curls framed a beauty such as he couldn't remember ever before encountering…at least not for a very long time.

For a moment she didn't reply, but remained staring up at him as if mesmerized. It only added to her appeal. Such an ethereal creature needed no words.

"Have I injured you, lass?" He had to speak; he couldn't continue to gaze at her without words.

"N-no, not at all." She ducked her head shyly. "If you'll excuse me, sir, my mother is waiting."

"For sure and certain." Standing aside, he stared after her as she scuttled off to where a farm wagon bearing a middle-aged couple waited.

She scrambled into the rear and took a seat that backed that of the older pair. The man clucked to his team, and they headed down the road that served as a street toward where he stood. As they passed, the older woman cast him a look that might have contained daggers had it been physical. The girl cast him a shy glance before returning her gaze to her hands clasped in her lap.

A dragon for a mother or I'll be branded a fool. He hefted his belongings and started off toward the tavern, struggling to put that beautiful young woman out of his mind. *Damn, but she reminded me of...*

He cut his memories short. Annie Burns had been a long time ago. Annie Burns had been his brother's wife, and now she was dead.

****

He pushed open the door and stepped into a room so dark it took him a few seconds to adjust his vision. When he did, he discovered a low-beamed structure with a plank floor, tables and chairs scattered throughout, and a bar at a far end not unlike many of such establishments he'd encountered in the Old Country.

This one bore a welcome difference. The floor had been swept, the tables cleared of any soiled tankards or dishes, and their surfaces wiped clean. An appetizing aroma drifted from a room at the rear. Beef stew, he reckoned, the aroma setting his gut rumbling. After weeks of salt meat and little else, he doubted if anything on earth could smell better at that moment.

There were no patrons, not unusual at this time of the morning. The sailors from Captain James MacTavish's ship would be flooding into the place that evening, he had no doubt, but first they'd be engaged in unloading cargo.

"Anyone to home?" He walked to the bar and dropped his sack on the floor.

"You're a tad early, sir." A massive man came out of the back room from which the tantalizing scent issued. Over six feet tall, he had broad shoulders, a barrel chest, and beefy, hirsute arms revealed by rolled-up shirt sleeves. Not a lad to be trifled with, Douglas decided. He noticed the man's shirt and apron were white and clean.

This place isn't the hell hole a lot of drinking establishments are back home. I could feel comfortable here.

"Good morning to you, sir." Douglas touched his cap. "It's not service I'm seeking. I'm new arrived from the Old Country and hoping to find employment. You wouldn't be in need of a lad not afraid of hard work, now, would you?"

The big man squinted over at him, letting his perusal run over him critically.

"Fresh off the boat, are you?" he asked.

"Aye."

"Have you ever worked in a tavern?"

"I know good wine from bad, I can measure out a dram of whisky or rum in a thrice, and draw a pint with the best of them. I'm also right good at making short shift of troublemakers."

"And what about cleaning? Are you willing to clean this place each night, to make sure it's presentable for first light?"

"I know how to use a broom and a mop."

"And what about horses? I have a stable out back with a couple of cobs of my own and stalls where customers can board their nags. Feeding and cleaning needs to be done out there."

"I'm a dab hand with beasts and no stranger to a manure fork."

"Well." The big man hesitated. "Another pair of hands around here would give me more time for my cooking. All right, you're hired…for the present…until I see how you work out. You'll get room and board and what I think you're worth at the end of a week. Do we have a deal?" He swung a big hand out over the bar.

"Sounds fair." Douglas clasped it.

"You can put your kit upstairs in the room at the end of the corridor," his new employer said. "It's small. I save all the bigger ones for guests. By the by, my name is Frank Miller."

"Douglas Smith."

"After you've put your goods away, come down and I'll put you to work, Douglas Smith." Frank Miller indicated a stairway to one side of the room. "But tell me," he continued as Douglas headed to do his bidding, "what made you look for work here? Most of the able-bodied lads head for the mills or the shipbuilding the minute they set foot on dry land. I'll tell you the truth, my lad. You'd find better pay there."

"I've no experience in either." He paused at the bottom of the stairs. "I have with spirits."

"Hie, now." The tavern owner stopped him on the second step. "Not given to drink, are you? I'll not have you stealing from me."

"I'm no' a drunkard."

"But you are a Scotsman?"

"Aye. Will you be holding that agin me?" Highland accent breaking through, he turned to face the man full on.

"No, no. Lord knows there're enough of them in this community. Do you maybe have kin here? Is that what brought you?"

"One place is as good as another. I decided to come to America and caught the first ship sailing west." He wanted no more of the landlord's questions. "Something smells right tempting."

"Caribou stew. I reckon you can stand a decent meal after weeks of salt meat and worse. I'll have a plate ready for you when you come back down. There's no work in a man with an empty belly."

"Thank you, sir."

He continued to the second floor, considering this small village, this Riverhaven, might be a fine place to settle down...if not for two matters. First, the problem of Clive Jones and his proposed victim, and second, the uncertainty of his reunion with his brother Brodie.

Chapter Five

"I tell you, he's another of those troublesome Scots." Hazel Green plunked a plate of meat and vegetables in front of her husband and returned to the hearth to fill a pair for herself and Morag. She was referring to the man Morag had encountered in the village. "You can tell at a glance he'll bring nothing good to this community. They should be banned from settling here. Those we have around us now should be run off." She handed Morag her meal and sat down opposite her husband with her own, her eyes flashing with self-righteous anger.

"That might make things difficult." Duncan Green spoke mildly as he chopped up potatoes and reached for butter. "Our lumber, milling, and shipbuilding trades are all run by Scots. And don't forget our minister and his family. They're from the Highlands, if rumors be true."

"Don't argue with me, husband! Remember how that scallywag Brodie MacMillan had the audacity to approach you for permission to court our Morag! Such brazen behavior! As if a young woman of our daughter's standing would have anything to do with an outlaw, a man whose background is as dark as the vilest thunderstorm."

"Mother, please!" Morag could stand no more. "Father forbade me to have anything to do with Brodie

MacMillan and I have done his bidding. Isn't that enough?"

"No, it isn't. He's still living close enough to be a danger. If I see him anywhere near you or this farm, I'll…I'll take your father's musket and shoot him!"

"Mrs. Green, calm yourself." Her husband's calm words sought to bring an end to her tirade. "Brodie MacMillan is married and, by all accounts, besotted with his wife and child. He's no threat to our daughter."

"We'll see." Speaking more reservedly but with the angry glint still in her eye, Hazel Green plunked her bottom down on her chair at the table. With vehemence, she began to carve up the meat on her plate.

****

Morag was forced to wait until the meal had ended and she'd helped her mother to clear away before she could escape to the privacy of her room and take up the book she'd been reading…the book she'd borrowed from the minister's wife.

The feelings the fictional couple's first meeting in the village street had aroused in the heroine as she drove her wagon out of town so closely mirrored Morag's own after bumping into that handsome stranger that she was astounded. With his Highland accent, he had not been unlike the hero of the book…tall, broad shouldered, narrow hipped, with a handsome countenance…except that his hair was black, the fictional hero's sandy…like Brodie's. In that brief encounter, he'd captured her romantic imagination as completely as the novel's hero had arrested that of the heroine.

But Morag had lacked the courage to look back at him with a smile and a hand raised in farewell as the book's heroine had. What might have transpired if she'd been so brazen? Might he have decided to seek her out, to find his way to their farm?

She went to the small mirror over her chest of drawers and gazed into it. She wasn't uncomely, she decided. Her complexion was good, her hair thick and glossy. And her figure... She ran her hands over the front of her gown and looked down at it. The mirror was too meager to allow her a full body perusal, but inspecting it as best she could, she decided her form was not unattractive. She wasn't plump like Maisey Manders nor scrawny like January Henderson. In fact, she believed she measured up decently against most of the village girls. Possibly, just possibly, a man like the handsome stranger might not find her unattractive.

What did it matter? She turned away from the mirror and her evaluation of her appearance. Unless the newcomer was the heir apparent to a title and a vast fortune, he'd never be allowed anywhere near her.

Her rosy imaginings faded. With a sigh, she returned to the pages of the book. There was no point in building daydreams about a man she'd met only for a moment...a man with whom she'd never be allowed to have any further association. Her romantic adventures would be between the covers of a book.

Chapter Six

"I'll have your attention, lads." Frank Mills clapped a hand on Douglas's shoulder and shouted out the request as the two men stood behind the bar in the crowded common room that evening. When the noise subsided, he continued, "This is my new man, Douglas Smith. He'll be working here. I advise you to treat him with respect or"—here he broke into a grin—"you'll have the pair of us to tangle with."

A mixture of laughter and chuckles broke over the room before the customers returned to their drinks.

"Another ale here, Douglas, me lad." A big, burly woodsman raised a hand at the bar. "And one for my mate as well."

"Right away." Douglas moved to pull the pair of pints as the two men resumed their talk.

He liked the easy way the customers had accepted him. As he moved about among them, he quickly gained a rudimentary understanding of the community through overheard conversations and gossip.

He learned that two major mills provided most of the employment and were in fierce competition. The Fowler Mill, run by Harry Wallace and Brodie MacMillan, was currently dominant because, aside from the lumber operation, it also housed the only grist mill in nearly a hundred miles. The MacPherson Mill, run by Culloden MacPherson and his partner Fletcher

Atkin, wasn't about to let this advantage in any way put them in second place in the timber trade.

"I reckon as how MacPherson is having a hard time calculatin' his books with his right-hand man Fletcher gone off to England," he overheard one of his customers commenting. "Might give us Fowler lads a leg up on him this summer while he spends time tryin' to figure out his finances."

"He'll be back soon, I hear," his companion continued the conversation. "I understand he and his wife only went to the Old Country for a short time…long enough for him to sign over the rights to his lands and title to his brother. Reckon as how he'll return in time to do the summin' up of the summer's work. How some ever, I hear MacPherson's taken on a new hand…name of Jones, new arrived from England. The lad bragged he's right sharp with figures"—he chuckled—"perhaps MacPherson won't be needin' Fletcher and his highfalutin wife when they return. May haps this new lad will be better and more to the boss's likin' than a dandy like Fletcher. Rumor has it MacPherson bailed Fletcher out of more than one mess his wagerin' got him into. Cully MacPherson might be feelin' it's time he dumped a gambler for someone more secure."

Douglas shoved the two tankards across the bar to the men, collected their coin, and dropped the payment into his apron pocket. So Jones had immediately sought employment with Culloden MacPherson, the second most important employer in the area. Was MacPherson the object of his revenge? But if so, what was he waiting for? Why not kill him right off and catch the next ship out of Riverhaven? No, it didn't seem likely the mill owner was his target. Jones may have taken the job merely to avoid appearing a suspicious layabout while he waited for the person he planned to make his real victim.

"Barkeep, whisky here. And none of that Irish piss, mind. Good Scotch."

Startled by the sharp command issued in a voice he remembered, he turned toward the end of the bar to see the man of his thoughts calling for his attention.

"At once, sir." Douglas reached for a bottle, deciding to try to engage Clive Jones in conversation in an attempt to find out who was the object of this mysterious man's animosity.

"Would this suit your taste?" He pulled the cork and held it out for Jones's approval.

The man sniffed the contents, then leaned back with an exasperated exhale. "If it's the best you've got, it will have to do."

"That it is, sir. Right from the Glenturret Distillery."

"I'll need a glass…a clean one if you have such a thing in this elegant establishment."

"Have you found Riverhaven to your liking?" Douglas took the requested item from a shelf, placed it on the bar and poured.

"For a time. I see you've found gainful employment." He cast a sneer over the words.

"Aye."

"Ah, well, to each his own." He quaffed the drink, slapped the glass down on the counter, and nodded to Douglas to refill.

"I'll take the bottle." He threw a coin onto the counter and snatched the whisky from Douglas's hand.

Carrying it and his glass, he moved off into the crowd.

"Rum."

Coming back to the moment, Douglas saw a white-haired old man holding out a tankard. He started. The fellow bore a striking resemblance to Artie Parsons, the Edinburgh vagrant who'd directed him to Riverhaven and his brother.

"You have coin?" he asked, guessing this ragtag creature had no means of payment.

"Ah, come now, laddie. Just a drop of your cheapest Jamaican brew. Surely you can spare it for a veteran of the wars."

"Here you go, Jonah." Frank Miller came up behind Douglas to pour a splash of liquor into the proffered cup. "One drink and one only. Mark that, Douglas. He gets no more tonight."

"Aye."

As Frank Miller replaced the bottle and moved off to serve other customers, Jonah Parsons squinted up at Douglas.

"You have the look of someone…someone I know well…someone who is as fine a gentleman as ever walked this…"

"Move aside, Jonah." A customer elbowed the old man aside. "Make room for lads who can pay for their drink."

Relief flooded over Douglas. He wasn't yet prepared to have his true identity known in Riverhaven.

****

"That man, the one who took a bottle of your best." Douglas confronted Frank Miller as they began the nightly cleanup. Alone in the tavern with his employer, Douglas had decided he must share what he knew about

Clive Jones and find out what his employer thought it best to do.

"Aye." The tavern owner paused in wiping off the counter to face Douglas. "What about him?"

"His name's Clive Jones. He came out on the ship with me."

"And?"

"We had a wee conversation one night. He asked me why I was coming to Riverhaven…I said one place in this new country was as good as another…and I asked him his reason."

"What did he say?"

"Revenge."

"Good God, is that all?" Frank Miller chuckled as he returned to his work. "A pillock like that…alone…coming out to seek revenge on someone here in Riverhaven? He had to be pulling your leg."

"Maybe. Still…" Douglas persisted.

"Look here, laddie…" Frank Miller paused in his work to put a big hand on Douglas's shoulder. "You'll find this place, this Riverhaven and its surroundings, has more than its share of former rogues and scoundrels…men and even a few women who led outlaw lives back in the Old Country, but who have come here to settle and live out their days peacefully. That's not to say, mind, they've lost any of their skills at self defense, so don't waste your time worrying about them."

"But against a pistol…or musket."

"Not to worry." Frank Miller turned toward his kitchen. "As I've said, our residents have lost none of their survival skills. I swear some of them must have eyes in the back of their heads. They're not likely to be run amuck by the likes of this Clive Jones."

He paused, put his hands on his hips, and drew a breath. "Nevertheless, if you feel the need to warn the community, I'd advise you to visit our magistrate, Captain Caleb Cameron. He's what passes as law and order in the region. You'll find him in his office and lockup at the end of the village street. Barring that, he'll be at the shipyard he owns with his friend Dunc MacDougal, farther down. You know…" Frank Miller rubbed a thoughtful hand over his chin. "He may need warning himself. He and Dunc were privateers in the recent past war. I've no doubt that profession made them more than a few enemies. Also, you say this Clive Jones is an Englishman. Both Cal and Dunc lived in England for a time and may have had a few incidents there."

"You're saying a number of people in this area have left grudges simmering in the Old Country." Douglas experienced a slight sense of relief. Maybe his brother wasn't the target of Clive Jones's revenge.

"Aye, aye, myself included in that number. Don't ask the reason." Frank Miller held up a hand, deflecting Douglas from any inquiry. "Now off to bed with you. We have a busy day tomorrow. I'll be wanting the stable cleaned first thing. I've been a bit negligent in that area."

****

Savoring the sensation of a bed that didn't roll, Douglas settled for the night in the small second-story room at the back of the tavern and laced his fingers behind his head. His couch, although narrow, had a comfortable straw tick, several quilts, and even a pillow. So far, so good. He'd arrived unscathed, in what he considered the safety of Riverhaven, secured work and a place to live. But what of that mysterious man with whom he'd shared the voyage? Upon whom was he seeking revenge? Could it be Douglas's own brother?

He rolled onto his side and pulled the quilt about his bare shoulder. His thoughts strayed back to that morning, when he'd bumped into a vision in the street. He closed his eyes and saw her again in memory…the angelic face, the raven-black curls, the trim figure. Coming only to his shoulder, she was like a delicate work of art in a faded blue gown and straw sunbonnet.

Frustration bubbled through him. Snatching up his pillow, he pummeled it into a lump. What chance had he, a former smuggler who'd lived in a brothel and now worked in a tavern, with such an ethereal creature?

Forget her, chust forget her, laddie. You've got all you can handle with a new job and new master, never mind looking out for the object of Clive Jones's revenge. That should be enough to keep your mind off the lass.

He thought sleep would come quickly, given the stability of his bed, but it didn't. When it finally took him away, his dreams were haunted by the face and form of a young woman with midnight black hair and a complexion that looked as soft and smooth as silk.

****

Douglas was up early the next morning. He washed, shaved, dressed with care, and combed his hair in an effort to make himself look worthy of serious consideration. He'd considered wearing his finery, that suit he'd purchased back in Scotland with visions of wearing it with pride once he'd made his mark in this new country, but decided against it. Frank Miller expected his stables cleaned and Douglas didn't think the tavern owner would appreciate him wasting time changing clothing.

"I'll be back shortly and get right to that stable cleaning," he informed Frank Miller as he passed him in the kitchen.

"Off to air your concerns to the magistrate?"

"Aye."

"Well, good luck to you…although I imagine you'll meet with the same thoughts I gave you last night. We're a community of former rogues and there's likely to be any number of folks across the Atlantic who'd like to seek recompense. They're simply not about to risk the cost and dangers of a sea voyage to execute revenge. This Clive Jones must be a rare one indeed, with a deep grudge simmering long and deep in his gut, to go to the expense and trouble."

****

At the plank door of the clapboard building with the sign "Magistrate" over the door, Douglas paused, hesitated, and finally knocked. Frank Miller's warnings of the futility of this visit rumbled around in his brain.

"Enter," a male voice ordered.

He stepped into a small, dusty office where a man with dark hair and broad shoulders sat behind a scarred desk. Seated in a chair near the door, another man of equally fine stature eyed him up and down.

"Captain Cameron?" Douglas closed the door after him.

"Aye."

"I've come…" The weakness of his case against Clive Jones all but overwhelming him, Douglas faltered before the man's steely gaze.

"Aye?"

"I've come to report a threat to a member of this community." There. The words were out. He had no choice but to continue.

"Oh, aye. And who, may I ask, is the recipient of this dire warning?" The two men came alert at his words.

"I don't know." A hotness spreading up his neck, Douglas spoke the truth. "A man I met on the ship aboard which I traveled to this country said his reason for coming to Riverhaven was revenge. He gave no name."

Chagrined, he saw both men visibly relax.

"What else did he say?" The captain leaned back in his chair.

"Only that his name is Clive Jones."

"What makes you think this Clive Jones is out to bring harm to someone here in Riverhaven?" The other man stood and moved to sit a hip on the corner of the magistrate's desk so that he might look Douglas squarely in the face. He spoke with a distinct Scottish accent. "British North America is a big country. He could have been headed anywhere."

"I understand that it is." Douglas was feeling more ridiculous by the second. "But he has remained here. He's taken a position at the MacPherson mill."

"Likely just another bit of London trash out to make a name for himself in the New World." Grinning, the man stood again and clapped a big hand on Douglas's shoulder. "Rest easy, laddie. I'd say this Clive Jones was pulling your leg. At any rate, most of us in Riverhaven are capable of taking care of ourselves."

"Mr. Miller has assured me of such, but I thought it my duty to give warning."

"Frank Miller? How is it he's advising you?"

"I work for him…in the tavern."

"Ah." The inflection in the response annoyed Douglas. Another layabout only fit to work in a tavern for free drink and a bed—he caught the thought. Unable to think of any words that would denigrate the conception, he ignored it.

"I chust thought it best to give warning," he said, struggling to keep annoyance out of his tone.

"And we thank you." The man's affable grin relaxed Douglas. "By the way, my name is Dunc MacDougal, and the stern lad behind the desk is the local magistrate Captain Caleb Cameron." He stuck out a hand.

"Douglas Smith." Douglas accepted the man's introduction. "I didn't mean to trouble you needlessly."

"Not at all." Captain Cameron stood, behind the desk, and also extended a hand. "Forewarned is forearmed, is it not, Dunc? We learned that lesson in the war."

"Highlander, are you?" Dunc MacDougal's attitude had become all-out friendly. "I hail from there, years ago, myself."

"Aye…years ago as well." He wasn't about to give out any unnecessary information.

"Well, then I hope to see you at the tavern soon. We'll have a pint or two."

Feeling this was a dismissal, even if a friendly one, Douglas nodded and went out. He'd done all he could to warn the residents, but he still felt an obligation to keep watch over his brother.

****

"You've done right fine work, laddie." Frank Miller clapped a hand on Douglas's shoulder. "You're welcome to stay on…if that's what you wish."

"I do." Douglas paused in wiping down the bar. It was well after midnight and the last customer had just gone on his way. After working at the tavern for a week, he'd grown comfortable with the place and his employer.

"Well, then, I'd best warn you." The big man placed large hands on his hips and drew in a deep breath that forced back his broad shoulders. "Two ships have been spotted coming up the river…one belongs to Captain James MacTavish, the other to Captain Charlie Duffy."

"Aye, so we'll be expecting a rowdy crowd tomorrow." Douglas went back to his work. "Nothing we can't handle, eh, sir?" He grinned at Frank Miller as he recalled how between them they'd already managed to eject the most boisterous customers.

"You did well, lad. But tomorrow the wagons from both this area's major mills will be arriving to load those vessels. Those from Culloden MacPherson's mill will be providing cargo for MacTavish's *Highland Lass* while those from the Fowler Mill will be providing the same for Duffy's *Avon Queen*."

"Oh, aye?" Douglas paused again, puzzled as he saw the concern registered in his companion's face.

"Those two mills are competitive…have been ever since Culloden opened his operation to compete with the Fowler one. Well, more than competitive. Downright combative. Now with both sides arriving in the village at once and with loads of lumber…" Frank Miller spread his hands, palms upward. "There's bound to be trouble. I suspect some of it will start in this very room. So"—he leaned his back against the bar and looked squarely at Douglas—"here is the plan. When I give the signal, you're to eject Brodie MacMillan, the leader of the Fowler group, while I'll throw out Culloden MacPherson. With their leaders out in the street, men inclined to start a donnybrook won't remain in here to break up my place. Understood?"

"Me? Eject Brodie MacMillan?" Douglas stared at his employer. "What made you come to that decision?"

"Laddie, you've not seen Culloden MacPherson." Frank Miller shook his head ruefully. "He's a bear of a creature, more of my build. Now Brodie MacMillan, while he's no small lad by any means, a dab hand with a sword and quick as a weasel, he's more your kind of opponent. I've watched how you handle rowdies, and I'm pretty sure you can handle MacMillan…at least long enough to see him safely out the door…if you take him by surprise."

"Mr. Miller, sir, I've tried my best to give good service." Douglas fought to find an excuse. He didn't want to meet his brother for the first time in years in this way. "I think you've discovered I'm no' a coward when it comes to takin' on customers who get out of hand, but this man MacMillan…"

"You've heard of him, then, lad? No doubt gossip in this room. He's got a reputation as a tough customer and more than a bit of a wild man when aroused…but trust me. I wouldn't be putting you up against anyone I didn't think you could handle. Now, enough said. We'd best get back to work. What with the crews from those two ships and local lumbermen due in town soon, we're in for a busy time. Just mind—when MacMillan and MacPherson are in here together and things appear to be heating up, I'll give the signal and we each throw out our man." Grinning, he punched Douglas in the arm. "And if you succeed in landing Brodie MacMillan out into the street, your reputation as one mighty lad will be established in this village."

As Frank Miller went into the kitchen, his words resonated in Douglas's mind. His resistance to his employer's orders slid away. Here was the opportunity to see if he could take his brother in a fight as Brodie had taken him all those years ago, the chance to even an old score. He rubbed the fist of his right into the palm of his left.

****

"I see you've brought in another load full of knots cut from timber as crooked as a dog's hind leg." Douglas looked up from where he'd been filling a tankard to see a tall, broad-shouldered man swaggering toward a table near the bar, where sat a bear of an individual dressed in buckskins, the man Frank Miller had already identified to him as Culloden MacPherson.

"Smart-mouthed as always, eh, MacMillan?" the big man responded.

MacMillan. Brodie MacMillan.

Handing the drink to the customer, Douglas wet his lips and stared. His brother had changed, become a man; there were fine lines about his mouth and eyes now, his countenance darkened, weathered from years in the elements. *But still, a good-looking lad with an impressive build. Not someone who would be easy to take down.*

"Well, at least none of it was poached from trees bearin' another man's mark." MacPherson's face contorted into hard, angry lines.

"Poached? Poached?" Brodie MacMillan crossed his arms on his chest and sneered. "I'll have you know, you backwoods bugger, the Fowler Mills have never taken in so much as a sapling from someone else's patch, while you…"

MacPherson leaped to his feet, fists clutched. "Son of a bitch!"

"Now!" Frank Miller hissed. "Get MacMillan the hell out of here."

As he bolted to handle the buckskin-clad individual, Douglas leaped over the bar. Lowering his head like a charging bull, he made for MacMillan's midsection. His unexpected attack catapulted both him and the other man across the room, through the open doorway, and outside into the dust of the street. Brodie MacMillan landed on his back with a gush of expelled air. It gave Douglas time to stagger to his feet, into the dominant position, before his opponent could recover himself.

"Bloody son of a whore!" Brodie MacMillan struggled to a sitting position, clutching his midsection. "You better not have broken any ribs, or I'll see you drawn and quartered!"

"You've only got the wind knocked out of you." A gush of satisfaction engulfing him, Douglas held down a hand to help him up. *Finally.* "I hold you no ill will, sir. I was only following orders."

"Argh!" Brodie MacMillan ignored the offer and staggered to his feet.

"Seems like you might have met your match,

MacMillan," one of the men who were spilling out the tavern door taunted. "Never saw you throwed on your backside afore."

"Shut your great trap, Jens!" he snapped back. "If you had half a brain, you wouldn't be workin' for the likes of MacPherson!"

"Seems as if he ain't done so well either," chuckled another man as Frank Miller propelled the big man out into the street.

"Gentlemen, you understand that I bear neither of you any hard feelings." The tavern owner stood in the doorway, big hands on his hips. "But I won't have you breaking up my establishment. If you wish to continue your differences here in the street, be my guest. Come along, Douglas. We've better behaved customers to serve."

"I won't be forgettin' this, laddie." Brodie MacMillan glared at Douglas. "You might just have been doin' your master's biddin', but no one gut-slams Brodie MacMillan without consequences."

For a moment the two stood facing each other before Douglas turned and strode back into the tavern.

"You acquitted yourself right well, my lad." Frank Miller slapped Douglas on the shoulder once the two men were behind the bar. "I never thought anyone could take Brodie MacMillan down without a major scrap. You've had some fighting experience, I can see."

"A bit." Douglas returned to pulling a pint.

"Aye, more than a bit, I'd say." Douglas looked up to see Dunc MacDougal grinning at him. "I've known Brodie MacMillan for some time now, and I've never seen anyone floor him…until tonight."

"Just doing my job. Ale?"

"Ale will do just fine." He waited while Douglas filled a tankard and shoved it toward him. As the noise of fighting erupted from the street, he raised it to his mouth and took a long drink.

"Shouldn't you be doing something to break that up?" Douglas gestured toward the door. "You're Captain Cameron's lieutenant, are you not?"

"Ah!" Grinning, Dunc MacDougal flapped a disparaging hand. "There's not much one man can do about it. Any road, those two bunches have been spoiling for a donnybrook. It will do them good…take some of the starch out of their drawers. Cal might be able to break it up by riding in among them and firing off a shot, but he's gone to Fredericton on government business, and I've no desire to go home bruised and bloody to my wife. She'd be right put out, I can tell you, and she's no' a lass to be trifled with."

"You're a wise man." Frank Miller grinned, heading into his kitchen.

"How well do you know Brodie MacMillan?" Douglas decided to take advantage of the nearly empty bar to learn what he could about his brother.

"Ah, well, he and I had one high old adventure a while back when he was being sent to Fredericton to stand trial. Instead of escorting him to the provincial capital like a good officer of the law, I guided him over the American border and let him 'escape.' When he was cleared of the charges against him, I fetched him back. The pair of us was near killed on the way back, ambushed by a couple of murderous pillocks who…"

"What were the charges against him?" Douglas interrupted.

"What? Oh, seduction, I think they called it. Later,

bastardry."

"So the man has a past…a past here as well as in the Old Country, that could make someone seek revenge on him?"

Dunc MacDougal guffawed. "A past? That's putting it mildly. His wife could fair write one of her novels about his goings on. And I understand she did…only she left out most of the bits for which he could still be held culpable." Narrowing his eyes, he looked over at Douglas. "You seem right interested in a man you just threw on his arse. Thinking he'll retaliate and you want to know what you're up against?"

"Aye, wondering what I'll be up against if he decides to take revenge." Douglas turned away and began to wipe down the bar.

Seduction. Bastardry. But not rape. And married not once but twice. Apparently his brother still had the power to entice whatever woman he chose.

Any desire he'd had to warn his brother about Clive Jones fell into the background.

****

"You've been doing some right fine work here, lad." Frank Miller clapped a big hand on Douglas's shoulder the following morning as he was sweeping the floor. "I reckon as how you could do with a bit of time off and a taste of fresh air. How would you like to go fishing?"

"Fishing?" Douglas paused, broom in hand, to look at his employer.

"Aye, trout fishing. I assume you know how?"

"Aye."

"Well, there's a fine stream fair bursting with beauties a short jaunt back in the bush. If you've a mind, take one of my cobs and try your luck. I'll even pay you for any of your catch beyond what you and I can eat. Customers are always ready for a fine trout dinner."

"I'd like that." Douglas leaned the broom in a corner, a grin crossing his face.

"Well, then, off with you, lad. I'll be wanting you back at the supper hour, mind. The stream I'm speaking of is between Duncan Green's farm and the Fowler Mill settlement. You'll have to turn off the main road for a bit to find it, but you'll know you've hit the right spot when you see an old cabin and stable near the shore. I'll give you better directions once you get Nellie saddled. You'll find my fishing gear in the back corner of the stable. Take what you think you'll need."

****

Douglas sank down on the mossy bank of the stream, drew up his knees, and rested his elbows on them. His basket was full of fat trout, the sun was shining, and there was a gentle, warm breeze to keep the flies at bay.

And he was abroad in daylight. Back in Scotland, he'd spent most of his waking hours in darkness, skulking along fog-draped shores, watching for the arrival of yet another ship or a contingent of redcoats. Barring those activities, he'd be posted near the door of the brothel, ready to handle troublemakers.

A contented smile curled his lips as he sucked in the fresh, unsullied scents of nature. Although grateful for his job at the tavern, he enjoyed being free of the smells of sweating bodies, flatulence, and stale spirits.

Thoughts of Frank Miller's establishment brought him back to the night when he'd expelled his brother.

His neck and shoulders still had twinges. Slamming into Brodie had been not unlike hitting a rock. A wry grin twisted his lips. No doubt about it, his sibling was one tough customer. And, no doubt about it, he, Douglas, had managed to get the better of him…even if the element of surprise had been involved.

Enough meandering. He stood and turned to look at the small log cabin Frank Miller had mentioned. Nestled in the trees a few feet from the stream, it had caught his eye before he'd begun to fish. Now it had his all-out interest. He'd had time to think as he cast his line time and time again and while he'd extricated fat trout from his hook. The rustic little homestead could be fixed up to make a snug home, he'd decided.

A home. The word sent a warm surge sliding over him. He hadn't had a home since he'd left his father's in the Highlands, but now he was in Riverhaven. He liked the area, the village and its people, and he had legitimate employment. Ambling around the small homestead, he took inventory.

Behind the little shelter was a ramshackle barn that must once have housed livestock…a cow, a dray, a few chickens. He could purchase a horse, a means of transport aside from his own legs, to get him to and from his work at the tavern. A bit of a clearing beyond the barn could be plowed for planting.

The cabin needed work. The plank door hung open on a single hinge, allowing access by a variety of smaller wildlife. A mouse skittered across the leaf-strewn floor and from the smell he reckoned some larger forms of tenants might have taken up residence.

He stepped inside to inspect the supporting beams. They appeared sound, as did the plank floor and log walls. A hearth filled with ashes, a bed built into a back wall, the mattress of which had been ravaged by wildlife, and a table with a bench and single chair comprised the contents.

He wasn't discouraged. He'd taken refuge in less welcoming dwellings. A bit of cleaning and repair could make the cabin a right fine place to live. Since its present owner seemed to have abandoned it, perhaps it might be at sale for a price he could afford. He'd ask Frank Miller about it.

Plans on how he might restore the small homestead in his mind, he returned to the bank of the stream, gathered up Frank Miller's fishing gear, fastened it and the basket of trout to the old horse's saddle, and led her up the lane to the main trail.

As he stepped out onto the roadway, he saw a woman crouching at its side. A basket on her arm, she was picking berries. When Nellie shook her head, rattling her bridle, she jerked to her feet and swung toward them.

When she faced him, his breath caught in his throat. It was the vision he'd encountered on his arrival. Even dressed as she was in a shabby sunbonnet and faded gown, she was an outstanding beauty.

"Mistress." Somehow he found his voice and managed to touch his cap.

"Sir." Avoiding his eyes, she dipped an awkward curtsy as she shrank away from him.

"Berry picking, I see." He fought to make casual conversation. Something in his chest had begun to pound a tattoo.

"Yes."

Have I frightened her? Bloody hell, what have I

done wrong? She won't look at me.

"I've been fishing." He jerked his thumb at the basket tied to Nellie's saddle.

"Did you have luck, sir?" She looked up shyly to meet his gaze.

"Very good luck. Would you like some?" As soon as the offer was out of his mouth, he felt stupid. Of course this beautiful lass wouldn't fancy carrying a string of dead fish along the road to her home.

"Thank you, sir, but my father has already secured a fine catch for our supper."

Good God, she's blushing. Although at first startled, Douglas realized he found pleasure in her reaction. After his years of living among brazen brothel women, this bashful creature enchanted him.

"Your father must have been fishing the same pool where I had such good fortune." He struggled to keep the conversation continuing. He had to know more about her.

"Perhaps. We live just down the road." She adjusted her basket on her arm, once more avoiding his gaze. "You must excuse me, sir. I have to be getting home."

As she made a move to walk past him, he wet his lips and took a plunge.

"I'm headed back that way. Would you be minding if I walked along with you? Or"—he blundered ahead—"you could ride Nellie. She's docile as a lamb, and I'll hold her bridle."

She glanced up sharply. What was it he saw in those wonderful blue eyes…apprehension, fear? Surely it couldn't be fear. He'd made no untoward moves, but perhaps he shouldn't have tried to engage her in conversation, never mind ask to accompany her, even to offer her a ride on the old cob. He didn't have the appearance of a gentleman, dressed as he was in his shabby shirt, breeches, and boots, and he most certainly didn't have the manners of one. Did she perhaps know he worked in the tavern and shoveled manure from its stable? Something hot began to flood up his neck.

Bugger all, am I blushing as well?

"Thank you, sir, but I'm accustomed to walking…alone." She turned away so that her face was hidden by the sunbonnet.

"Verrae well." He swung onto Nellie, his words sharper and filled with more of a Scottish brogue than he'd intended. "I bid you good day, Mistress…?" He couldn't contain his desire to know her name.

She didn't reply at once, but as she walked past him she murmured, "Green, Morag Green."

"Douglas…Smith. Your servant, ma'am." He used the only gentlemanly form of address he knew before touching his heels to Nellie's sides and sending the old mare off down the dusty road at a shambling trot. He wished he was riding a fine, prancing stallion that he might amaze her with his horsemanship…since he obviously hadn't impressed her with his verbal dexterity.

Chapter Seven

Walking along after him, Morag allowed her gaze to settle on his broad shoulders and straight back. A fine figure of a man she'd once heard such a person described. The thrill of excitement his sudden appearance had aroused still fluttered inside. Seeing him again after their brief encounter on the village street had been a great surprise, but he was as handsome as she remembered, and he had a lovely smile. Surely there could be no harm in such a man.

The thought spurred her imagination and she carried her wishes further. She should have accepted his invitation. He'd have had to assist her to mount. How would those strong brown hands have felt about her waist as they lifted her onto the mare? Would he then have vaulted up behind her, his arms going about her to hold the reins? The blush that had begun during their encounter was spreading to suffuse her entire body.

Stop it at once, Morag Green! Such thoughts are shameful! Mother would be appalled! Mother would…

Chagrined, she pulled a wry face. Mother never understood. Mother never wanted her to meet any young men. None in the small community were good enough for the daughter of judgmental Hazel Green.

If I'm ever to find happiness with…a man, I must cease to be cowed by Mother. As Mrs. Morgan said, recognizing the love of your life and sticking to him takes courage. I must find courage…if I'm ever to enjoy the company of a man…like Douglas Smith.

****

As Douglas was passing the end of the lane that led to what Frank Miller had described as the Green farm, a dappled gray bolted from behind the barn and charged toward him, a rope dangling from its halter.

Reflexively he drew Nellie crossways at the end of the lane and leaped to the ground.

"Whoa, whoa!" he ordered, raising his arms and blocking the horse's path. "Easy, easy."

He grabbed the trailing rope. After a few moments of battle, he managed to bring the mare to a prancing stop.

A man with a decided limp came shambling up from the farm buildings.

"You caught her," he gasped as he arrived to join them. "I'm right glad she didn't run you down. She's a fractious creature. I rue the day I bought her."

"Nothing a bit of training won't settle." Douglas managed to bring the mare to a standstill. She stood trembling and sweating beside him. "She's a right fine animal." He ran a hand appreciatively along her arched neck.

"Yes, well, fine to look upon, perhaps." The man, tall but grizzled and stooped in the shoulders, reached to take the rope from Douglas. The horse shied away from him. "She's nothing but a great trouble to me."

"She's not suited to farming," Douglas continued, soothing the animal with his hands. "I'll wager she's more fit to being swift under a saddle than before a plow."

"Flighty creature!" The man took the lead and gave

it a sharp yank. The mare jumped away from him, eyes showing their whites. "I'll be taking her back to Walter and saying good riddance to her. He can shoot her for bear bait for all I care."

"Walter the blacksmith, who owns the livery stable?" Douglas, through dealing with customers in the tavern, was becoming acquainted with many of the village's residents.

"Yes, that's the one. For now, I'll turn her out into the pasture and leave her there until he can fetch her. I'll not go risking life and limb to take her back to the village. Lord knows, I had enough trouble bringing her out here. I should have known right then she was a bad one. Walter said he got her off a ship. Her owner had died on the voyage and the captain was looking to cover his passage by selling the creature."

"Father." Her voice made both men turn to see Morag hurrying down the road to join them. Involved with the horse, they'd failed to notice her approach. "What has happened? Is Lady all right?" She stepped past the two men and went to lay a hand on the mare's sweating neck. The animal lowered her head and nuzzled the young woman.

"It seems Miss Morag has a way with beasts." Douglas wet his lips and tried to speak casually, but this image of the beautiful lass tenderly calming the mare sent a rush of feelings flooding through him. He handed the animal's lead rope to her father.

"Yes, well…" Then, realizing the stranger had recognized the woman as his daughter, the man swung on him, eyes narrowing. "You know my girl, sir?"

"We met up the trail a bit," Douglas replied, recognizing the farmer's expression as changing to one of suspicion. "I was coming up from the brook... fishing." He indicated the basket strapped to the old mare's saddle.

"I was picking berries." Fearful apprehension was evident as Morag turned to indicate the contents of her basket. "We spoke for but a moment, Father."

"Yes, well, I'll not have you dallying with strangers. Get on up to the house. Your mother has chores for you."

"But what about Lady? If you'll take my basket, Father, I'll lead her back to the barn. She behaves for me."

"Go!" The farmer's command snapped out at her. After a final furtive glance at Douglas, she scuttled off down the lane.

"And you as well." He swung back on Douglas. "I'm obliged to you for your help with the mare, but I'll not have my daughter accosted on the road."

"I did no accosting." The accusation brought a quick rebuke from Douglas.

"Get!"

"Verrrae well." Douglas swung back onto Nellie. He must look the right tramp with his shabby clothing and shambling old mare. "I can take this beast back to the blacksmith, if you wish."

The farmer hesitated a moment, then handed the lead rope to Douglas.

"Take her, take her. Tell Walter I'll be in to get my coin back in a day or so."

He turned and limped toward his farm buildings.

Douglas turned both horses down the road toward the village but couldn't resist glancing back. Across the fields, he saw Morag had paused and was looking after him. He raised a hand in farewell. After a furtive glance to see if her father was watching, she shyly returned the gesture. Then she hurried off down the lane to the farmhouse.

A warmth spread over him as he clucked the old mare to a fumbling trot. She'd waved to him. Did that mean…? He brought himself up short. What was the point in speculating? A respectable lass such as Miss Morag Green had no business associating with such as Douglas Smith.

The gray mare had come up beside him. Her nose nudged his leg.

"Ah, lassie, you're a good beast, I've no doubt. All you need is a bit of understanding." He looked down at the animal. "And I think I'm just the lad to give it to you."

****

At the blacksmith shop, he dismounted and tied both horses to the outdoor hitch rail. Advancing into the hot interior, he addressed the big man working at the forge.

"Mr. Walter, I've brought back the gray mare you sold to Duncan Green." He waited until the man had ceased hammering a bit of hot iron and turned to acknowledge his presence.

"Oh, aye?" The man known simply as Walter squinted over at Douglas from beneath bushy eyebrows. "Found her wantin', did he?"

"She wasn't what he desired in a beast."

"So I'm stuck with the damned thing." Annoyance frowning his face, the blacksmith looked out to where Douglas had left the pair of horses tied. "Ah, well, maybe I can sell her for bear bait."

"Or I could take her off your hands." Douglas faced him squarely.

"Could you now?" Walter narrowed his eyes as he looked back. "Would you be willin' to pay what Duncan Green paid?" He named a figure Douglas thought fair.

"Aye. I chust have to go to the tavern and fetch the coin." He started to leave, but turned back. "Do you want me to leave her here until I return? If you'll trust me, I'll take her to the stable with Nellie and she'd be out of your way once and for all."

"Take her, take her." Walter waved a disparaging hand as he returned to his work at the forge. "The sooner I see the last of that troublesome creature, the better."

Outside, Douglas caught up Nellie's reins and the gray mare's lead rope and headed up the street toward the tavern. A grin stretched his mouth. He'd had a fine day. Success at the trout pool, the discovery of the small homestead, a chance meeting with Miss Morag Green, and now the acquisition of the first real property of his life.

"Come along, Lady," he urged the mare. "We'll be keeping the fine name Miss Morag gave you. I think it fits you right down to the ground."

Chapter Eight

Morag hurried along the dusty road, then off onto the trail and over the bridge that led to the manse and church situated on the small island in the river between her home and the village. She had to see Mrs. Morgan, to talk to her. If she didn't confide in someone sympathetic to her feelings, she was certain she'd burst.

"Why, Morag, my dear, how lovely to see you." The minister's wife greeted her at the door with a bright smile. "Do come in. My, my, you look as if you've run for miles."

"Mrs. Morgan, I've met someone," she gasped as the woman guided her into the same room where she had spent her previous visit. "And he's…"

"Quietly please, child." Mary Morgan put a finger to her lips. "Edward is working on his homily." She indicated a closed door across the foyer.

"Oh, of course." Morag moderated her tone and took the chair her hostess indicated.

"Now," Mary said, closing the door to the room and taking a seat. "Tell me all about him."

Morag launched into a narrative that stretched from her first meeting with Douglas on the village street to her most recent encounter.

"Mrs. Morgan, do you think he might be the one?" she ended, heart pounding in anticipation of the woman's response.

"He could be, dear, but you don't know him yet. A couple of casual meetings are hardly cause to get involved seriously."

"Yes." Deflated, Morag clasped her hands in her lap and looked down at them.

"Now, now, don't be discouraged by my words. He could well be the right man for you. You simply must get to know him, to discover what kind of person he truly is. He's a newcomer, you said?"

"Yes, from Scotland, by his accent. That makes the situation worse. Mother has a terrible prejudice against such people."

"Hmm." Mary Morgan leaned back in her chair and furrowed her brow. "It would seem the next step is for us to learn more about this young man. And I know just the person to discover his character." She stood and moved to open the door, then crossed the hallway to do the same at the entrance opposite. Morag glimpsed the reverend, shirt sleeves rolled, bent over an untidy desk.

"Mrs. Morgan"—Morag breathed the words—"you said Reverend Morgan must not be disturbed. You said…"

"This is an important matter, my child," she said, glancing back at the younger woman. "Edward, we have need of you," she continued, turning to address her husband.

The clergyman looked up at his wife, exasperation for a moment crossing his countenance before he stood with a rueful sigh.

"Of course, my darlin'," he said. "What do you desire?"

Chapter Nine

"Here." Frank Miller flung a clean white apron at Douglas. "You'll be serving the customers this noon time. I've these fine fish to attend." He turned back to sprinkling seasoning on the dozen trout Douglas had caught, now spread on the kitchen table. "And there are your first clients." He jerked his head in the direction of the common room.

"Women?" Moving to view the clientele, Douglas received a surprise. "In the tavern…unescorted? And dressed…?"

"Those two are quite the pair." Frank Miller chuckled. "The taller one would have to be. She's Brodie MacMillan's wife. The other is her sister."

Wife! His brother's…wife? He stood staring at the beautiful, titian-haired woman. A shaft of jealous anger shot through his heart. Wasn't it enough that Brodie had stolen Annie Burns from him? What right had he to another lovely woman when he, Douglas, had had only the company of brothel whores? Bloody hell, why should he concern himself about protecting the brother who'd beaten him to a pulp when he was but a young lad and called him that miserable name? To hell with Brodie MacMillan.

Fastening the apron about his waist, he strode toward the women's table. He had to admit they were outstanding beauties, even dressed astonishingly as they were in breeches, boots, shirts, and jerkins.

"Ladies"—he hoped his voice sounded congenial, not tinged with bitterness—"what may I get for you this fine summer's morn?"

"Are you the gentleman who sent my husband reeling out into the street?" The one Frank Miller had identified as his brother's wife looked up him, a twinkle in her bewitching green eyes.

"If you're married to Brodie MacMillan, mistress, I plead guilty. I will, however, inform you that I did so on the orders of my employer."

"Oh, have no fear, Mr. Smith—I believe is your name?" She looked the question up at him and when he nodded, continued. "I'm not here to chastise you. Rather, to thank you. My husband has been in need of taking down a peg or two. I much prefer it to be done at fisticuffs than with swords or pistols. Now, what is your fare for the day?"

"Trout, mistress, fresh caught and shortly hot from the fire, served with new potatoes, the first of the season's crop, Mr. Miller informs me." Douglas relaxed into a congenial grin. This was a lady he could easily come to like.

"Wonderful. We'll enjoy such a meal."

"Very well, mistress, within minutes."

"Oh, and, sir," the second woman called as he turned away. "A couple of tankards of your best ale. Riding this warm morning has left me parched."

"Aye, mistress, at once."

An astonishing pair of women if ever he'd met such. Douglas appreciated their free spirits and their unusual manner of dress, but as he held plates for Frank Miller to fill with trout and potatoes, his mind strayed back to the shy beauty picking berries by the roadside and the furtive wave with which she'd favored him.

****

"Would you know who owns the wee cabin and barn near the trout pool?" Douglas made the inquiry as he and Frank Miller ate their own dinner in the kitchen after their midday meal customers had departed.

"Peter Fairly." The tavern owner mumbled, his mouth full of trout. "Why do you ask?"

"The place seems to have run to a bit of neglect." Douglas cut into a mealy potato and reached for butter. "I was wondering if it might be for sale."

"Ah, thinking of settling here now, are you, lad?" His companion paused in his eating to grin over at him.

"I like the location." Douglas shrugged. "And I have a wee bit saved from my work back in the Old Country. I believe I might be able to afford it…if it's offered at a fair price."

"Are you planning on leaving my employ? That cabin is a fair distance from the village. You'd have a long walk, morning and night. My lending you Nellie wouldn't help much. She's as slow as molasses running up hill in winter."

"It's not fit to live in now. I'd spend my Sundays fixing it up. It would be winter before I could consider having it ready…and even then only if I was able to put away in enough firewood to see me through the cold months. As for transport, I've chust bought myself a mare with a bit more get up and go than Nellie." He paused to look apprehensively over at his employer. "I'm hoping you'll let me stable her here until I get things fixed up a bit. You can take the cost of her keep out o' my pay."

"My, my, you are in a settlin' frame of mind. I'll not be charging you to have your animal in my stable. You've done a fine job of keeping my barn clean and its occupants fed. Continue to do such a fine job and that will be sufficient."

"I'm grateful. Now, as to that homestead…"

"That parcel of land lies between Duncan Green's farm and the Fowler Mill holdings. You'll have no trouble from the Fowler holdings, but on the other side…Duncan Green's not a bad fellow, but that wife of his! A fair tartar if ever there was one."

"And the daughter?"

"Ah, now, lad, don't go telling me you've got an eye for the fair Morag? You can put any ideas regarding that young lass right out of your head. Hazel Green thinks no one less than a crown prince is good enough for her precious girl. She wouldn't welcome a tavern lad sniffing around."

"I've no aspirations regarding Miss Morag. As for her mother, I couldn't be less concerned. I know how to stay clear of trouble."

"Well, I reckon, then, as how we can do business."

"We? I thought you said a lad named Peter Fairly laid claim to it."

"Aye, but Pete has gone west on the fur trade, taking my barmaid Molly with him. He left his place for me to dispose of…at a fair price. I'll be pleased to have you staying on in Riverhaven. Now, let's talk terms. What can you afford? I reckon most any offer will do, seeing as how the place is going to rack and ruin."

Douglas had calculated carefully what he could afford to put out for the homestead and stated his offer.

"Aye, well, I reckon that will do." Frank Miller leaned back in his chair. "What have you in mind for it? Even if it's become a tad overgrown, there's a fair chunk of arable land attached. A man could make himself a tidy sum planting potatoes, carrots, turnips, beets, and the like for sale to the lumber mills and camps. If it's one thing this community is sorely lacking, it's farms and farmers to provide vegetables and grain. Right now, we're importing most of it from Maine because everyone around here is anxious to get rich quick through timber and shipbuilding. But mind you, laddie, come January, those lumber camps will pay top dollar for root plants…dried beans as well. Do you know anything about farming?"

"A bit. When I was a wee bairn, I lived on a farm." Frank Miller's question dredged up memories of being a young lad on his father's holdings.

"Well, then I reckon it will come back to you. If not, I'm sure Ezra Gardiner would be more than willing to give you a bit of advice…and maybe even a bit of seed to get you started. Now we'd best get back to work. Although there isn't a vessel newly docked or lumber coming into town to be shipped, we always have a few folks wandering in to wet their whistle and maybe have a plate of food."

They stood, picked up their plates, utensils, and tankards, and headed back into the kitchen. Douglas's thoughts were occupied with this new possibility Frank Miller had offered. A farmer. He liked the idea. Working the land, making an honest living. And maybe someday with a pretty wife by his side.

****

"A tankard of your best ale, laddie." Brodie

MacMillan swaggered up to the bar and issued the order.

"The same for me, if you please." His companion, a tall, broad-shouldered man with a thatch of dark red curls joined him.

"Damn it, Lex, that lady wife of yours is giving you the manners and airs of a gentleman," Brodie scoffed.

"And sadly yours hasn't." A wry grin curled the corners of the second man's mouth.

"She loves me just as I am…a bit of a wild lad. Bartender"—he leaned across the counter toward Douglas as the latter placed a tankard in front of him—"you have the look of someone I once knew. I've been puzzlin' over it ever since you knocked me on my arse. The lad I'm thinkin' of even bore the same Christian name."

"And who might that be, sir?" Keeping his head lowered, Douglas felt his heart rate quicken. He wasn't yet sure he wanted to make himself known to his brother. He pretended to center his attention on filling a second tankard.

"Where did you get that scar?" Douglas looked up to see Brodie focusing on the U-shaped mark on his right forearm below his rolled-up sleeve.

"Fell on a horseshoe hot from a forge when I was too young and foolish to keep clear." The lie had come so quickly he couldn't believe he'd fashioned it.

"I remember a young lad gettin' such a brand once." Brodie looked with narrowed eyes at Douglas. Was his brother about to recognize him? A pounding began in his chest. "Ah, well, it was a long time ago." Brodie took up his drink. "He was but a bairn when last

I saw him. A right pain in the arse, he was. He's been dead these many years, and I'll not be mournin' him." He headed toward a table.

So my family thinks I died...and my brother isn't sorry. Inwardly Douglas heaved a sigh of relief as he shoved a second tankard across the bar to Brodie's companion, the man identified as Lex, with more vehemence than necessary. *I'll be wise to keep my own counsel...at least for the time being.*

Chapter Nine

Morag was setting the table for their noon meal when her father arrived, dusty and weary, from a trip to the village. He'd taken a broken plowshare to the blacksmith to be mended. It had been no easy task, hefting the instrument into the back of his wagon, especially with that game leg.

"What news, husband?" Her mother turned from where she'd been stirring a pot of chicken stew on the hearth. Morag felt a corner of her mouth curl in a bit of a sardonic smile. Hazel Green was forever alert for gossip. "Are any new ships come in? Any new arrivals? What of Captain Cameron's wife? Has she given birth yet?"

"No, no, and no." Duncan Green sank down on a chair by the door to remove his dusty boots. "But that new lad, the one working for Frank Miller in the tavern, has purchased Peter Fairley's place."

"What!" The word was a shriek from his wife as she faced him. "Sold the Fairley place to that ne'er-do-well!"

The bowls Morag had been about to place about the table dropped to its plank surface with a bump. Douglas Smith was to be their…her neighbor. A thrill that was a combination of excitement and apprehension gushed over her.

"What can Frank Miller be thinking, letting such a

man buy the land abutting ours," her mother continued her rant. "Why, he'll be within a stone's throw of this house! Husband, I demand you drive me into the village this very afternoon. I'll have a word with Frank Miller. I'll see that he revokes the sale. I'll see…"

"Mrs. Green, the transaction has already been completed." With a weary exhale, Duncan Green pulled off his second boot and stood. "And I'd hardly call a near mile from this house a stone's throw. There's a hayfield and good stand of pine between the Fairley place and our farmyard. Now, I'll be obliged if you'll serve up some of that stew. I'm hungry and tuckered, but I have to get back to work as soon as possible. Hay don't mow itself. Morag, I'll be glad of your help."

"Of course, Father." Something that felt like butterflies were fluttering inside as she went to fetch her own meal from the hearth.

A neighbor! Douglas Smith was to be their neighbor.

"He's also purchased that fractious mare I couldn't abide." Duncan Green looked over at his daughter. "Paid good dollar for her, Walter told me."

"Mr. Smith bought Lady?" Morag's astonished pleasure told in her words.

"That he has. Maybe he'll be able to put the creature to some use."

"I'm sure he will." Morag pretended to concentrate on her meal. She didn't want them, especially her mother, to see her delight.

****

Involved in his morning duties, Douglas didn't at first notice the big, broad-shouldered man, dressed in black except for a white shirt open wide at the throat, when he walked into the tavern the following day. When he did, he paused in wiping a table to address him.

"Good morning, sir. What can I get for you?"

"Two pints, if you please, laddie." He sat down at a clean table and stretched beneath it long legs terminated by knee-high black riding boots.

"Oh, aye, right away, sir." Douglas strode behind the bar to comply.

"Sit down." The newcomer startled Douglas with the request when he returned to the table with a pair of tankards. He indicated the chair across from him and shoved one of the drinks in its direction.

"I thank you, sir, but Mr. Miller would not approve." He started to turn away, but the stranger's voice, suddenly thick with Scottish accent, stopped him.

"Dunnae greet, laddie. Frank and I are old friends. He's not about to deny you a few minutes with your minister."

Douglas swung back to stare at the ruggedly handsome man, so casually dressed. *Minister?*

"Reverend Edward Morgan. Dunnae look so taken aback, laddie." Grinning, the big man took off his straw hat and ran his hand though the thatch of red curls revealed. "I'm no' here to lecture you on the evils of drink."

"I wasn't afeard of that, sir." Taking the indicated chair, Douglas pointed to the ale in front of the minister.

"I'm not against ale or whisky…in moderation." The clergyman paused to take a long drink before continuing. "Aw, my, but that hits the spot. Some days a man is sore tried and must relieve his hurts."

"Aire you hurting today, sir?"

"No, just feeling a bit uncomfortable with my current mission. My guid wife has sent me to inquire as to your intentions regarding Miss Morag Green."

"My intentions…?" Flummoxed, Douglas didn't know how to reply.

"Aye, laddie." Reverend Edward Morgan leaned back in his chair and eyed Douglas with a calculating eye. "It appears the young lady has expressed an interest in you…to my wife, mind, not me. And she…my guid wife, that is…has decided I must evaluate you and see if you're worthy of this fine lass. Now…" He pulled himself up and leaned across toward Douglas, eyes narrowed. "How do you feel about Miss Morag? I'll get right to the crux of the matter."

"I…I…" Caught off guard, Douglas could only stutter.

"Come, come, laddie, this is not the Spanish Inquisition."

"I…I think she's the most beautiful lass I've ever seen…the finest of ladies." Words began to come, honest words, the only ones he could use when it came to Morag Green. "A man would have to be a swine not to hold her in the highest regard."

"Aha. I can only conclude that you do…hold her in the highest regard?" Edward settled back in his seat.

"Aye, the highest."

"Would you consider courtin' the lass with honorable intentions?"

"No, sir—" Catching the clergyman's disapproving glance at his quick response, he stumbled on. "That is, I am not in a position to consider myself deserving of such an honor. I work here…in a tavern. I clean the stable."

"But I understand you've recently purchased a cabin and a tidy bit of land near the Green farm. Surely that shows intent to settle and build a life…a life a man might share with a loving wife."

"It's but a ramshackle place." Douglas toyed with the handle on his tankard. "Hardly a house where a woman of refinery could be expected to live."

"You're working on it steadily, are you not?"

"Yes, and maybe in a year or two…"

"Aye, well, I've heard enough." Edward Morgan quaffed the last of his ale and stood to wipe his mouth with his sleeve. "My, that was fine stuff. Whoever decided it was only decent for a clergyman to have a bit of wine and brandy on his premises definitely wasn't of the ilk." He turned and headed for the door. "There's a church fete on Saturday week…a ceilidh. Feel welcome to attend." He paused at the entrance and turned back with a sly grin. "Miss Morag Green will be in attendance."

Astonished, Douglas watched him leave. The last statement gave him to understand that he'd passed muster with the minister. A gush of happiness rushing over him, he snatched up his tankard and quaffed it down in a single drink.

But as he stood and gathered up the two vessels to return to the bar, his euphoria began to fade. What he'd told Reverend Edward Morgan had been true. He couldn't court Morag Green with so very little to offer.

Furthermore, the man didn't know Douglas's past. Would he want one of the village's fairest (to Douglas's mind the fairest) to be involved with a former thief, smuggler, and brothel inmate?

****

"Before I've been here long, the weeks t'was scarely three,

A farmer's lovely daughter did fall in love with me.

She told me that she loved me and she took me by the hand,

And shyly told her mother that she loved a shanty man.

Oh, daughter, dearest daughter, you grieve my heart full sore,

To fall in love with a shanty man you never saw before.

Well, Mother, I do not care for that, so do the best you can,

For I'm bound to go to be with my roving shanty man."

Stripped to the waist, Douglas sang the song he'd learned in his smuggling days as he swept dirt from the cabin. Suddenly a sense he'd come to possess during his outlaw days, that of knowing when someone was watching him, made him whirl toward the door.

Bathed in a ray of sunlight filtering through the trees, Morag Green stood at the end of the trail that led to his homestead. Released from the bonnet that hung on ribbons down her back, a thick mass of shining black curls fell over her shoulder. Against the variegated greens of the surroundings, the white dress she wore made her look even more ethereal than he remembered. Sunlight striking a jar she carried in her hands turned its contents to the brilliance of rubies.

The words of the song he'd been singing, words she'd no doubt overheard, caused heat to gush up the back of his neck.

"Mistress Green." He found his voice, snatched up his shirt, and hastened to the doorway. "Good morning." He struggled the garment over his head.

"Good morning, sir." She bobbed a small curtsy. "I understand you're to be a neighbor."

"That I am." He glanced ruefully back over his shoulder at the neglected cabin. "It will take a fair bit of doing, but I hope to make it fit before the snow flies."

"It is a sturdy place." She was looking at him, blue eyes turning his innards to jelly. "Perhaps the barn could become fit for livestock once again…with work."

"I'm afraid I'll not make much of a farmer yet," he said. "But I have purchased a mare so that I might have transport…that mare your father disliked."

"Yes, my father said you did."

"She's a good lass," he said relaxing enough to let his Highland brogue show through. "I couldn't let her be sold for meat. All she needs is…"

"A gentle hand and a caring heart." She startled him by quickly finishing his sentence.

"Aye."

"I believe you can provide both, Mr. Smith. I'm pleased Lady will have a good home." She extended the glowing jar toward him. "I've brought you some of the jam I made with the berries I was picking the day we met."

"That's right kind of you, Mistress." He reached to accept it. Their fingers touched on the glass surface and their eyes met. A pleasurable sensation flooded through Douglas. Beautiful blue eyes touched his soul and warmed it to the core.

It lasted only a moment. She pulled back abruptly,

lowering her gaze.

"I'd invite you in for tea, but I'm afraid my house hasn't yet become fit for such." He glanced ruefully behind him and struggled out of the situation. "And I haven't any tea." He flavored the last bit with humor.

"That's quite all right, Mr. Smith. Mother and Father will be back from church soon, and I must have dinner ready for them. I bid you good day."

"You chose not to accompany them?" he called after her as she started down the trail.

"I begged off with the excuse of headache." She cast a smile back over her shoulder that he saw carried a hint of mischief in it.

He grinned in return, then watched as she hurried off down the trail, a warm happiness engulfing his innards.

Chapter Ten

I visited him! I talked with him!
Morag's heart did wild upbeats as she scurried down the forest trail to the road. The fact that she'd lied to her mother about having a severe headache, too severe to attend church that Sunday, seemed well worth any chastisement she might suffer as a result. He'd looked so handsome, so virile...she blushed to even think the word she'd learned in her reading of Mrs. MacMillan's book...but he did.
Oh, my! It has such a forbidden tone.
As she reached the road, she paused to draw a deep breath of the wonderful summer's day. Could anything be more perfect, more thrilling! She whirled around twice, arms outstretched in a small dance. Then she set off toward her home, humming a little tune...not the one she'd caught him singing but still making equally happy sounds.
Back at the farmhouse, she set the table and cut up bread, meat, and cheese for her parents' midday repast. Meal preparations complete, she went to her bedroom to lie down, in preparation to facilitating her ruse of illness. As she glanced into the mirror above her chest of drawers she was horrified to see that she was flushed—glowing, actually. That would never do.
Panicked, she rushed back to the kitchen, snatched up a basin, and ran outside and across the farmyard. At

the ice house beyond the barn, she hacked bits of ice from a block with a pick her father had left for the purpose and put them into the pan. In a desperate flurry, she raced back to the house, wrapped the ice in a piece of toweling linen, and hurried back to her room to lie down on the bed, the cold pack against her bright cheeks.

Perhaps Mother will mistake my heightened color as due to a slight fever. Perhaps...

She could only hope.

Chapter Ten

Douglas dressed with meticulous care. He'd bathed in the stream where a curve in its travels had fashioned a deep pond, scrubbed his hair with a vigor that all but uprooted it, shaved closely and carefully, and taken out his best clothes, the clothes he'd purchased in England with money gleaned from the sale of one very fine barrel of Dos MacLintock's smuggled wine.

As he viewed himself in the small scrap of mirror resting between two timbers on the wall, he drew a deep breath and hoped he looked respectable. He'd never been to a church function since he'd been a lad, and never in this country, but he assumed a man was expected to wear his best.

Aye, well, now I must endeavor to make a good impression on the folks of Riverhaven...the folks who don't know me from the tavern, that is. Especially I must try to behave properly before Miss Morag.

He left the cabin, being careful to place the bar across the door. While he had little worth stealing, he didn't want wandering wildlife to get inside and destroy all the work he'd done to make the little place habitable.

He strode out to the stable and saddled Lady. Early that morning he'd brushed her until she looked every inch worthy of her name. When he led her outside and swung aboard, he could at least feel confident he was riding one of the finest-looking mares he'd seen so far in the community.

Chapter Eleven

The ceilidh was in full swing when Douglas rode across the bridge and into the church yard. One of the men spotted him and nudged the person next to him. It had a ripple effect. Soon, it seemed, everyone had paused to stare at him.

Attracted by the hush that had fallen over the gathering, Morag glanced up from where she was sitting beside her mother on the ground in the church yard. Dressed finer than any of the men at the gathering and riding an animal with a thick arched neck and prancing hooves, Douglas Smith was breathtakingly handsome.

Oh my!

She could barely believe this was this same man she'd encountered on the trail, a string of fish hanging from the saddle of an old mare or that she'd interrupted as he, disheveled and glistening with sweat, cleaned his ramshackle cabin.

With a sudden pang of something she didn't at first recognize as jealousy, she saw Tilly and Sarie Gardiner, daughters of her mother's friend Lillian Gardiner, staring at him in ill-disguised awe. She comforted herself with the fact that *she*, Morag Green, had had meetings with him in private. *She* had a distinct advantage over these two silly, simpering girls.

"Welcome, welcome, laddie." Morag watched as

Reverend Morgan got up from where he and his family were seated near the Greens and went to greet him. "I'm delighted you could come. Tie your mare over there in the trees and join Mrs. Morgan and our daughter and me for supper. My guid wife has made enough for a small army."

"I thank you, sir." Douglas swung to the ground and gave the minister a respectful nod. He flashed Morag a quick, furtive smile. Catching her mother's stern expression, she dared not respond. She cast her gaze downward to the plate in her lap.

As Douglas led his mount off to join the other horses tethered in the shade of pine trees, conversations that had stilled at his arrival resumed. The minister's welcome appeared to have garnered acceptance for Douglas. Morag dared to venture a quick glance at his retreating figure.

"Don't go looking at that man!" Her mother gave her a sharp nudge. "What will people think?"

"But, Mother, Reverend Morgan welcomes him. Surely…"

"Surely he's dressed as a London dandy, flaunting himself before all the silly young women of the community. I hope and pray you have at least a modicum of common sense that will allow you not to act in a similar fashion. Now, eat your supper. And when the dancing begins, keep your eyes off him. I don't want him encouraged to think he is welcome to ask you to partner him."

Chastened, Morag made a pretense of focusing on her meal, but whenever her mother became distracted into conversation with one of the other women, she took the opportunity to steal a glance. Once he caught her look and smiled.

She allowed her lips to curl slightly at the corners before quickly returning her attention to the slice of ham on her plate. Smugness settled over her. In spite of the Gardiner girls' best efforts, he hadn't cast a single glance at Tilly or Sarie.

She also noticed, as the evening progressed, men going over to welcome Douglas…men who probably had made his acquaintance at the tavern and liked him. Even Morag's father joined the group. They greeted him with bonhomie, but the women stayed their distance until Mrs. Morgan made a point of calling several over to meet him. Once acquainted, they seemed quite content to remain chatting with the handsome newcomer who appeared to be charming them no end.

Only Morag and her mother remained apart. When the minister and his wife beckoned them to join the group, Hazel Green stubbornly shook her head and busied herself with clearing away the supper leavings. Morag had to fight with all her willpower the urge to disobey her mother as she watched the two Gardiner girls simpering close to him and favoring him with coquettish smiles. She was on the verge of violating her parent's wishes when her mother's harsh words stopped her.

"Mind, when the dancing starts, remember what I said. You're to stay away from that creature," Hazel Green snapped as Morag replaced bread and cheese into a basket. "I'll not have you anywhere near him."

Morag didn't reply. Too many emotions were swirling around in mind and body.

****

"I fear I may have made a horse's ars...a mule's behind of myself," Douglas commented as he sat on the grass, sharing the Morgans' supper. He'd had time to peruse the other picnickers and realized that while they were neatly and cleanly dressed, none of the men sported the excellently tailored outfit he did. "I have but one decent suit of clothing, and I thought..."

"Nothing for which you should apologize, Mr. Smith." Mary Morgan was quick to respond, making him wonder if he looked as awkward as he felt. "I'm sure if any of the men had such fine clothing, they'd be only too glad to show it off."

"And you're not alone." Edward Morgan jerked his head to a family group several yards away from them. "Just look at Harry Wallace. While his getup is not so spanking new as yours, he's as well turned out."

"Truly, that is Harry Wallace?" His attention distracted from his discomfort, Douglas looked over at the handsome, well dressed man seated beside a beautiful auburn-haired woman and surrounded by a bevy of young people and children. "Once known as Highland Harry and now the owner of the largest saw and grist mills in miles? I've never seen him in the tavern."

"Aye, that's him. You're not likely to see him in your place of business. He's the image of respectability now, married, with nine children and a wife he adores."

"Nine? Are all those his? Surely some of the older ones..."

"Are stepchildren he and his wife Margaret took over parenting after their birth parents passed. And those mills aren't really his, he'll be quick to tell you. He and Brodie MacMillan are simply holding them in trust for the children of the man who started the enterprises. Only the two youngest, those rambunctious little dark-haired boys, are his and Margaret's biological children."

"He's made a right-sized change in his life." Douglas drew his gaze away from the happy family.

"As have most of us." Reverend Morgan reached to take his wife's hand and smile fondly at her. "Riverhaven can be a place of miracles, my lad." He turned his attention back to Douglas. "Anything you truly want can be yours with persistence and hard work."

"It's a shame Fletcher Atkin and his wife haven't yet returned from England." Mary cast Douglas a teasing glance. "Then you'd have no reason at all to be concerned about your attire. Mr. Atkin always dresses elegantly on such occasions as this. I assume that when he returns, he'll have even more finery for both him and Isabella."

"He's the man who once attempted to court Miss Morag?" Douglas recalled, feeling relieved that this man with his fancy clothing and renounced title was married.

"Yes, but he hadn't a chance"—Mary Morgan grinned over at him—"once Hazel discovered he'd been a bit of a lad back in the Old Country. Of course, that was before she learned he was also an aristocrat. Had she known that fact, she'd have been making Morag a wedding gown as fast as she could."

"Mr. Douglas." A small hand tapped him on the shoulder. "Your mare is right bonny. Might we visit her?"

"If your parents will allow." He smiled at the

Morgans' four-year-old daughter, the Highland inflection that mirrored her father's warming his heart. She wasn't losing her heritage, at least not entirely. Even her looks, so like her mother's, spoke of the hills of Scotland.

"Of course." Mary Morgan smiled. "I'm sure Mr. Douglas will take good care of you."

"She's a dab hand with beasts." The minister grinned proudly. "I swear she'll be riding as well as her mother and me afore long."

"Verrae well, then." Douglas got to his feet and was startled as a small, warm hand was placed in his. A wonderful sensation, this gesture of trust. What would it be like to have his own child looking to him for guidance, believing in him to love and protect her? As the little girl drew him in the direction of the horses, his longing for a home and family swelled.

"She's a bonny beast." When they arrived at the place where the mare was tied, Iona looked up in admiration at the animal. She released Douglas's hand, and before he could stop her she was at Lady's head, speaking softly to her in Gaelic. Douglas made a move to pull her away, then stopped. Lady had lowered her head and was nuzzling the little girl as she continued to coo softly in the Highland tongue.

Her father is right. She does have a dab way with beasts.

"What is her name?" She looked up at Douglas.

"Lady."

"Lady. A perfect name for such a fine lass."

"I agree."

"Mr. Douglas, someday will you let me ride her?" Iona turned to him, blue eyes bright with the desire of the request. "Mother and Father only have a team of plodding Percherons. They ride them sometimes, even though Father says it takes a heaven-sent miracle to get them into a gallop. But this lass"—she touched her hand to the mare's nose—"can run like the wind, I'll reckon."

"Again, this will depend upon your parents' permission, but for now"—he caught her up in his arms, astonished at how light she was, and swung her onto the mare's back—"I doubt it requires such just to sit upon her as she stands tethered." And to the animal he said, "You stay right still, now, Lady. You have a very important passenger."

Looking down at him, the child drew a deep breath. A radiance of pure delight cast an almost ethereal expression over her small face.

"Oh, Mr. Douglas, this is wonderful." She leaned forward to pat Lady's arched neck. "It's like being close to heaven."

"I doubt your father would describe it as such." He grinned up at her, her pleasure washing down over him. "You can only sit a few minutes more. Then we must be getting back to the others."

"Of course, Mr. Douglas." The words came out regretfully. "But you must promise you will ask my parents to allow me to ride Lady some day…really ride."

Later, as he lifted her to the ground and she once again inserted her hand in his to return to the picnic site, he knew as never before that what he wanted most in the world was a family…a family like Edward and Mary Morgan possessed.

****

Douglas was enjoying himself. In the evening's warmth, he'd shed his coat, vest, and neck cloth, as had other men who were wearing similar attire, and settled in to enjoy the general camaraderie. He'd never been part of such a community gathering, never thought he would be admitted into one. Now here he was, welcomed by nearly all the residents...aside from the family which he most wanted to find him acceptable...and having a good time.

As he helped the men pile up kindling and logs for a bonfire, he cast furtive glances to where Morag and her mother were sitting. Duncan Green had joined the men in the work with only a curt nod of acknowledgement toward Douglas, most likely warned to do no more by his wife. Still, Douglas knew this was the life of which he longed to be a part...being a neighbor and friend to respectable, hard-working people, sharing their good times and their bad. If he had Morag by his side, it would be perfect.

Stop dreaming, laddie. Chust be content with the present.

He jumped back as the heap of wood burst into flames, sending sparks up into a sky darkening with early evening and brightening with shy stars beginning to peek out into the night. The men gave whoops of satisfaction.

When they quieted, the soft tones of a fiddle echoed out into the gloaming. Douglas turned to see Brodie MacMillan seated on a stump, pulling a bow across the strings of an instrument.

Startled, Douglas stared at his brother. Memories rushed back...memories of their father teaching them to play an old violin, of their mother sitting by the hearth and smiling as she watched her husband's efforts. Brodie had always been the more adept. He, Douglas, had never had his brother's gift for creating music.

Jealousy rose like bile in his throat. Brodie MacMillan had it all...a beautiful wife, a son, a partnership in the largest business in the area, and the skill of a talented musician.

"Dancing will be commencing shortly." Frank Miller at his elbow, a tankard in his hand, spoke softly. "Just what a young buck such as yourself will enjoy. But a word in your ear, laddie. Stay away from the Green lass. I've seen that dragon of a mother casting nasty looks your way ever since you arrived. Antagonizing her will only lead to trouble. We don't want that here on church grounds, now, do we?"

"No, no, of course not." He looked down at the tankard his employer held and sniffed. "Rum? I thought that since this was a church event..."

"You've got the nose of a bloodhound when it comes to spirits, laddie." Frank Miller's broad face lighted up with a grin. "To all appearances, and especially for the ladies' benefit, it's plain cider, but some of us have added a bit of extra flavor...merely a wee drop here and there, mind, and the lads are careful not to overindulge...just enough to put magic in their feet for dancing. Most of them are either too shy—the single ones, that is—or too awkward to dare to attempt a reel or a jig cold stone sober."

"Does the Reverend know of this...subterfuge?" Douglas glanced over at the big, red-haired man joking with a group of men.

"Now, I'm not one to go telling tales, laddie, but if you stuck your sensitive nose near his cup, I'll wager you might get a whiff of good Jamaican juice. He's a wise man, our minister." He chuckled. "He knows exactly how to handle parishioners such as these. That's how he manages to fill his church each Sunday. Now, mind what I say, young fellow." He leaned close to Douglas. "Stay away from that Green girl. Don't court trouble."

He saluted Douglas with his tankard and moved off into the crowd.

Douglas knew he had to obey. He couldn't be the cause of trouble at this gathering. Not after the minister had been sufficiently trusting to invite him, had even trusted him with his only child.

****

Douglas was dancing with Tilly Gardiner. Morag fidgeted as she sat on the family's blanket, watching him weaving about the fire amid the other dancers. The fact that he moved more gracefully than most of the other male participants only served to rankle her further.

Where had he learned to dance? She'd guessed him to be a country boy from a farm in the Highlands. Now, she was seeing a different side of him, what with his fine clothing and dancing skills. If she'd had any aspirations regarding him, the level of his sophistication on this evening shredded them to rags. Perhaps his father was a laird in the Highlands…not as fine as an English aristocrat, but still of a much higher station than she, Morag Green, frontier farmer's daughter.

No, no, that could not be the answer. No laird's son would have come to this country to work in the tavern and shovel manure in its stable, to attempt to make a home from a ramshackle cabin and barn. There had to be another answer.

A man of mystery, that was Douglas Smith. The idea made her tingle and sent even more resentment spewing through her veins toward the pudding-faced Tilly Gardiner.

Chapter Twelve

What can she be thinking?
As Douglas whirled around the fire with Tilly Gardiner, he cast an occasional furtive glance at Morag sitting primly beside her mother. Did she care that he was dancing with another lass, even if it was with a simpering, foolish one? If not for her parents, would she dance with him?

The next instant what he saw made his gut contract. Clive Jones, dressed as fine as he, Douglas, had been before he'd shed his outer wear, had joined the circle of onlookers around the fire. For a moment, he stood perusing the group. His attention finally fell on *her*. Morag, as if feeling his gaze, turned in his direction. Smiling, he advanced toward her.

Douglas tripped as he saw the man bow politely to the two Green women and had trouble keeping even half his attention on the dance as he watched Jones engage in genial conversation with them.

Stay away from her, you London dandy! Bloody hell, stay away from her!
Brodie rendered a last few bars of music and the dance ended. Douglas bowed to his partner and led her back to her parents, barely aware of what she said or how he answered. After he'd returned her to her family, he strode to the table where cider was being ladled out and procured a tankard of the refreshment. He took a

long drink, his attention focused on Morag and Clive Jones.

"Easy, lad, easy." Frank Miller had arrived at his side and was following his gaze. "Don't get yourself in a fluff. If the lass truly prefers you, it will all work out, trust me."

"But that pillock… God only knows who he's planning to take revenge upon. It could be Miss Morag's father."

"And it could all be a bluff, a taunt to make you raise a false alarm in the village. Here." The tavern owner pulled a flask from inside his coat and, after glancing around to make certain he was unobserved, splashed a dollop into Douglas' tankard. "Enough to calm you down, but not enough to put you in fighting form." He tucked the container away and patted his chest over its hiding place. "Have no fear about the young lass. Her mother will see to it that man doesn't get anywhere near being alone with her daughter."

Still perturbed, Douglas let his gaze roam elsewhere on the group around the fire in an effort to disarm his ire. He saw the man who had been pointed out as Harry Wallace get up from where he'd been seated with the beautiful woman Douglas assumed was his wife. With a slight limp, he strode over to where Brodie had paused in his playing. They spoke for a moment, and Brodie replaced his fiddle under his chin and drew the bow slowly across the strings to produce a beautifully sensuous sound. Quiet fell over the gathering as Harry Wallace returned to his family and held down his hand to his wife. The smile she cast up at him shot envy coursing through Douglas. To have a woman, your wife, look at you like that!

She got to her feet as Brodie's music, a gentle, lilting melody, wafted out into the softness of the summer night. Hand in hand, the couple made their way to the center of the dancing space. Harry Wallace, tall, handsome and commanding, swung his wife into his arms, and shortly they were whirling gently around the fire, gazes locked in loving expressions.

So this was the former outlaw Highland Harry, father of nine children, and husband to this beautiful chestnut-haired woman. Douglas watched as the couple circled the dance area several times. Finally others began to join, imitating Harry and his wife's steps, but with a lot less grace and confidence. Maybe it was possible for a man with a less than savory past to find peace and happiness here. Maybe Riverhaven held such a possibility for him.

His hopes smashed to a halt at what he glimpsed through the dancers.

"Sweet Jesus!" Involved in taking a swig, he choked.

Clive Jones was leading Morag out to dance, taking her in his arms as the new dance required.

"Well, well," Frank Miller scoffed. "That foolish mother has seen fit to let her partner that bit of English flotsam. I always said Hazel Green had the brains of chicken. She must be hoping he'll turn out to be another aristocrat in disguise like Fletcher Atkin."

"And well he might be." Douglas, flushed with suppressed anger, struggled to regain his composure.

"Aye." Frank Miller's response was another scoff. "The likelihood of that being the case is as rare as hen's teeth."

"You say she'll be safe from him with her

parents?" Douglas swilled the remainder of his spiced cider as he waited for his companion's reply.

"As safe as if she were guarded by a regiment of redcoats."

"Then I'll be leaving." Douglas returned his tankard to the table and strode off toward his mare.

"Lad…"

He ignored Frank Miller's call. He could no longer passively bear the sight of Morag in another man's arms. Pausing only long enough to scoop up his discarded clothing from where the Morgans sat watching the dancing, he headed off to retrieve his mare.

"Douglas…lad." The minister's call slowed him only long enough to try to make a polite reply.

"I thank you, Reverend, ma'am, Mistress Iona, but I must be going."

He strode to where Lady was dozing among the trees, untied her, and vaulted onto her back. Swinging the startled mare toward the bridge, he urged her into a gallop. Her hooves thundering over the planks mirrored the pounding in his chest.

Back at his homestead, he stabled Lady before heading into the cabin with long, fierce strides. Once inside he shed his finery, all but ripping it in his haste. Naked, he headed out into the night that was now sultry and cloying and alive with buzzing insects. At the pool in the stream, he waded in, its coldness bringing a gasp to his lips although it cooled the heat raging through his body.

Even so, it failed to erase the image of Morag in Clive Jones's arms. He scooped handfuls of liquid over his head and willed himself to be reasonable. He had to get a grip on his feelings for the lass.

   She'd never be his.

   He had to come to terms with the reality.

Chapter Thirteen

"Father, will you be needing the team this afternoon?" Morag finished clearing away the noontime meal as she glanced furtively in her parents' direction.

"No, child. Why do you ask?"

"I should like to use Brown to learn to ride." She barely knew how the question managed to get past the apprehensive lump in her throat, but seeing Douglas dancing with Tilly Gardiner had made her bold, had inspired the idea that she must find some new, outstanding way to make him notice her. He was an expert horseman and apparently enjoyed riding. Her becoming proficient on a horse and able to join him in this activity had burst to mind as a wild possibility.

"Ride? Whatever gave you that daft idea?" Her mother swung on her.

"I understand all accomplished English ladies ride." She forced out her strongest argument. "Mrs. Atkin is a fine rider, and so is Mrs. Anna Wallace, Alexander Wallace's wife. There have been rumors that she was a lady back in the Old Country."

"Mrs. Wallace, indeed! Ran away with her father's groom to come to this country...and well before she married him."

"But Mrs. Atkin—" Courage surged through Morag. She wasn't about to give up. "She's married to a man who could have been a lord if he'd chosen."

"Humph! She may have come close to being an aristocrat, but she came to this country as a mail order bride intended for that barbarian Culloden MacPherson." The woman narrowed her eyes as she looked at her daughter. "I hope this sudden desire to learn to ride hasn't been as a result of seeing that tavern worker arrive at the church fete on a half-wild horse."

"No, no, of course not." Morag was surprised how easily the lie surfaced. "It's just that…well, Mr. Jones hinted he might ask me to go riding…if he can find a suitably safe horse. I should like to at least be able to stay on the animal and guide it."

"Mr. Jones?" Hazel Green's outlook softened. "Well, he does appear to be a fine English gentleman."

"There's that old sidesaddle we brought with us from Yorkshire." Duncan Green astonished his daughter by speaking up. "It's yours, Mrs. Green, you'll remember."

"I brought it because I had visions of our being able to purchase a decent riding animal." Hazel spoke with asperity. "I had no idea the money my father invested in you would be spent on this farm and a pair of plodding drays."

"Well, that's no reason why our girl shouldn't make use of it." He stood and started to limp toward the door. "I'll put it on Brown, daughter," he said as he went out, "but you'd best put on your oldest gown. He hasn't had a good grooming in days."

****

Morag stood beside Brown and wet her lips. She'd driven the gelding Brown and his mate the grizzled gray White harnessed to a wagon, but she'd never climbed on the back of either one. Suddenly it seemed a long way up. Brown glanced around at her and wriggled his hide near the saddle. Although unaccustomed to the device, he had apparently accepted it with only mild surprise.

"Use the fence." Her father, holding the horse's bridle, had stopped the animal beside the cedar rails of the pasture behind the barn. "In the Old Country there'd have been a mounting block, but here we have to make do."

You can't continue to be a coward, Morag Green. Not if you want to have any chance at attracting Douglas Smith.

After an undignified scramble she managed to get her bottom into the old saddle, her right leg hooked over the horn. Nervously she gathered up the reins her father had shortened for her convenience.

"Is this how I should sit, Father?" She looked down at him. "Is this how Mother looked when she rode?"

"Aye, aye." A slight smile crinkled his weathered face. "She was a right sight to see, back in those days."

Again, as it had many times in the past, the question as to why her parents had married crossed her mind. Such an ill-suited pair. Had they once been in love? Had something happened to sour that feeling?

"Walk on, Brown."

Her mind rushed back to the present at her father's command to the horse. The big dray moved slowly forward, no faster than if he were pulling a loaded wagon.

"Circle the field, daughter," Duncan Green called after her. "Get the feel of it. Give him directions in the same way as when you drive a wagon."

As she headed away from her father, keeping close

to the cedar rail fence that enclosed the field and moving down its length toward the trees at the far end, she experienced a gush of something fresh and exhilarating. Seated high on the gentle horse in a tattered old saddle that more than a single mouse had nibbled over the years, she got her first taste of the joy of riding. How much more exciting it must be once one had mastered the technique and could go galloping freely wherever one chose. An image of Douglas Smith entering the church yard on his beautiful, prancing mare flashed across her mind. Someday she'd be able to ride as well as he, she told herself confidently.

But as she turned Brown back toward her father waiting by the paddock gate, her fine dreams shattered. It was a long way from riding a plodding dray to managing a spirited creature like Douglas's Lady. Perhaps she, Morag Green, was destined to a life of slow, unromantic drudgery.

****

Early Sunday morning Douglas took Lady out for a run. The mare was a delight to ride. After working hard between the tavern and his small homestead, he decided he needed a bit of pleasure.

At first he let her have her head and race along the trail toward the Fowler Mill, but before topping the rise that Frank Miller had said crested the facility, he turned her homeward. He wasn't yet ready to make a visit to his brother's community or chance an accidental meeting.

Lady, contented with having had a good run, settled into a brisk trot. Unwilling to yet abandon the pleasure he was having in the ride, he passed the lane to his own farm and continued on down toward the

109

village. If he was being honest with himself, he thought with a wry grin, continuing to exercise Lady was only a small part of his desire to ride farther. Although Morag would most likely be at church with her parents (she'd hardly risk not attending twice) a desire to be in the vicinity of where she spent her hours overwhelmed him.

As he came in view of the farm, he received a pleasant surprise. In the pasture by the barn, he saw the object of his dreams. Perched on one of her father's draft animals, she was circling the enclosure, the dray plodding beneath her. What was she up to? Definitely she had no destination in mind, turning about the fenced area as she was.

Learning to ride? That had to be it. Her cautious progress could indicate nothing else. And sidesaddle at that. Good God! She needed instruction before she injured herself.

Heedless of interference by her parents, he turned Lady into the lane and arrived at the paddock just as she was turning the gelding back toward the gate. Her eyes widened as she saw him, and he recognized embarrassed confusion in her expression.

"Good morning, Mistress," he said as he halted Lady by the fence and she drew rein on the other side. "A fine day for a ride, is it not?"

"Yes, yes, that it is."

"Would you care to ride out with Lady and me?" he asked, then immediately recognized his faux pas.

Bloody hell, what a stupid suggestion, when it was obvious the lass was a rank beginner.

"No…no, I thank you."

"It's a brave thing, riding in a sidesaddle." He

struggled to make up for his inappropriate remark. "I've never been able to understand how lasses manage to stay aboard the blessed devices. It's much easier astride."

"I believe you're correct, Mr. Smith. I've only ridden astride once in my life, and that was with Mrs. MacMillan on her lovely white mare." His comments apparently easing her chagrin, she managed a shy smile.

"Well, then, let's get you started on that better style." He glanced toward the house. "Your parents are from home?"

"At church. I said I'd stay home and care for our cow. She's been poorly. They used White and the small driving wagon for transport."

"I'll wager you didn't tell them you were planning a ride while they were gone?" Grinning, he swung to the ground, led Lady to the gate, and brought her inside.

"Not exactly…well, no, I didn't." She seemed to be relaxing as she cast him what he could only call a slightly mischievous smile. He grinned as he refastened the gate.

Aye, perhaps she's coming around…ready to step a bit outside her mother's control.

"Well, then, let us get on with a practical riding lesson." Douglas took the dray's reins from her hands, swung them expertly over the animal's head, and tied them to the fence. Turning back to her, he held up his hands to lift her down. She hesitated only a moment before accepting his assistance. She felt a feather in his grasp.

"Now," he said, standing beside Lady and making a cup of his hands. "Give me your foot, grasp the saddle front and back, and up you go."

"She'll stand quite still?"

"Quite still."

"Very well."

She put her foot into his cupped hands, grasped the saddle front and back, and let him hoist her upward.

Once she was aboard, he passed her the reins. He felt the tremor in her fingers as she took them.

"There's naught to worry about, lass," he said softly, forgetting in his concern to address her as mistress. "Lady may not have behaved well as a farm animal, but she's perfect trained to the saddle. Any road, I'll be holding her bridle and walking right beside you. Now, off we go."

He heard her soft intake of breath as he started to lead the mare around the paddock. A thought shot through his mind.

Could I ever make her gasp with desire? Sweet Jesus, *lad, get a hold of yourself! She's a lady, a real and true lady. Be content with the moment, you fool.*

And there was joy in the moment. Watching her delight as he led the mare carefully around the paddock, seeing her eyes bright with excitement, gave him a rush of pure pleasure. And reminded him of his manners.

"That jam you kindly gave me"—he squinted up at her in the sunlight—"it was right fine. I thank you again."

"I should have brought bread as well…that you might have it to spread over."

"Mr. Miller…my employer at the tavern…he gave me a spoon. I fair lapped it up."

Bloody hell, can I sound any more like a barbarian! Lapped it up! Has my brain turned to muck?

"I'm glad."

"Would you be comfortable if I took her to a trot?" he asked after they'd rounded the field twice.

She wet her lips, adjusted herself in the saddle, and nodded. He clucked to the mare and started her off at a slow trot, jogging along beside her. A sudden peal of laughter from Morag pleased him right down to the core. He'd never heard her laugh. The sound sent a surge of happiness through his soul. He glanced up at her to see her face bright with joy.

"Please, Mr. Smith," she said after they'd gone round the field twice at a trot, "you must be weary. That will be enough for today."

"Never fear, lass. I've run much longer and harder than this and not lost my breath." His statement, spoken simply to reassure her and without thought, reminded him of who he truly was…a fugitive from British law.

"At any rate"—she shifted in the saddle—"I'm sure you must have other plans for this lovely day and are impatient to get on with them. You're probably eager to work on your homestead."

"You're perhaps becoming weary."

He moved to the mare's side and held up his hands. Much as he hated to see those glorious moments end, he knew her parents would soon be home from church, and he must not be found alone with her.

Lifting her down, he was again struck by her slight weight. To a man accustomed to hefting kegs of liquor, she was a feather.

"I'll help you put this fine lad back into his stall." He indicated Brown standing docilely by the fence, casually swishing flies with his tail. "Too many insects about to put him out to pasture."

"Of course." She hurried to open the gate to allow

him to lead both horses out of the field.

A farm girl, that's for sure. Knows just what has to be done and ready to do it. Such as would make a perfect wife for a homesteader.

Memories unexpectedly gushed forward to dim his enjoyment. Former smuggler, thief, and brothel resident, and now tavern worker and stable hand. He had absolutely no right to think himself a fitting companion for beautiful, innocent Morag Green.

As he put the big dray back in its stall, he kept averting his eyes. She was so naïve, so lovely, so unaffected by her beauty he believed angels would have to be very special to compete with her.

When he'd finished and accompanied her back outside, he paused before mounting Lady.

"I hope I can help you again." Unlikely as the suggestion was, it was the best he could manage.

"I thank you, Mr. Smith, but I doubt that will be possible." She dropped her gaze. "My parents…"

She looked up at him, eyes begging him to understand.

With perhaps even just a tad of longing? He dared not allow himself to read too much into her glance.

"I understand." He gathered up his mare's reins and mounted. "I wish you good morning, Mistress."

He swung Lady about, away from those bewitching eyes. Putting his heels to her sides, he sent her galloping down the lane to the main trail. He must not come again, he must not allow himself to be alone in her company. It was far too dangerous.

Chapter Fourteen

The storm spat rain against the shutters, but inside his cabin, in front of the fire, Douglas was warm and dry. He'd spent so many nights abroad at the whims of the elements that he had a fine appreciation of what he was experiencing. Tomorrow he'd have to be up early and hurrying back to the village to his job at the tavern, but tonight this small cottage, coupled with memories of his morning spent with Morag Green, warmed his soul.

He leaned back in one of two rocking chairs he'd purchased, together with a chest of drawers from the cabinet maker in the village, and took in his snug surroundings. He'd scrubbed the old table, bench, and chair that had been part of the cabin's original furnishing until they were free of dirt. Along the wall opposite the hearth was his bed with its fresh mattress of spruce boughs made comfortable by its caribou hide covering. A pillow, quilts, and blankets he'd purchased at Angus Harris's store completed its inviting ambience. Near as comfortable as he'd been as a child back in the Highlands.

He rubbed a hand over his right forearm, encountering the slight rise that was the U-shaped scar. He remembered the day their father's stallion had kicked him, leaving a deep, bloody horseshoe impression. He also recalled how Brodie had pulled him out of further danger from thrashing hooves, and later taken the blame for their being too close to the animal they'd been ordered never to approach. He'd admired Brodie back then…tall, handsome Brodie with his mother's sandy curls, his swaggering, self-confident manner.

His thoughts travelled back to other memories, how on a wet spring day in the hills and heather beyond their family farm, his hero worship of his brother had come crashing down. They'd fought savagely that morning until, battered and bleeding, Douglas had fled the only home he'd known, vowing never to return.

Dusted and done. He shrugged those memories aside and returned to his contented perusal of his small home. On the mantel, a pair of empty whisky bottles held candles that provided light aside from that emanating from the fire. A kettle sat on the floor nearby, ready to make tea…tea he'd purchased at Angus Harris's store in anticipation of having it ready if Miss Morag ever visited again.

He scoffed at the sheer ridiculousness of the idea. Looking over at the table which held a single plate, mug, and eating utensils supplied by Frank Miller, he resigned himself to his lot. He should be content with a tidy bit of a homestead and food enough to ward off anything near the hunger he had once experienced.

He picked up a flask from beside his chair and took a drink. He'd never taken much to drinking, but this was the kind of night a man could fancy to unwind with a wee dram. In a few minutes, he'd put a final log on the fire, strip off his clothes, and fall into bed, comfortable and secure against the rain and wind buffeting his new home.

The only troubling bit was that he knew he'd toss and turn at first, as visions of the unattainable Morag ruffled his peace. Visions of Clive Jones boldly accosting her and her mother at the church ceilidh still rankled his mind. But why should it? What had he to offer a woman—any woman, never mind a paragon such as Morag Green. Still, his mind—and body—couldn't help longing, aching, desiring. Memories of her joyfully riding Lady at a shambling trot around the meadow, of the wonderful sound of her laughter, didn't help.

"Mr. Smith! Mr. Smith!" Her voice, accompanied by a hammering at the door, wrenched him out of his thoughts. "Oh, dear God, Mr. Smith! Father has been injured!"

In an instant he was on his feet, stumbling across the cabin and pulling the door open to admit the lady herself. With a drenched cloak covering her head and body, clutching a lantern, she stared in at him, eyes wide with terror.

"Come in, lass, come in." He reached out to draw her into shelter and shut the door on the storm. "Whit's that you're saying? Your father has been hurt?"

"Yes, yes, grievously, I fear!" She stared up at him out of a blanched face. "He was trying to cover a hole in the barn roof to keep out the rain when he slipped. Mother and I carried him into the house and laid him on the bed. He hasn't opened his eyes nor spoken since!"

"I'll come back to your house with you, lass, but I'm no' a doctor. I don't know whit…"

"You can ride a horse!" Her eyes implored him. "You can ride swiftly to fetch Mrs. MacMillan! It's only a few miles farther down the road! Oh, please, Mr.

Smith, I'm begging you!"

He could no more ignore the appeal in those beautiful, frightened eyes than he could fly.

"Very well." He snatched up his coat and cap. "Stay inside. I'll come back for you."

"No, no, I have to get back to our farm! Mother needs me. Please, just fetch Mrs. MacMillan."

Looking down into her desperate expression, he paused.

"All right then," he agreed finally. "Give me directions."

In gasping breaths, she complied.

When she'd finished, he took her arm, drew her out of the cabin, and barred the door. When he turned back to speak to her, to caution her once more, the bobbing light of her lantern told him she had already started back down the trail through the woods to her home.

Shaking his head, he headed to the barn to fetch his mare. Miss Morag Green might appear meek and mild, but when a crisis arose, she had the courage and strength to do what was needed.

****

He slid from the mare's bare, wet back, slung the reins over her head, and bounded up the steps of the cabin to which Morag had directed him as the home of Brodie and Louisa MacMillan. The storm-blackened night hadn't made it easy to find. At the plank door, he pounded on the panel. Inside, a dog barked, then snarled.

"Whit…?" He recognized Brodie's voice. "Who is it, and whit do you want at this time of night?"

"It's Douglas Smith. There's been an accident. Duncan Green has been bad hurt."

The door was yanked open and his brother stood before him, wearing only breeches, his hair tousled. He held a great white dog, or was it a wolf, by a collar. The animal showed a wide expanse of white teeth, a growl rumbling in its throat.

"Duncan Green's been hurt?" Brodie squinted out into the storm. "Hush, Jasper, hold your counsel," he quieted the animal. The creature settled to a low mutter.

"Aye, bad hurt. He fell from his barn roof and hasn't opened his eyes or spoke a word since. Mrs. Green and her daughter would be much obliged for your wife's help."

"Brodie, what is it?" Her golden-red hair a soft cloud about her shoulders, Louisa MacMillan came from the bedroom, pulling a robe about her.

Bloody hell, what a beautiful woman! He hadn't realized the full extent of her appeal that day in the tavern when she'd been dressed in breeches, her hair hanging in a queue from beneath a cap.

"Smith here says Duncan Green has been bad hurt and needs your help."

"Come in, Mr. Smith. Please wait while I dress and gather up my medical supplies. Brodie, saddle Snow." She whirled and strode back into the room from which she'd emerged.

"I'll fetch her horse," Douglas said. "I'm fair soaked to the skin already, and"—he paused as a baby wailed from the second chamber—"I reckon you have duties here."

"Aye." Brodie started to turn toward the sound, but paused to glance back at Douglas. "Hers is the white mare." He paused, then continued, "You've done a good deed this night. I'm hopin' the Greens will be

119

fittin' grateful."

****

"How is he?" Douglas asked the question the moment Morag answered his knock on the kitchen door at daylight the following morning. After stabling Louisa MacMillan's mare and Lady, he'd spent the night in the barn. He'd told Louisa he'd be there if she needed him, and she'd acknowledged his offer with a curt nod.

"He's awakened, but very weak." Her lovely face, pale and with dark circles under her eyes, told the tale of a long, anxious night. "Mrs. MacMillan is still with him. She says he'll recover, but he'll need at least a week in bed, and then only light work for another two."

"Well, I'd call that right good news." Douglas heaved a deep breath.

"Yes, it is. Nevertheless, there is farm work to be done…and the wheat in the lower field is ripe for the harvest." She forced a weak smile. "I expect we'll manage. Now, I have yet another favor to ask of you."

"Aye?"

"Mrs. MacMillan will be leaving soon and asks if you will saddle her mare."

"Aye, aye, no trouble at all." He started to turn away, but her words stopped him.

"Mr. Smith."

"Aye?"

"I've not had time to prepare a proper breakfast, and Mother is engaged with Father, but there are bread and butter and a fresh pot of tea. Mrs. MacMillan is partaking at the moment. You're most welcome to join her."

"I thank you, Mistress, but I'd best be getting the lady's mare saddled and be on my way. I have to be at work at the tavern soon."

"Bread and tea are a poor recompense for what you did last night. I wish there was some way I might repay our debt to you for your valiant ride to fetch Mrs. MacMillan."

"You might call me Douglas." He faced her squarely, letting a soft grin curl his lips.

"That's hardly…" she began.

"It will be more than enough, Mistress." This time he did swing away and head for the barn, whistling.

****

"I'm wondering if I might trouble you for a bit of leave from my job." Douglas faced Frank Miller as the pair was cleaning up from the noon meal crowd.

"To work on your homestead?" The big man, involved in gathering up plates and utensils, glanced over at him.

"No, no." He avoided his employer's eyes and continued to wipe the table top. "It's just that…"

"Just that what?" Frank Miller had paused in his work and was all out staring at him.

"I've told you Duncan Green was bad hurt last night."

"Aye?"

"He's got wheat standing in the field, ripe for the harvesting. Tomorrow, once it dries out from last night's rain, would be fair time for cutting."

"And you're thinking you can cut it and gather it into sheaves, all on your own?" The tavern owner headed for the kitchen with the plates. "You'd need a crew of able-bodied men to do that up in a day."

"I don't have a crew of able-bodied men." Douglas followed him, annoyance rising. "All I've got is me, and I intend to do the best I can."

"Aye, well, we'll see about that." Frank Miller went to the hearth, where a large roast was on a spit, and gave it a turn. "Riverhaven may have more than its share of former rogues and rebels, but it comes together whenever one of us is in need of help. Wait until tonight, laddie, and you'll see what I mean. Now get on with your work and don't waste time worrying about Duncan Green and his grain."

Puzzled, Douglas headed into the kitchen to set about the task of washing dishes.

****

Douglas was pulling a pint for a customer that evening when Frank Miller reached under the bar and pulled out a pistol. Douglas watched as the man checked its prime. The tavern was well filled and noisy but nothing to warrant taking armed action.

When his employer raised the weapon and fired it into the boards above his head, Douglas shied back. The room instantly quieted as all eyes turned to the big man brandishing the pistol.

"Gentlemen, now that I have your attention…" A snigger ran through the crowd before Frank Miller continued. "I will bring a bit of news to your notice. Duncan Green has been sore injured in a fall from his barn roof. He will not be able to work for a few weeks, and his wheat is ripe. I know most of you are done with harvesting, but we must get together to help out the Green family."

A slight mutter ran through the room.

"I know, I know," the tavern owner was quick to continue. "He let it go longer than he should have, missed out on the round of harvesting, and now most of you are busy at other autumn tasks, but that's no reason for us not to help. Didn't he help out with your gathering?"

"He were late puttin' in his crops," a burly man spoke up. "He were too busy fixin' up that house of his to suit that vixen of a wife."

"That may be so," Frank Miller continued, humor in his tone, "but all the more reason to help the poor soul."

Laughter broke out.

"All right, Frank. We'll be there bright and early day after tomorrow…once things have dried out a might. And we'll round up the teetotalers who aren't here tonight." More laughter erupted.

The customers went back to their drinking. Douglas was left staring in amazement.

"Hie, there, laddie, another pint, if you please, and one for my friend."

A customer's request brought him back to the moment.

"Aye, aye, right away, sir." He hurried to comply, a warm feeling inside. Frank Miller had been right. This community of rogues and rebels came together when the need arose.

****

Douglas paused to wipe sweat out of his eyes. The sun blazed down on the harvesters laboring with scythes in the Green family's wheat field. Hot work and no doubt about it, but an honest endeavor, something he realized he enjoyed and appreciated. He sucked in a deep breath as he returned to swinging the implement.

"Hie, there, laddie." He stopped again, this time at the sound of his brother's voice. "You're doing a right fine job…for a bartender. Almost as if you've done such work before."

Turning, he saw Brodie MacMillan. Shirtless and glistening with sweat like himself, the millwright leaned on his scythe and grinned at him.

"I've laid my hand to many tasks over the years."

"Aye, I imagine you have." Brodie narrowed his eyes as he looked at Douglas. "I'd wager your past would make an interestin' tale."

"As perhaps would your own."

"Ah, so you've been listenin' to tavern gossip." Good humor brightened Brodie's expression. "Well, I'd advise you to take it all with a grain of salt. A man's past deeds often heighten over the years…and ales." He returned to swinging his scythe at the standing wheat. "Now, we'd best get back to work, rememberin' a prime law here in Riverhaven—A man's past is his past."

****

At midday Douglas sat on the ground in the shade of the farmhouse, his plate filled with potatoes and carrots covered with melting butter and slices of meat in some kind of a sweet sauce, the likes of which he'd never eaten. Who would have believed meat in a sugary gravy could be so tasty and tender?

The other workers were similarly situated, enjoying food from the huge pots on a table constructed of planks and sawhorses near the farmhouse door. Women kept bringing more and more containers from the kitchen, leaving Douglas to wonder at how they were managing on this warm day in a room that must have been seething with heat from the wood fire required to cook so much food.

"How do you find it?" Jerking a thumb at the meat on Douglas's plate, Brodie MacMillan came to sit down beside him, heaping bowl in hand.

"Right good, but I'm hard pressed to know what it is."

"Moose meat boiled in maple syrup. Harvested in early spring, it can be right tough and not much of a pleasure to eat, but cooked this way…" Brodie smacked his lips and used his fingers to pull a piece from the large portion in front of him. "Laddie, you can't get better. The Indians taught us the trick." He stuffed it into his mouth.

"Aye," Douglas replied vaguely, his interest taken by Morag, who'd come out of the house carrying a tray of sliced bread.

"But I'm thinkin' you've got sweeter thoughts on your mind." Following Douglas's gaze, Brodie chuckled.

Douglas returned his attention to his food, embarrassed that his brother had caught him staring after Morag.

"Hardly," he muttered.

"Come, now, laddie, it's only natural for a young buck such as yourself to have eyes for the lovely Morag." Brodie finished chewing the meat and began to cut up potatoes and carrots. "Too bad that witch of a mother makes it next to impossible for a man to court the lass. She's wastin' away, and that's for sure. She needs a good man…such as yourself."

"But, as you've said, her mother will have none of it."

"Aye, well, never give up hope, laddie." Brodie squinted him a conspiratorial wink. "Where there's life, there's hope." He pointed to Douglas's forearm. "By the by, that scar looks more like you got kicked by a horse than that you fell onto a bit of hot iron."

"It was a long time ago." Douglas rolled down his sleeve and stood. "I see they've brought out pies. I haven't had a piece of one in a dog's age. Do you want me to fetch you some?"

"Aye, aye, that you can."

But as Douglas moved away, he caught the wondering curiosity in his brother's tone.

****

At the tavern, Douglas moved among the tables, gathering up deserted tankards and wiping tables. The harvesting had been finished at the Green farm. The work had been hard, but he'd gotten to see Morag both in the fields as she worked stacking sheaves and later around the meal tables. Although he'd refrained from making open conversation with her, they'd exchanged a word here and there and looks…ah, those looks.

Lost in remembrance, he moved to clear a table close to the door. Four men sat nearby, glasses in hand, the bottle of whisky three of them had purchased in the center of the table. The fourth man Douglas had come to recognize as a ne'er-do-well named Michael Kelly. The man spent his time conniving to garner free drinks on the pretext of having a crippled right arm, but Douglas had seen him using it as well as the left when he thought no one was looking. The man regularly became loud and offensive when gone in drink, and Douglas had been forced to remove him from the tavern on several occasions. Tonight, fueled by whisky provided by his companions, he was nearing that point.

"I tell ya, lads, that Green girl is nothing but a

tease." Michael Kelly's words brought Douglas up short. He continued to wipe down a nearby table, but his ears became peeled to the drunkard's remarks. "She's given every man in this here village one of her sly smiles, then bustles off to hide behind that bitch of a mother's skirts. But I know for a fact"—he leaned across the table in pretended confidence toward his companions—"that Brodie MacMillan once had eyes for her…and we all know that bastard. He never gives up until he gets what he wants." He leaned back in his chair, a smug grin on his dirty, bearded face. "So I'm thinkin' the fair Miss Morag likely isn't so pure anymore."

Douglas could stand no more. Dropping the cleaning rag, his hands grabbed Michael Kelly by his shirt front. Knocking over the drunkard's chair, he yanked him to his feet.

"Shut your filthy mouth!" he snarled. "Miss Green is a lady."

The attention of all the tavern customers turned on the pair.

"Ah, so you have eyes for the little whore," Kelly taunted over yellowed teeth. "Mind you don't let Brodie MacMillan know you have a taste for his bit on the side, or you'll be gettin' the right trouncin'."

"You think so, do you?" Swinging the staggering man about, Douglas grasped him by the shirt collar and seat of his pants and propelled him to the door and out into the street.

Watching Kelly fumble about in the dust as he struggled to orient his whisky-fuzzed mind sufficiently to get back on his feet, Douglas stood in the tavern doorway, chest heaving. *Miserable, foul-mouthed bugger!* When he turned back into the tavern, it was to the applause of the customers.

"Good for you, lad!" one shouted. "That fella is a bit of trash if ever there was any."

Ducking his head, embarrassed by the cheers that followed, Douglas returned to the bar to resume his duties.

"I'm right sorry, sir," he muttered to Frank Miller, who stood, hands on his hips, looking at him.

"No need to apologize, laddie." The tavern owner slapped Douglas on the shoulder and grinned. "Kelly is nothing but a troublemaker. It's high time he got thrown out on his arse."

"He landed on his belly." A corner of Douglas's mouth curled as he relaxed at his employer's attitude.

"Well, arse end up or down, I'm hoping it will keep the lazy bastard out of here for a day or two. It's too much to expect it to last forever. Now, let's get back to work, lad. That bit of excitement has made our customers right thirsty, I'll reckon."

Chapter Fifteen

"Mrs. Green, have you learned what happened in the tavern last evening? I made Ezra harness the team the moment he told me about it."

Involved in making her bed with fresh sheets, Morag heard Lillian Gardiner, her mother's friend, burst into the kitchen below.

"What is it? Mrs. Gardiner, sit yourself down. I swear you're red as a ripe tomato."

Morag moved to the top of the stairs to listen. When she'd heard the woman's wagon drive up faster than usual she knew something was afoot…usually local gossip. The bit of information the woman carried this morning must be particularly virulent to bring her out so early in a rush.

"Well, dear, my Ezra stopped in at that infamous tavern in the village for a drink—of water, mind—last evening on his way home." The woman settled smugly into her narrative. "While he was there, a right donnybrook broke out between that new fellow Douglas Smith and Michael Kelly."

Morag's breath caught in her throat. Had Douglas been injured?

"Not surprising." Morag heard her mother sniff disdainfully. "Michael Kelly is nothing but a troublemaking layabout. And as for that Douglas Smith…well, what can you expect of a Highlander?"

"Of course, my dear. But you'll never guess the cause of this altercation."

"Some drunken disagreement, I'll wager."

"It was your daughter."

Morag's hand flew to cover her mouth.

"My daughter!" Morag heard her mother's cry of horrified disbelief. "But why? What could those two despicable men have to quarrel about concerning my girl? She barely knows either, surely..."

"My dear Mrs. Green, it makes no sense that two men would come to blows over a woman with whom they're not at least casually acquainted. It appears"— and here Lillian Gardiner lowered her voice so that Morag had to venture onto the top step in order to hear—"that Michael Kelly made some disparaging remark about Morag being involved with Brodie MacMillan...in more than a casual way. Mr. Smith took exception to the accusation."

"Good God!" Morag heard a chair scrape the floor and guessed her mother had jumped to her feet. "What an abominable thing to say! As if I'd let my daughter anywhere near that reprobate!"

"Then perhaps you won't be holding Douglas Smith entirely at fault for defending your girl's honor?"

"Holding him at fault? For brawling over my daughter's good name in a house of ill repute?" Hazel Green's words were a shriek. "God in heaven, I'll never be able to hold my head up in this community again!"

"Mrs. Green, I'm sure talk of this incident will soon pass away." Morag caught the false comfort in Lillian Gardiner's tone. "Some other bit of infamy regarding Brodie MacMillan will shortly raise its head to stifle the memory of this nonsense."

"Yet you thought it sufficiently important to have your husband harness your team—a team he no doubt could be using to better purposes—and rush over here to share the news with me!"

"I thought you should know."

"Of course you did! You've always been eager to defame my Morag because she's a hundred times more beautiful than your two ugly hens of daughters! You feel safe spreading tales of tavern disputes over my girl because you know no man will ever come to fisticuffs over *their* honor!"

"Well, I never!" Again Morag heard furniture scuff. "And here I thought I was doing you a favor, giving you the news before you heard it elsewhere, giving you time to come up with a tale to refute this story. Forewarned is forearmed. I'll be going, Mrs. Green, and you may feel safe, knowing I will never inform you of such demeaning events again."

"Morag!" The door had barely slammed behind Lillian Gardiner when her mother's voice, shrill with anger, summoned her. "Come down here this instant!"

"Yes, Mother?" Morag obeyed, her heart pounding, but less, she realized, in trepidation of what her parent would say than with the thrill of it all. Douglas Smith had done battle in her defense. Surely nothing could be more romantic.

"Morag, I'm sure you overheard what that obnoxious woman has said." Her white-faced mother stood in the center of the kitchen, trembling hands clenched at her sides.

"Yes, Mother." Morag wet her lips and struggled to look contrite.

"I can only pray that her words about your being in

any way involved with Brodie MacMillan in the past— or God forbid, presently—are lies, bold-faced lies."

"Of course, Mother." *Only in my imagination...in the past...before Douglas.*

"Will you swear on the Bible?"

"Yes, Mother."

Hazel Green strode into the parlor to return with the thick, black volume.

"Swear." She thrust it toward her daughter.

"Mother, don't you trust me at all?"

"Swear."

"Very well." She placed her hand on the book. "I do so swear."

"Thank you." The words implied very little of gratitude. She headed back into the parlor with the Bible. "Dear God, how are we ever to be viewed as respectable again?"

"I'm going out to milk Bessie." Morag picked up a pail. "It's past her time."

Swinging the container, she headed for the barn, a song in her heart. Perhaps she was on her way to becoming a woman of Louisa MacMillan's ilk...a woman who could inspire a man to fall in love with her to the point of taking to his fists to defend her good name.

At the barn door, she had a sudden inspiration. Setting aside the pail, she cast a furtive glance toward the house. The next instant she was dashing down the woods path she'd used to summon Douglas on the night of her father's accident. She had to know if he'd been injured defending her good name, she told herself, as she ran through the dew-wet undergrowth of early morning.

Down in her heart, she had to admit it was an overwhelming desire to see the hero, the man who had done battle for her. She hoped he hadn't already left for work at the tavern.

As she burst noisily into the clearing beside his cabin, she saw him placing the bar across its door. Lady stood saddled and waiting a few feet away as he turned to leave.

"Miss Green." Startled, he faced her. "Whit are you doing here?"

She was relieved to see he appeared unharmed. At least his handsome countenance bore no traces of a battle.

"I came…" She stuttered out the words, breathless after her run. "I came to see if you'd been injured. A neighbor"—the confession nearly choked her, but she managed to continue—"arrived at our farm this morning…to say you'd been involved in a fisticuffs"—she grappled to continue—"at your place of work." She avoided saying tavern. It seemed crude and unpleasant, hardly the site where a knight errant would do battle over his lady love.

"Aye, well, hardly." He threw the reins over Lady's neck, then paused to turn to her, a somewhat rueful grin curling his lips. "I put out a customer who was being unruly."

"Oh." Suddenly embarrassed by her rash arrival, she wet her lips and rubbed her hands together.

"May I offer you a ride back to your farm?" He stood aside to indicate the stirrup on the mare's left side.

"Oh…oh, no, I thank you. It's a pleasant morning for a walk through the woods," she refused his offer, although the dew-wet skirt of her gown belied the statement.

She swung and headed back the way she'd come. His voice stopped her.

"I thank you, Miss Morag." His remark, thick with that intoxicating Highland brogue, brought a tingle rushing through her body. "I've not had anyone care about my well-being in many a moon."

Overcome by his soft words, she started back down the trail to her parents' farm. She refrained from looking back until she heard him mount the mare and start off at a brisk trot down the lane to the main trail. Only then did she dare to glance back and, through the trees, watch him ride away.

He cared that she'd cared. Did this indicate he might feel still more for her?

With a wistful sigh, she hurried back toward the waiting cow. She couldn't tarry, wrapped up in fanciful dreams. She had to get back to her home and concoct a tale of how Bessie had escaped from the barn and how it had taken her some time to capture and milk the errant bovine.

Chapter Sixteen

"Mr. Smith." Douglas turned back to the bar, from where he'd been placing bottles on a shelf, to see Duncan Green limping across the deserted tavern.

"Yes, sir, how can I be of service?" Surprised by the man's first appearance in the facility since he'd come to work there, Douglas faced him squarely.

"I've come to thank you, young sir, for your help since I've been injured." The man wet his lips and glanced around the room nervously.

Afraid his wife might catch him here. Douglas hazarded the guess.

"No thanks are necessary, Mr. Green. I was only doing my duty as your neighbor."

"Well, nevertheless, your efforts are much appreciated." He placed his hands on the counter and again wet his lips.

"May I get you a tankard of ale?" Douglas didn't know what to say in the ensuing pause.

"No, no." Duncan Green looked down at his boots and shuffled his feet. "It's just that"—he finally looked up—"my wife...and I...want you to stay away from our daughter. It's a hard request to make, after all you've done for us, but you're..."

"A Highlander who works in a tavern." Douglas snapped out the man's reason.

"Look here, lad..." The man fumbled and, in spite

of his stating a request that Douglas stay away from Morag, Douglas felt sorry for him. He'd been sent on a most distasteful mission and was in a miserable position.

"Sir, let me assure you, I respect your daughter as the fine lady she is," he replied, drawing himself up to his full height. "I would cut off my right arm before I allowed harm to come to her or wrong her in any way, but I think it's up to Miss Green to decide with whom she wishes to keep company."

"Then you won't agree never to accost her again?"

"Accost? I dunnae like that word. I would never confront her in any way she felt threatening or inappropriate. Nevertheless, if the lady wishes to speak with me of her own free will, I will not deny her that right."

Duncan Green met Douglas's unflinching gaze. Finally, he lowered his own with a sigh.

"I can see that's the best I'll get from you." He turned and limped toward the door. At the entrance, he stopped and turned back. "But I feel confident you are a man of your word and one who will respect a lady. I bid you good day, sir."

****

Douglas halted Lady on the brow of the hill overlooking the valley that held the Fowler milling operations. Curiosity to see in daylight the business in which his brother held an interest had prompted him to ride out to view it. The night he'd come to fetch Louisa MacMillan to care for Duncan Green had been pitch dark, his view blurred by heavy rain fogging his vision.

On a Sunday such at this day, with most of the valley's inhabitants at church or resting, the mills stood idle, but he could envision it engulfed as a hive of activity. A prosperous-looking establishment with its mills and a number of log houses and outbuildings, it was a community unto its own.

Annoyance swelling his chest, he turned Lady back toward his meager homestead. Some day, he vowed, he'd have a fine place to call his own.

As he trotted the mare homeward, charcoal clouds roiled overhead, swallowing up the hot, humid summer's day blue sky. Thunder rumbled, making Lady toss her head. *Damn!* Wet weather wouldn't be conducive to working on the stable roof. He'd also been hoping to start building a privy to make the place more civilized.

Ah, well, with just him and Lady living there, being civilized wasn't a priority. There would be time for the niceties once the necessities had been seen to.

A jagged bolt of lightning rent the sky. Lady began to prance.

"Whoa, easy, lass." He spoke softly to the nervous mare. "We're near home. I'll have you snug in the stable in no time." To quell her nervousness, he allowed the animal to break into a slow, cavorting gallop in the roll of thunder that followed the flash.

As the first splashes of rain assaulted him, he saw her. Huddled under a massive pine, she clutched a basket in her arms. A stricken expression suffused her face.

"Mistress Morag." He drew rein, leaped to the ground, and hurried to hunker down beside her. "Are you all right?"

"Th…the storm." The explanation stuttered from blanched lips. She looked up at him, eyes wide.

"Ah." He understood. He'd not been overly brave in violent summer storms as a lad. "Hiding under a tree is not a safe place, lass." He spoke softly, as he had to the mare, Highland brogue thick in his tone. "Come." He dared to reach out and place a hand under her elbow. She was trembling as she allowed him to help her to her feet. "We'll not have time to make your father's farm before this storm gets outright nasty. We'll shelter at my cabin."

She hesitated, staring at him. Was she more afraid of the storm or him? A following bolt of lightning and crash of thunder settled the question. She cringed into his arms, her face hidden against his chest. Her small, warm body sent a gush of sensations coursing through him.

Sweet Jesus, lad, get a grip.

"Come." Fighting down his impulses, he indicated the mare standing still but shaking her head nervously. "You ride Lady. I'll lead her."

She paused, glancing from him to the animal. "I...I...can't..." she stammered.

Before she could finish, another bolt of lightning lighted up the dark sky and rain burst with great bucketing force over them. She cried out as she again sheltered against him.

"For sure and certain you can," he shouted above the noise of the storm. "You've done it afore. You know Lady is a gentle soul. She'd not harm you for the world. And give me that thing." He took the basket from her arm and let it slide up along one of his. Before she could protest further, he caught her about the waist. "Throw your leg over her back," he instructed. "Hang onto her mane."

He hoisted her onto the animal.

"Guid, verrae guid." Rain cascaded down his face as he looked up at her and mustered a grin. "We'll be at my place in a thrice, safe as two bugs in a rug."

Her white face gave a slight twitch of acknowledgement. He took the horse's bridle and, jogging by the mare's side, led the animal at a trot toward his cabin. Once in his dooryard, he lifted her to the ground.

"Go inside," he instructed, raising his voice to be heard above the wind, rain, and rumbling thunder. "I'll chust put Lady in her stall and be right in."

She hesitated only a moment, then amid a flash of lightning and a roll of thunder, she darted off to do his bidding. He watched as she removed the bar and scuttled inside. Once he saw her safe, he hurried the drenched, nervous animal to the shelter of the barn.

After he'd seen her stabled, he darted through the storm and into the cabin.

"Heavens!" he gasped, leaning back against the closed door. "Whit a wild day!"

She didn't reply. Standing by the dead hearth where he'd left logs and kindling at the ready, she had her arms wrapped about her. She was shivering violently. Her drenched garments clung to her slender body. A pitiable sight, she brought every protective urge in his body rushing to the fore.

"Sit yourself down." He stepped forward to indicate one of the rocking chairs. "I'll light a fire."

She didn't accept his invitation. Instead she stood watching as he knelt by the hearth to strike flint and steel. Sparks flew, and shortly, flames began to lick up from among the dry kindling and logs.

He stood to watch the fire catch. When he was convinced it would grow, he stepped back and turned to her with a satisfied smirk.

"There. We'll be warm in no time."

"Thank you." She favored him with the shadow of a tremulous smile.

Chapter Seventeen

Morag couldn't believe it. Here she stood in *his* cabin, her thin summer dress drenched so that it molded to every curve of her body. In the firelight illuminating the small building's interior, *he* smiled down at her with all the charm Brodie MacMillan had once held in her most romantic fantasies. No, that was not true. Douglas Smith's appeal was much more potent. His gentleness and caring wasn't greatly overwhelming, yet he was somewhat frightening, with the mysterious shadows of a genuine roué coloring his background as Brodie's had been.

"You must get out of that wet gown." He broke the moment with a shocking idea. "I have a shirt…a clean shirt…that reaches to my knees. It will cover you near to the floor while I dry your clothing by the fire."

"No!" The word burst from her involuntarily. Her hand flew to her throat. How could he suggest such a thing?

"Lass, lass." Again that mesmerizing soft Highland tone that made her innards flutter. "I'll turn away while you change. I promise you, appearances to the contrary, I do know how to behave as a gentleman in such a circumstance." His lips quirked into a gently teasing curve before he sobered. "You'll catch your death if you remain in that drenched getup."

"And what of you?" She found she could construct

a question. "You're drenched as well."

"I've spent more time than you can imagine soaked to the skin, and lived." He took down a long shirt from a peg on the wall. "But you—" He held the garment out to her. "You are a refined lady who I can believe has never spent a single night at the mercy of the elements. Now, no more protesting. Put this on while I stare into the fire."

He shook the garment in front of her. Their gazes met. She could find no ill intent in his outlook, only sincere concern. Gingerly, she accepted the shirt.

"Verrae guid." He turned his back to her and focused his gaze on the burning logs.

The shirt felt softer than she'd expected for a worker's garment. And dry. Wonderfully dry. She turned her back to him and put her hands to the top of her dress. Shortly it fell, together with her undergarments, to the floor about her feet. Heart beating a wild frenzy, she scrambled into his shirt and let the garment slip down over her body. It offered welcome relief from the cold sogginess of her soaked clothing. She smoothed it down around herself. Turning back toward the fire, she saw him, naked to the waist, hanging his wet shirt up near the flames. A small gasp escaped her lips.

"A thousand pardons, mistress." He glanced in her direction. Hastily he crossed the room and reached for another shirt suspended on a peg. "I thought it would take you longer to change clothing." He pulled the dry garment over his head before turning to grin sheepishly at her. "Of course, I'm afraid you've previously seen me *déshabillé*, as the French would say."

Nervously wetting her lips, she could think of no

appropriate reply.

"Come, sit by the fire." He once again indicated the rocking chair. "I'll hang your…clothing…" He hesitated as he looked at the tangle of her discarded items. "Just here, where they'll dry quickly."

With a swipe of his hand, he gathered up the garments and carefully shook them out so that they might get the full benefit of the warmth. As she seated herself and watched his careful spreading out of her gown and chemise, disturbing ideas invaded her mind.

He's done it before. How many other women has he rescued in a storm? How many others has he invited to disrobe in his presence? How many others has he…? She could not allow the train of thought to continue. Instead she spoke.

"Mr. Smith, may I ask you a question?" She could contain it no longer.

"Aye?"

"Is it true you came to fisticuffs with Michael Kelly…because he made a disparaging remark about me?"

"Aye, I'm afeard it's true." He sat down opposite her. "I'm right sorry, Miss Green. Your name should never have been spoken in a tavern."

"But you were not the first to do so, is that not true?" She looked over at him.

"Aye."

"And you were only defending my good name."

"I didn't succeed, though, did I?" He heaved a deep breath. "Perhaps if I hadn't interfered, things wouldn't have gotten to the point that they did, and a story would not have spread."

"Nevertheless, I thank you." She looked demurely

down at her hands. "It…that is, it reminded me of how the knights of old defended ladies' (she deliberately avoided saying 'their ladies') honor."

"Dunnae go painting pretty pictures of it, Mistress. It was a wee bit of a tavern scuffle, nasty as they all are."

Lightning glared, illuminating the interior of the small cabin with a ghastly light, and thunder crashed with an intensity that made the building shudder. Morag cried out and leaped to her feet. The next moment, she was in his arms, sheltered against his broad chest, one strong hand gently stoking her hair.

"Hush, hush," he said softly. "It's naught but a summer storm. You're safe with me, lassie."

He drew her closer, cradling her to him. As their bodies came full length into contact, Morag couldn't suppress the gasp that rose up her throat. The sensations aroused as he pressed her to him made her head spin. Her reality whirled into a mesmerizing place of astonishing feelings of erotic pleasure. In her most romantic dreams, she'd never conjured anything like it.

Could this be love?

The passion in his blue eyes when she looked up at him gave her to believe she was not alone in these wonderful moments of magic. When he lowered his head to kiss her, she soared away into a place of magic. The flash of lightning and cannonade of accompanying thunder that punctuated the moment were beyond her concern.

"Forgive me." As the thunder rumbled off, he stepped back to rub his hands on the back of his breeches.

Stunned, Morag felt as if ice water had been

thrown over her. Why was he apologizing for what had been the most wonderful moments of her life?

****

Guid God, what did I do? I had no right.

"I…I'll make tea." He stumbled out the only words he could find to alleviate the awkwardness.

He reached for a pot of water beside the hearth and put it on the spit over the flames. Lightning again lighted the room, but this time with less intensity. The storm was moving away. Out of the corner of his eye, he saw she merely flinched.

Perhaps feeling safe here with me. Although how she could, after I behaved like a randy…

"Allow me, Mr. Smith." She came to kneel beside him. "I'm quite skilled at making tea."

Is she forgiving me?

"I'm right sure you are." He stood, took a small tin box from the mantel, and handed it to her. "I never mastered the task."

As she turned her attention to the chore, he settled back into his chair. She was willing to move on, to put his unfortunate behavior behind her. In spite of his regrets for his actions, he couldn't suppress the warm feeling suffusing his chest. First that kiss and now watching her doing the wifely duty of preparing tea… He willed this time to stretch out forever.

"Mr. Smith." Shortly she'd stood from the hearth, a steaming pot in her hand. "I see but one cup on your table. Do you have more?"

"No, but dunnae fret." Instantly he was on his feet and taking one of the candles from the flask on the mantel. "You use it, lass. This"—he held up the empty bottle—"will suit me right down to the ground." A dash of embarrassment flashed over him as he realized how poorly equipped his home truly was.

"Very well." She hesitated only a moment. "Place it on the table, please. It will make pouring easier."

"Oh, aye, aye." He hastened to do her bidding, then watched as she poured tea first into the cup and then, with a skill he admired, into the flask.

"I fear I have no milk or sugar," he said as he picked it up. He tried to refrain flinching at the heat of the tea burning through the handle-less container.

"I'm quite comfortable with it as it is."

Her confidence as she moved past him to reseat herself by the fire pleased him intensely. What if someday she would be actual mistress of his home?

Stop meandering! He brought himself up short, took a quick swig of the hot tea, and stifled a choke as it burned his mouth.

"Is it too hot?" Her concern made him wince more than the scalding liquid. "Or perhaps, too strong? Mother always says I add too many leaves to the pot."

"No, no—" He gulped to retain normal speech. "It's fine...perfect, in fact. I've never tasted better. Would you like some bread? I have bread...and butter." He indicated the sideboard.

"No, thank you. Hot tea is all I could ask for after such a wetting. Come, please. Sit by the fire with me."

Taking the other rocking chair, he obeyed.

Silence, except for the remains of the storm moving away, invaded the cabin. Finally she spoke.

"You said you were frequently cold and wet," she finally asked softly. "Were you often from home?"

Slowly he placed his tea flask on the floor and stared down at it. *How should I answer her? I dunnae want to lie.*

"I've not had a place to call home for a goodly number of years," he replied.

"You've been on your own?" The sympathy in her beautiful blue eyes encouraged him to continue.

"Aye, since I was a young lad."

"What of your parents?"

"Dead."

"Have you no other kin?"

"None as would be worth mentioning."

"How sad." He saw genuine sadness in her eyes. Afraid of his reaction, he hastened on.

"You get used to it," he muttered gruffly. "And…" He forced a grin. "You have more than a few adventures."

"It appears you're planning to make a home here." She also managed to change the tone of their conversation as she let her gaze roam over the cabin. "You've made a fine beginning at repairs and furnishings."

"I hope to make it a decent place to live before the snow flies. There's a whale of a lot to do. I must repair the barn and lay in hay for my mare. Then I'll have to get a supply of firewood to warm this hovel." He looked around the cabin.

"It's far from a hovel." She was quick to correct him. "It's already a tidy, snug shelter. You've made a world of difference."

"Thank you, miss, but I fear it's far from what you're accustomed to." He took a swallow of tea from the flask. In spite of its unorthodox container, now that it had cooled, it tasted good, the best he'd had in ages. He liked tea.

"Father and Mother came to this country shortly before I was born." She focused down into her cup. "Father had received a legacy back in England. It made it possible for him to purchase land, build a house—the house we're presently living in—and a barn. He also purchased stock and thus set our family up in farming."

"You were fortunate." Douglas drew a deep breath. "While I, too, came here with a bit of coin, I fear it's likely nowhere near that which your father had. Buying the mare and purchasing this bit of a homestead is about all I can manage…at present."

"But you have your wages from…your place of employment." She glanced furtively over at him.

"Ah, aye, but they're not great. I mainly work for a room, food, and a place to keep my mare when I'm engaged at the…tavern."

He stumbled out the last in a more subdued tone.

"It's honest labor." She surprised him by replying. "Mr. Frank Miller is a respected member of the community…no matter what my mother says. My father declares him to be a pillar of Riverhaven, a fine and honest business man."

"And how do you feel about…my place of employment?" The question was out before he could stop it.

"The same." She stuck out her chin and held her head up. "Honest work is honest work."

"Aye." The word came out softly as he dropped his gaze to his hands…hands that had been party to more than their share of nefarious deeds.

"But now you plan to be a farmer." She took up the conversation with a new brightness that brought his attention back to her lovely face. "It's a hard life, but a rewarding one." She smiled at him.

"Aye, my feelings exactly." Enthusiasm came into his words. "Mr. Miller has suggested that what this area needs is a good market farm, one that can supply produce to the mills and lumber camps. He believes there is a good living to be made by whoever invests in such an endeavor."

"I agree, oh, indeed I agree." Her zeal for the subject delighted him.

He found himself falling into a description of future plans, of his ideas on how the land might be cleared, on what crops he saw as the most profitable, on how he could stretch his remaining capital to buy a team of drays, a plow, wagon, and seed. The passion he saw reflected in her eyes encouraged him to keep pouring out his thoughts until finally, feeling more than a trifle embarrassed, he paused.

"What marvelous plans," she breathed.

"Then, you no' think I'm daft?" He sought approval from her as he'd never sought it from anyone in his life.

"Of course not. I love farming. Your future will be full of achievement and pleasure."

"You love farming?" A flutter of hope winged about in his chest.

"Definitely. I enjoy getting up in the early morning when the dew is on the grass and going out to milk Bessie and collect eggs. And the seasons! How I enjoy the changes of scenery and tasks on our farm. Tilling, planting, harvesting—all bring their rewards."

Engrossed in conversation, they barely noticed when the storm ended. It rumbled away into the distance as they continued to sit in front of the low-burning fire savoring the tea. Douglas drew a deep breath, hoping she felt as happy and content as he did.

"You make a fine cup of tea," he said finally.

"Thank you. I do believe I am much more adept at it than I am at riding." She cast him a twinkling glance that utterly bewitched him.

"Given a bit of practice, you can become a right fine little rider. You have the hands and seat for it."

The moment the last was out of his mouth, he cursed himself. Surely a gentleman didn't mention such as a lady's seat, even if he were referring to her proficiency in the saddle.

"Forgive me, Mistress Green." He fumbled for words. "I've no' the manners of a gentleman."

"I'm complimented that you think I have the hands…and seat for riding." This time she all-out grinned at him. "To become as skilled as Mrs. MacMillan would give me great pleasure."

"And given permission, I'd take great pleasure in teaching you…me and Lady."

They smiled at each other.

The moment was fleeting. Pounding at the door ended it. When Douglas lifted the bar, Duncan Green, flanked by two burly men, burst inside.

Chapter Eighteen

"You'll be off to Fredericton as soon as I can arrange transport." Hazel Green fussed about the hearth, her face contorted with outrage. "I'll not have a child of mine the center of finger-pointing and crude remarks. Out of sight is out of mind, my mother always used to say, and…"

"And your father as well." Duncan Green spoke up suddenly. The remark brought an abrupt end to the tirade. He gave his wife a knowing glance.

"Well, at any rate, Morag must leave Riverhaven. In the provincial capital, where no one knows of this disgrace, she might have at least a chance at finding a decent husband."

"I won't go." Morag, seated beside the hearth mending an apron, said softly but with such resolution both parents turned to stare at her. "Douglas…Mr. Smith and I have done nothing wrong. I refuse to be sent away with him in prison for something of which we're not guilty." Although she was trembling, she stood and stuck out her chin in what she meant as a defiant gesture. "In fact, if you persist in this plan, I'll say we *did* behave…inappropriately."

"Morag!" Her name was a shriek from her mother's lips.

"Child, you wouldn't…" Now even her father was dismayed.

"I would." She swallowed hard, then continued, "The only way I will go in peace and make no embarrassing allegations will be if you both agree to have the charges against Mr. Smith dismissed and any hint of guilt expunged from his name."

"Charges dropped…?" Hazel Green stared at her as if thunderstruck.

"Those are my terms." She gathered up her mending and, head held high, headed for the stairs and her bedroom above. "I advise you to consider them most seriously."

Somehow she managed to march out of the room and up the steps. But once in the sanctuary of her bedroom, she dropped onto her narrow bed, limp and spent.

****

"Mrs. Morgan, please excuse me, but I had to come." Morag gasped out the words as she stood panting on the manse doorstep.

"Come in, my dear, come in." Mary Morgan took her arm and drew her inside, out of the wild wind buffeting the surroundings. "We'll have tea."

Morag took the time it required to follow the minister's wife into the warm, cheerful room and be seated to regain her breath and some of her composure. In her wild dash from her home, she hadn't been able to decide how to begin or what to say once she'd reached Mary Morgan.

She needn't worry. Mary Morgan allowed her to recover while she went to fetch tea and a plate of scones. When she'd returned with a tray, Morag had decided what she had to say.

"Mrs. Morgan," she began as the woman seated

herself at a small table and poured tea into a pair of cups. "By now, I'm sure you've heard what transpired at Mr. Smith's cabin and you most likely also know he's been put in the village jail."

"Yes, sadly, I am aware." Her companion handed her a cup, sympathetic concern reflected in her expression. "I'm so very sorry. It's been a terrible time for you…and Mr. Smith."

"Mrs. Morgan, I tell you Mr. Smith did nothing untoward." She leaned toward her confidant, fervently hoping she could convince her of the true state of the affair. "He simply rescued me from the storm. He took me to his cabin because it was closer than our farm, and he gave me dry clothes and…"

Here she stumbled as memories of that kiss, that all-consuming kiss, flooded her mind. Mary Morgan waited silently as she gathered her thoughts to proceed.

"He did kiss me, Mrs. Morgan." She decided to plunge ahead with total honesty. She could do nothing else if she hoped to enlist this woman's understanding and compassion. "And…" She stumbled over the continued confession. "And I was willing to allow for more."

"But he stopped." Her companion's voice was soft.

"Yes." Morag dropped her gaze to her teacup. "I'm not sure why. Perhaps he found me too bedraggled from the storm, unattractive, perhaps…"

"Perhaps, and most likely, he stopped out of respect for you." The minister's wife reached out to cover Morag's hand with hers. She waited a moment before continuing. "Do you love him, Morag?"

Morag looked up to meet her companion's sincere, searching eyes and could find no other reply.

"Yes, I do, but the only way my parents will dismiss the charge against him is if I go to Fredericton and promise to stay there until I've found a suitable husband." She paused, reluctant to tell the minister's wife of her rash intimidation, but finally burst out, "Mrs. Morgan, I threatened to spread the tale that…that Mr. Smith and I had truly done what they were accusing us of if they persist in their plans to send me away."

"Oh, child, that would be terribly rash." Mary Morgan reached out to cover her hand with hers. "You must realize that would make matters even worse for Mr. Smith."

"I do…now…but at the time I was so angry, so upset…"

"Then let's put that possibility aside." Mary Morgan leaned back in her chair. "Given what you've told me, I can only assume from his actions that Mr. Smith has similar feelings toward you."

"Do you really believe so?" Morag couldn't keep the eagerness out of her tone as she looked at the other woman.

"I do. But"—she drew a deep breath—"we have a conundrum, don't we? Mr. Smith is in jail on a charge of seduction and your parents are dead set against your ever seeing him again."

"We?" Morag quickly caught at the pronoun in the woman's first sentence.

"You and I. We must put our heads together and come up with a solution to this problem. Never fear, my dear. You won't be alone with this trouble. And I think I know just the man to enlist in our efforts. Help me harness our team, and we'll head off to consult him."

****

As they drove down the rutted wagon road toward the Fowler Mills, Morag glanced sideways at the woman handling the team and wondered about her. Mary Morgan was certainly not what one would expect in a minister's wife. She most definitely had a mind of her own and was quite ready to act as her conscience dictated.

"Why have you chosen Mr. MacMillan to help Douglas?" Finally, Morag could contain the question no longer. She'd been astonished when her companion had told her of her choice of allies as they harnessed the team, but she had managed to hold her counsel until now. "I know he's had…experience with the law…but still…"

"That's exactly the reason." Mary Morgan paused for a moment before glancing at her companion. "Morag, I've no doubt you've heard rumors about my past as well as my husband's."

"Yes."

"Well, most of them are true. Edward and I were rebels back in the Highlands. For a time we rode with Brodie—Brazen Brodie he was known as in those days, and Harry Wallace known as Highland Harry. My name was Iona—thus my daughter's name—and Edward was Lachlan Cameron." She threw Morag a smug smirk. "We were a formidable foursome."

"So if Brodie MacMillan's past is the reason for choosing him to help Douglas, why not Harry Wallace…or even your husband?"

"Because, my dear, both Harry and Edward have become respectable members of the community. Brodie has not. He continues to circumvent authority when he sees the need"—she clucked to the sauntering team—"and that's exactly the kind of man we need at the moment."

****

Mary Morgan drew her team of Percherons to a halt in the mill yard of the Fowler mill. Some of the workers not involved in running the saws paused to stare at the two women. A yell from Brodie MacMillan, who'd noticed the visitors as he stood beside the great saws, sent them back to work. When they were once more engaged in their tasks, he strode down the ramp toward the wagon, brushing sawdust from his clothing.

"Ladies"—his demeanor changed from tough boss to affable friend as he approached—"whit can I do for you?"

His shirt was soaked with sweat, his hair tousled, yet as he grinned up at them, he lacked none of the blatant charm that had once sent Morag's pulses racing. Now, with Douglas in peril, that impulse was all but gone. Still, he was a handsome, virile creature…

"Brodie"—Mary Morgan got right to the point—"we've come to enlist your assistance…to employ your skills and knowledge."

"Oh, aye?" He squinted up at them, suspicion crossing his countenance. "And whit might they be?"

"Is there somewhere we might talk…privately?"

"There's no one to home at my house. Louisa and the bairn are spendin' the day with Margaret Wallace, makin' preserves." Agile as a cat, he leaped into the back of the wagon.

"You lads!" he shouted to the workmen. "I'll be gone for a time, but I'll not tolerate any slackin' off, you hear?" Turning to the women, he grinned. "You have to keep those Irishmen on their toes, mind. Drive on…Iona."

Shortly, Morag and Mary were seated in the MacMillan cabin.

"Tea?" Brodie gestured toward the embers on the hearth.

"No, thank you, Brodie," Mary Morgan replied.

"Well, then, I'm right glad." He heaved himself into a chair opposite them. "I never quite got the knack of makin' the brew. Now, whit can I do for you charmin' lasses?"

"Douglas Smith has been accused of accosting Miss Green. He's been charged and thrown into the jail."

"Whit?" Brodie MacMillan lurched forward on his chair. "Bloody hell—excuse me, ladies—has Cal taken leave of his senses? Douglas is a good lad, a decent lad, if ever I met one."

"Of course he is." Mary Morgan's tone was undeniable. "But Mr. Green…or Mrs. Green, to be exact, is insisting on such charges being laid. Morag, here, the supposed victim, swears Douglas made not a single reprehensible move. He behaved as a perfect gentleman when they were trapped in his cabin during that summer storm yesterday. Her parents simply won't allow her to have her say. Brodie, we have to find a way to help Douglas, or he could face a serious prison sentence…or perhaps a flogging."

"And so you've come to me, rememberin' as how I have firsthand experience in such matters." A sardonic grin curled his lips.

"Yes."

"Why didn't you go to Harry?" He stood and went

to the cupboard to take down a flask. "As head of the Fowler operations, he has a lot of influence in this community."

"Because—" Mary stood and went to stand beside him at the sideboard. "We...I thought this was a situation you were best qualified to remedy." As he took down a cup and splashed whisky into it, she reached for two more and put them in front of him.

He looked at her for a moment. Then, a corner of his mouth quirking, he poured a measure into each. Mary turned to Morag and handed one to her.

"Sip on this," she said. "You've been through so much. It will steady your nerves."

Morag hesitated, then raised the cup to her lips. How wrong could it be, with the minister's wife offering it?

The sharp taste made her grimace and jerk back.

"A bit of a shock the first time." Brodie MacMillan grinned at her. "But you'll find it right fortifyin' in a pinch. From the color of your pretty face, I'm right sure this is one of those moments." He took Mary's arm and drew her back to sit at the table with Morag and himself. "You ladies enjoy your wee dram and let me reflect for a bit."

Chapter Nineteen

"Got yourself in a bit of a scrape, did you?" Brodie MacMillan swaggered into the cell area of the small jail and closed the door that separated it from the magistrate's office behind him.

Without getting up from the straw pallet that served as his bed, Douglas glared up at the visitor asking the inane question.

"Bloody hell, I feel right naked." Fingers hooked into his belt, Brodie came to stand close in front of the bars. "Cal, actin' like an ass of a magistrate, demanded I give him my sword and pistol before I could see you. You'd think"—he grinned—"that I'm some kind of threat to keepin' you incarcerated. I've been in there more times than I care to recall, you might have heard. Maybe he's afeared I've mastered the way to get out. Any road, not a nice place to spend a lad's time."

"Then why did you come?" Annoyance filled Douglas's retort.

"To see what I can do for a fellow Highlander." He drew a deep breath that swelled him up until he looked as if he were lord and master of the situation. "Now…" He drew confidingly close and spoke in a soft voice. "I could break you out of here in two shakes of a lamb's tail and see that you got a fair head start for the border, but I'm guessin' that you'd rather I cleared your name so that you can once again take up with the fair Morag."

"Small chance of that." Douglas guffawed. "Even if I could get the charges against me cleared away, there's no way her parents will allow me within a mile of her."

"Now, now, don't go despairin'. There was a spell I couldn't even dream of bein' with Louisa for the rest of my life. Then a bunch of stuff happened and now she's my wife and mother of my bairn."

"You've been lucky." Douglas didn't relinquish his place on his pallet as he replied with sarcasm.

"Lucky and clever as a fox in a henhouse. Now, listen, laddie, I'm goin' to ride out to Duncan Green's farm and talk sense to the man…without that harridan of a wife around. I'll be remindin' him he owes you for settin' up that harvestin'."

"Frank Miller did that."

"Aye, well, you set the wheels in motion, didn't you? And dunnae forget, it was you came for my wife after Duncan's accident."

"Nothing more than was my duty."

"Ah, aye, your duty. Well, well, enough. I'm ridin' out to the Green farm just now. I'm sure Miss Morag will defend you. Furthermore, I know Duncan will appreciate a dram of good Scotch whisky." He tapped on a swell in his vest pocket, winked, paused, and finally squinted in at Douglas to ask the question. "You truly didn't do anything untoward, did you, laddie?"

"Whit! You come here, offering to help me, and yet you ask such a question?"

"Simmer down, simmer down. I had to ask. You're a young buck livin' alone, and Miss Morag is one lovely lass." He paused before continuing. "Her mother's not let her talk to Captain Cameron to give her side of the story. The old witch says the lass is too upset to be questioned on such indelicate matters. Fancy a wee dram?" He pulled a flask from the pocket he'd indicated previously and held it through the bars to Douglas.

"Aye." Douglas pulled himself to his feet and crossed the cell to accept it. He yanked out the stopper and raised it to his mouth.

"That'll help for a bit." Brodie accepted the flask when Douglas handed it back to him. "Now I'm off to set the wheels turnin' to get you out of this foul-smellin' dump." A grin spread across Brodie MacMillan's face. "You've not got the look of a lad who'd have to resort to force to get a lass's attention. I reckon as how you might be half decent-lookin' once you're cleaned up and put in proper clothes."

"Argh!" Douglas snarled his disgust.

"Dunnae despair." Brodie turned and headed for the door. "I've a feelin' Duncan Green will listen to what I have to say. Cal, let me the hell out of here," he bellowed to the magistrate. "I've spent more than enough time in this stinkin' hole."

****

"On your feet, Mr. Smith." Captain Caleb Cameron entered the prison area and strode to Douglas's cell. He carried a metal ring with a collection of keys dangling from it. "You're being released. The charges against you are being dropped."

Startled, Douglas stumbled to stand from where he'd been sitting, dozing, on the cell floor, his back against the wall. He watched with disbelief as the magistrate inserted the key and opened the barred door.

"I'm free to go?"

"Yes. Duncan Green has lifted his claims against you…on a condition."

"Condition?"

"That you never attempt to see his daughter again and that you conscientiously avoid all contact with her in the future. I've a document drawn up in my office that you're to sign before you leave this building. Do you agree?"

Douglas hesitated only briefly before nodding.

It's for the best.

"Good, very good." The magistrate selected a key from the ring and thrust it into the lock on the cell.

Suspicious of this turn of events, Douglas moved cautiously out of the cell and faced the captain.

"This isn't some treachery?" he asked, narrowing his eyes to assess the magistrate. "You've not got a pair of soldiers waiting outside with muskets ready to bring me down the minute I stick my nose out of this place?"

"You may have suffered under such perfidy in the Old Country, but here, under my jurisdiction, you have nothing to fear on that score. Now"—the magistrate stepped back—"into the office and the signing of your pledge. Afterwards, I'd advise you to get yourself off to the tavern and a bit of soap and water."

"Aye, aye." Douglas caught a twinkle of humor in the eyes of the otherwise stern-faced official.

"Oh, and Mr. Smith." The captain's words stopped him as he reached the door to the office area.

"Aye?" Without looking back, Douglas paused with his hand on the latch.

"It shouldn't be all that difficult to keep the terms of your release, since Miss Morag is shortly to be shipped off to Fredericton."

"Shipped off to…?"

"You heard correctly."

With a sinking feeling in his gut, Douglas opened the thick plank door and walked out of the jail.

Shipped off to Fredericton, hundreds of miles beyond his reach. Shipped off, more than likely, to meet what her mother considered a suitable man. He sucked in a deep breath. *For the best. Morag Green deserves a husband chosen from among respectable men.*

In the small office, the magistrate shoved a document across his desk.

"Sign," he ordered.

Douglas gave him a disparaging look before reading the contract.

"By this document, I, Douglas Smith, agree never to have contact, casual or otherwise, with Miss Morag Green, spinster of this county, daughter of farmer Duncan Green and his wife Hazel. Violation of this agreement is punishable by imprisonment and possible deportation."

Bloody hell!

"Well? Are you unwilling to sign? Am I to put you back in that cell?" Captain Cameron dipped a quill in ink and held it out to him. "Or are you unable to read and write?"

"I'm no' an ignoramus," he snapped, the terms of the agreement he was being forced to sign roiling a sickness in his gut. Grabbing the quill, he scrawled his name across the bottom of the page.

"Obviously not," the magistrate said mildly. "Now, off with you. I've a shipyard to run."

"So you're free, laddie." Grinning, Brodie MacMillan greeted him the minute he stepped from the building that housed the magistrate's office and the jail.

"Aye." Surprised, Douglas stopped.

"Good, good. Only that harridan of a mother would push forward such foolishness. Of course, the father laid the charges before Cal, but I strongly suspect he was forced to do so by that bitch…beg pardon…witch of a wife. Now, how about a pint?" He slapped Douglas on the shoulder, affability lighting up his face.

"Verrae guid." Relaxing, Douglas lapsed into his Highland brogue and fell into step with Brodie to head toward the tavern. *What the hell. Life went on. No sense brooding about what would never be.*

"But first…" His companion chuckled. "Maybe a bit of a wash…and a shave."

****

"I'd like to know what made Duncan Green drop the charges against me." A half hour later, washed and in clean clothing, a tankard of ale in his hand, Douglas sat in the tavern, deserted at the early morning hour except for himself, Brodie, and Frank Miller.

"Ah, the man chust came to his senses." Brodie quaffed a long drink.

"With a boot in the arse from the manager of the only grist mill in a hundred miles." Frank Miller chuckled.

"Whit?" Douglas looked sharply at Brodie. "Whit's he saying?"

"Nothin', nothin'." Brodie focused on the drink in his hand.

"Tell the lad, Brodie. He deserves to know." The tavern owner pressed the point.

"Ah, verrae well." Brodie continued to stare into his ale. "I may have suggested the Fowler mill might not be available to grind Duncan's grain this autumn if certain daft charges weren't lifted against a Highlander friend of mine."

"Why would you go to such lengths…for me?" Astonished, Douglas stared at the man.

"Because I was once in your position, because I know how it feels to be falsely accused." Brodie looked up at him. "Prison is no place for an innocent man…or even a guilty one"—he cast his companions a mischievous quirk of his lips—"dependin' on what he's supposed to have done. Any road…" He slanted Douglas a sideways glance. "I had a visit from Miss Morag and the minister's wife. Mistress Morag declared you'd done no wrong and Mrs. Morgan supported her. On such strong evidence, I could hardly, in good conscience, allow you to remain incarcerated."

"Morag…Miss Green went to the minister's wife…on my behalf?"

"Aye." Brodie cast him a conspiratorial wink. "It appears the lass has more than a tad of feelings for you, laddie…and the courage to act on their behalf."

"Not that it matters." After a moment of elation at the news that Morag had gone to lengths to intervene on his behalf, Douglas dropped his tone as he recalled the paper he'd signed in the magistrate's office. "I've signed a pledge never to see her again."

"Dunnae despair, laddie." Brodie stood, slapped on his cap, quaffed the last of his ale, and headed for the door. "True love always finds a way."

"Thank you," Douglas remembered to call after him.

Without turning back, Brodie waved a hand as he strode out into the street.

"I owe that man." Douglas shook his head ruefully. "I owe him a great deal."

"Aye, well, no one can ever honestly accuse Brodie MacMillan of not having a good heart." Frank Mills stood and picked up the empty tankards. "But mind, laddie, he can be, at times, a law unto himself. Don't get yourself too involved with him."

Chapter Twenty

Morag folded clothing slowly and placed the items into the battered trunk that had once carried her parents' possessions from the Old Country many years before. It had been several days since she'd heard from either Brodie MacMillan or Mary Morgan. At first she'd told herself that even if Brodie had come up with a solution to their quandary, he could not ride out to her parents' farm with the news. But Mary Morgan could. Therefore she deduced her going to Fredericton offered the only solution to seeing Douglas freed.

She paused as she heard her mother greeting someone at the door. Mary Morgan's voice brought her instantly alert.

"Morag." Shortly her mother was calling up the narrow stairs. "Mrs. Morgan is here. She wishes to speak to you."

"Yes, Mother." Eager to learn the purpose of the woman's visit, she dropped the gown she'd been folding and hastened down the steps.

"Morag, my dear." Mary Morgan, dressed in a plain cotton gown and faded sunbonnet, stood from where she'd been sitting at the kitchen table. She held out both hands and Morag took them. She was exhibiting the calm demeanor suitable to a clergyman's wife, but Morag guessed there was some underlying reason for the visit. Her heart began to beat faster. Had

Brodie managed to free Douglas?

"My husband has reminded me that I had not visited you since your recent ordeal," she said solicitously, but Morag caught the sly wink she cast at her behind her mother's back. "I do apologize. May we walk together? Perhaps I can offer some restorative counsel."

"Yes, of course." Morag could barely contain her curiosity. "Mother, may I walk with Mrs. Morgan?"

"I suppose." Hazel Green's permission came out slowly. "But mind, don't go far. You never know what kind of creature might be lurking about."

"I'll take good care of her, Mrs. Green, never fear." Mary Morgan took Morag's arm and guided her toward the door.

"A moment." Hazel Green stopped them. Morag had all she could do not to cry out in impatience.

"Yes, Mother?"

"Your sunbonnet." The woman pulled one from a peg by the door. "Just because of the recent… unpleasantness…that's no reason to neglect your complexion. You'll want to look your best in Fredericton, mind."

"Yes, Mother." Morag took the worn hat and pushed it onto her head.

"Well?" Once they were out of hearing distance of the house, Morag swung on her companion. "What news? Has Mr. MacMillan managed to help Mr. Smith? Has…?"

"Patience, child, patience." She smiled. "Yes, he has. Your Mr. Smith is free."

"Praise be!"

"I understand, however, that it was under the

condition that he's never to see you again. He had to sign a pledge to that effect."

"Never see me again?" Morag's joy plummeted.

"My dear, there was no other way. Surely you don't want him to continue in prison and face charges that would see him held there for months, perhaps years?"

"No." The word faltered out. "But never…"

"Don't despair too quickly on that count, child." She touched Morag's hand as she cast her a conspiratorial wink. "You must give Brodie time."

****

"Farewell, daughter." Duncan Green handed his daughter up onto the cargo wagon.

"Right pleased to have your company, Miss Morag." Dunc MacDougal held the reins to the team of drays and smiled at her as she joined him on the plank seat. "It's a long drive to Fredericton."

"You mind your manners, Mr. MacDougal." Hands on her hips, Hazel Green stood on the doorstep, her face puckered into a warning frown. "You might be an officer of the law, but I've not forgotten you were a pirate."

"Privateer, ma'am, privateer in the defense of this country. You will admit, I've been a model citizen for a goodly while now." He met her nastiness with a cold, eye-narrowed look. "A married man with a wife and daughter and an interest in a flourishing shipbuilding business. I'm a highly trusted lad these days. Being a government courier is part of my duties as Captain Cameron's lieutenant. This trip to Fredericton, as you know, is to carry important documents to the lieutenant governor."

"Doesn't such an officer usually ride a swift horse?" Hazel Green gave him a critical look.

"I fair cannot abide such a means of travel." He heaved a deep breath. "You're right fortunate I have an aversion to riding and am available to give your daughter safe transport. Never fear." He patted a pistol stuck into his belt. "I'll see she's kept as secure as if she were at home in your kitchen."

"Very well." Hazel Green gave him a last haughty look before turning her attention to her daughter. "Mind you behave, my girl. Mrs. Baker is doing this family a great favor by agreeing to take you on and introduce you to the best elements of the city's society."

"Yes, Mother." Morag spoke contritely, but she caught the sly glance Dunc MacDougal threw her. What did it mean? Anticipation mixed with apprehension began to creep through her veins. Was something afoot? Had Brodie MacMillan formulated a plot whereby she might see Douglas again? She reined in her hopes. That would be too wonderful.

"Walk on." Dunc MacDougal flapped the reins over the backs of the team and turned them out of the farmyard.

"Safe journey," Duncan Green called after them.

Morag swung on the seat to wave farewell to her parents, but her father stood alone. Her mother, her mission accomplished, had apparently returned to her chores in the kitchen.

If I am ever blessed with a child, may I never treat it as coldly as my mother treats me.

"I'm right glad to see you've brought quilts and blankets, Miss Morag." She became aware that Dunc MacDougal was speaking to her as they turned out onto the trail and west in the direction of the provincial capital. "We may have to spend one night under the stars if this team doesn't make it to the coaching house by dusk. It's fortunate we got an early start, so we just might manage to get there. Have you ever slept outside?"

"No, but I fancy that, on a fine night, it might be a lovely experience." She thought of Douglas and the nights he had confessed to spending in the open and longed to know more of his past. Not that anything about it would change her feelings for him. She simply wanted to understand and appreciate every aspect of the man who'd won her heart.

"Aye, aye, that it is." He heaved a sigh. "That's what I miss about sailing…being able to come up on deck on a clear night and see the stars dotting the sky like tiny candles, to feel the spray on my face and lick salt from my lips."

"Tell me about it." Her thirst for tales of adventure whetted, she urged him on.

"Well…"

****

"We're being followed." They'd been driving for several hours when Dunc MacDougal halted the team around a bend in the trail to listen.

"Highwaymen?" A mixture of apprehension and excitement dashing through her, Morag breathed the question. Afraid, yes, but also longing for an adventure, she glanced back over her shoulder.

"Here…" He handed her the reins and pulled the pistol from his belt. "Keep a tight rein on them." He jumped to the ground, checked the prime of his weapon, then, putting a finger to his lips to indicate silence, he slipped out of sight into the trees.

Struggling to contain the shaking in her hands, heartbeat thumping at the back of her throat, Morag took a tight grip on the pair of drays and prayed.

When a familiar white horse with its rider leading a second mount appeared around the bend, her breath came out in a gush of relief. Brodie MacMillan.

"Hie, there, lass, where's your driver?" Grinning, he drew up beside the wagon. "Gone to answer the call of nature, or"—he glanced tauntingly about—"took off at the first sign of trouble?"

"Bloody hell, Brodie!" Dunc stepped from his hiding place. "I fair thought you'd forgotten us. I was afeard it was a genuine highwayman that was on our track. Whit kept you so long?"

"My guid wife was curious as to why I wanted to ride her mare." Brodie swung his mount to face the other man. "She was right suspicious. Still is, I reckon. It took a deal of storytellin' to satisfy her questions. Now I'll just be takin' the lass back to the manse and the chaperoning of Mrs. Morgan."

"I thought you would be taking Miss Morag back to her home. Damn it, Brodie, you can't go dragging Mrs. Morgan into this plot. If Cal finds out…"

"And how is Cal goin' to find out? Iona—I mean Mary—knows how to keep her trap shut, as does her husband."

"Brodie MacMillan…" Frustrated, Dunc shook his head. "Your middle name must be trouble."

"Ah, now, Dunc, that's a bit harsh." He dismounted and indicated the docile animal on the lead rope. "Just see what precautions I've taken to assure Miss Morag gets safely back to Riverhaven. I've brought Frank Miller's Nellie for her transport. The creature's only vice is that she's one slow, ploddin' bit o' flesh. And I'm ridin' my wife's lovely, quiet Snow, even though, as I've told you, it took a book of stories to quiet my wife's suspicions. I couldn't chance ridin' Vixen. That young filly would scare the daylights out of Nellie. You see how thoughtful I've been."

"And chust what reason did you give Frank for wanting to borrow that old nag?" Dunc frowned up at him.

"Do you no' think Frank is more than willin' to help Douglas and this lass?" Leaving the two horses ground-tied, he held up his hands to lift Morag from the wagon. "Come along, lass. We're wastin' daylight."

"Sweet Jesus!" Dunc rounded the wagon to jump up to the seat and take the reins. "How many more citizens of Riverhaven have you dragged into your plot?"

"That's pretty much it." Brodie shook his hands impatiently as Morag continued to hesitate. "Lass, come along, we've no time to waste."

Dozens of butterflies seemed to be fluttering in her chest. She was caught up in an intrigue her mother would utterly condemn, with two men of colorful, even outlaw backgrounds. Throwing caution aside, she accepted Brodie's assistance and allowed him to swing her to the ground.

As he placed her on the ground, she realized she'd become a part of an adventure that could rival anything in a book. A thrill of excitement coursing through her body, she recognized that by her actions she was very likely becoming another of Riverhaven's rogues.

"Come along, come along," Brodie was urging as

he held his hands cupped into a stirrup to boost her aboard the brown mare. "I've got to get Snow back to my wife or, like what happened to the horses in a story she once read me—Cinderella, I think it was called—she'll turn the innocent beast into a mouse or some such. You must know Louisa has the reputation of being a witch."

Grinning at her, he winked. As she scrambled onto Nellie, she realized he was enjoying the adventure and wasn't in the least worried about the consequences.

"I'll be seein' you, laddie." Brodie gathered up Nellie's lead rope and swung into Snow's saddle.

"Probably sooner than I'd like," Dunc muttered and clucked to send his team shambling forward. "Good luck to you, Miss Morag," he called back.

"Thank you, Mr. MacDougal," Morag replied, her words a broken stutter as Brodie urged the white mare into a brisk trot and Nellie was forced to follow. Clinging to saddle and mane, she prayed she'd survive this escapade.

"Tell me if the pace is too much for you, lass," Brodie said as he brought her animal up beside his.

"No...no, I'm fine," she replied, trying to keep the bumping out of her speech.

"Guid, verrae guid. We'll keep a steady pace. I have to get back to the mill afore dark. You do realize that what I said about my wife turnin' this mare into a mouse was a jest? She's no more a witch than you or me."

"Of course."

"Guid, verrrae guid. I wouldn't want any more tales to be put about."

As Morag became more accustomed to the quick

pace, she glanced at the man slightly ahead of her. Handsome and daring, he also had a cavalier attitude toward life that at times frightened and appalled her. Although she recognized him as having a good heart when it came to helping out friends and neighbors and an affable personality that charmed people after even the briefest of acquaintances, the more she came to know him, the more she realized he wouldn't have been the man for her. His freewheeling actions and devil-may-care attitude weren't character traits with which she could have lived.

Douglas, on the other hand, while he embodied all the laudable characteristics of her rescuer, was a kindly man, stable, and exuding a calm, reliable personality. Although he was able to defend himself and the honor of anyone he cared about—she recalled the confrontation in the tavern he'd had with Michael Kelly—he did not go seeking trouble…or adventure, as Brodie would have labeled his escapades. He was a man who would make a strong, dependable husband and loving father to children…

"Are you doin' well, lassie?" Brodie's words broke into her thought and she started.

"Yes…yes, I'm fine."

"Daydreamin' were you?" He grinned back at her. "Wool-gatherin' about the lad Douglas?"

"No…that is, not really."

"Don't be shy, lass." He chuckled. "When a lad or lassie is in love, it's right and natural."

Embarrassed, she didn't reply and focused her attention on staying in the saddle as Brodie urged the horses to an even quicker trot.

Chapter Twenty-One

"Good evenin' to you, sir." Brodie strode up to the bar. "A pint of your best ale."

"Right away." Douglas was quick to comply, but as he thrust the tankard toward his brother, he caught a twinkle in his eyes that cast a shadow of apprehension over him.

What is he up to now?

"The minister's wife would like to see you"— Brodie leaned across the counter and hissed to Douglas—"right away."

"What? Why?"

"I have no idea." Brodie shrugged, but the feigned innocence in his outlook was not lost on Douglas. "Just seemed right urgent to me."

"I can't go." Douglas looked around at the room filled to capacity with locals and the crew of two ships newly docked.

"Certain sure you can." Brodie rounded the bar and took a position beside Douglas. "I'll take over here."

"I don't think…" Douglas tried to protest, but his brother was shoving him on his way.

"Go along. Everything will be fine. You lads," he bellowed to the customers, "swill down what you've been nursin' and belly up to the bar. We're sellin' drinks, not gossip."

Good-natured chuckles and laughter followed

Brodie's urging. Douglas, shoved out into the room by his brother's hand in the middle of his back, shook his head ruefully. What would Frank Miller say when he came out of the kitchen to find Brodie tending bar? But the minister and his wife had been kind to him. If she needed him to do her some service, he had to comply.

He headed to the stable and saddled Lady. In the gloaming, he cantered the mare to the manse.

At the door, he ran a hand through his hair, brushed his shirt and trousers, and rubbed first one boot and then the other on the back of each calf. Assured he'd done the best he could to make himself presentable, he knocked on the door.

"Mr. Smith, come in, come in." The clergyman himself answered and bade him a hearty welcome.

"I thought your wife…that is, I thought…" Words stumbled out as Edward Morgan drew him inside.

"Ah, a wee bit of a subterfuge." The big man drew back a step to grin at Douglas. "If you'll just go into the drawing room, I'll be with you shortly."

He opened the door, thrust Douglas inside, and withdrew, closing the panel after him.

The young woman who stood facing him took his breath away.

"Morag." He breathed her name. "Whit…?"

"Douglas." His name came out softly in the candle light.

"I was told you were"—he hesitated over the words *shipped off* and substituted—"sent off to Fredericton."

"It was not my choice." She looked over at him, and he saw the truth in her words. "It was my mother's decision. Mr. MacMillan…rescued me and brought me

177

back to Riverhaven."

"Brodie MacMillan?" His brother's name came out in a gush of astonishment.

"Yes." It was only then that he became aware of the minister's wife, who'd been seated in a shadowy corner of the room. She stood and advanced toward him. "You must keep it a secret, Mr. Smith. I'm sure you don't want to see Mr. MacMillan arrested."

"Oh, aye, never fear, mistress." Douglas stuttered out the promise. "Nary a word of such will pass my lips."

"Now"—she moved to the door—"as mistress of this house, I have duties. I will leave you two alone, but have no doubt, Mr. Smith. This is a modest home. If you behave in the least inappropriately, I'll be able to hear, and you'll be cast out as fast and furious as you've thrown customers from the tavern." The twinkle in her eyes cast doubt on the seriousness of her warning.

"Aye, mistress."

"Very well, so long as you understand." Closing the door after her, she left the room

"Oh, Douglas, I'm so sorry!" Morag's words gushed out the moment they were alone. "I tried to tell Father and Mother nothing happened between us that day in the storm, but they…Mother especially… wouldn't listen."

"Dunnae greet, lass." Stifling the urge to take her into his arms, he clutched his battered cap until his knuckles whitened. "I would never blame you." He paused, then couldn't refrain from asking, "You said Brodie MacMillan rescued you. How…?" He stared at her, remembering how Frank Miller had warned him not to get too involved, how Brodie could at times be a law unto himself.

"Mother had decided it was time to send me to Fredericton to find a suitable husband. Mr. MacDougal was taking some government documents there. My father convinced Mother I would be safe in his care since he is an officer of the law and a married man."

"And so you started out with him?" Jealousy began to roil in his belly. The thought of Morag alone with the big, good-looking Scotsman on what he guessed could be a two-day journey wasn't easy to accept.

"Yes." His expression must have revealed his annoyance, because she dropped her gaze to her hands.

"When did my"—he caught himself before he said *brother*—"Brodie MacMillan come into the picture?"

"We'd gone a half day's journey when he caught up with us." She looked up again. "He had planned the idea most carefully. He must have guessed I wasn't much of a rider, because he brought Nellie for me to ride on the return journey to Riverhaven."

"That poor old nag!" Douglas guffawed. "It's a wonder you got here."

"Mr. MacMillan is a thoughtful man." This time when she spoke, there was an edge on her tone. "He cares about me…about us."

"Oh, does he now?" As the entire scenario came into focus, Douglas spoke sharply. Here was his brother once again interfering in his life…a fresh, new life for which he held out glowing hopes. "Well, if he cared so much, he might have used his brain. Morag, when your parents learn of this, he and I will be in no end of trouble. Do you not know, kidnapping is a hanging offense?"

"I'll tell them I came back of my own free will, I'll

tell them…"

"And that will no doubt have as much effect as when you told them nothing happened between us in my cabin!"

"Well, then, what exactly would you have me do?" This time there was spirit in her words, exasperated annoyance.

"Go home at once. Tell your parents you refused to go with Mr. MacDougal. Tell them that you've spent the entire time here with Mrs. Morgan."

He swung to leave the room. Her words stopped him as surely as a musketball.

"I love you, Douglas Smith."

"Don't say that, lass." His back to her, he swallowed hard, drew a hand across his mouth. "You dunnae know me."

"I know all I need to know." She rushed across the room to lay a hand on his arm. "I know you're a good, kind man…a man who was willing to help my family when they needed it although they'd done nothing to warrant your assistance…a man who wouldn't take advantage of a woman even when she was at her most vulnerable."

"Bloody hell—" Quivering with repressed emotions, he swung on her. "Back in the Old Country, I was a smuggler and a thief! I lived in a brothel! Now I serve ale in a tavern and shovel manure in a stable. Do you still see fit to say you can love such a man?"

He shrugged free of her hand and strode out of the house. As he swung onto Lady, his chest ached, a sensation so unfamiliar he didn't at first recognize it until tears trickled down his cheeks.

****

Morag stood as if frozen in the middle of the minister's drawing room. Douglas had repudiated her love. The confession of his life back in England had done nothing to deter her. She'd guessed he, like most of the residents of Riverhaven, had a shadowy past, but she also felt certain he'd begun a new life in the community. It was the fact that he hadn't replied in kind to her confession of love that had thrust a dagger through her heart.

"Dear girl, what is it?" Mary Morgan, followed by her husband wearing a white surplice and carrying a Bible, returned to the room. "You're as white as a ship's mainsail."

"Douglas doesn't love me." She sank into a chair, too numb to further stand with the stabbing pain she was experiencing.

"What?" the minister's wife looked at her, eyes wide. "Did he say as much?"

"No, but he didn't reply in like when I told him I loved him." She clutched her hands in the folds of her skirts until the knuckles whitened.

"Don't let that distress you overmuch." The minister stepped forward to smile down at her. "I'm a good judge of character, and I'm right sure Mr. Smith has only backed away because he doesn't feel worthy of you."

"Doesn't feel worthy…?" Morag stared at the clergyman. "A man who rode for help when my father was seriously injured, a man who saw to it that our crops were harvested, a man who rescued me from a vicious storm, a man who defended my honor in a physical altercation, a man who spent time alone with me on more than one occasion and yet made no untoward advances? How can you then say…?"

"Hold, lassie." Edward Morgan put a placating hand on her arm. "I said *he* feels unworthy, not that I think him such. What I do believe is that he's a young man desperately trying to make a new life for himself, a respectable life. His only fault is that he's trying too hard." He stepped back from her to put an arm about his wife. "An ancient poet said it much better than I, don't you remember, my love?" He looked fondly down at her. "I once quoted it to you before I rode off on an…adventure."

"I do." She smiled up at him. "I believe it went something like this—'I could not love thee, dear, so much, loved I not honor more'…the words of one Mr. Richard Lovelace. It was a cunning way to manage to ride off without me."

"It was a venture which I deemed too risky for even your brave heart…and you were with child at the time."

"You think it's Douglas's desire to be respectable, to do everything right, that kept him from staying with me, from perhaps saying he loved me?"

"As I've said, my dear, I'm a good judge of character, and I'll wager—" He glanced down at his wife as she gave him a nudge. "And I sincerely believe that is the only impediment to his declaring himself to you."

"I want to believe you, Reverend." Morag looked at the clergyman. "With all my heart I want to believe you."

"Then do." With a sigh, he turned away, still clutching the Bible. "I must say, I am a bit disappointed. Here I am, all dressed up for a wedding and none about to happen…today."

"Don't worry, my dear," his wife called after him as he headed into his study across the hall. "Soon, very soon."

Chapter Twenty-Two

Douglas put his heels to Lady and headed her off down the trail, away from the manse, at a dead run. His thoughts churned faster than the mare's flying hooves. She'd said she loved him. Bloody hell, how was he to deal with such a declaration? In his meanderings, he'd fantasized hearing those words. Now that she'd made them a reality, what was he to do about it?

As he neared the lane that led to his homestead, he slowed the animal to a trot. Running this lovely beast into the ground was no way to respond to what should have been the answer to his fondest dreams.

"Sorry, lass." He patted the mare's damp neck. "This is no way to treat a fine companion such as you, but my brain is fair addled."

He rounded a bend and drew rein abruptly as, in the darkness, he recognized Brodie MacMillan riding his red mare.

"Hie, there, laddie." Brodie greeted him, grinning. "You've been ridin' hard…like a man who's just come from a warm moment with his lass. When's the wedding to be…or has it already happened and you're but comin' home to make sure the place is fit for your bride?"

"You abducted her." Douglas ground out the words, anger flushing through him. "You set up that meeting at the Morgan house. Damn you to hell, Brodie

MacMillan. Now you've got me involved in a kidnapping."

"Ah, cool yourself." Brodie's good humor didn't flag. "Cal's not about to put that charge on you, since Dunc MacDougal will testify it was me who did the deed. The lass will also deny she was taken by force. What with her stayin' at the minister's house, Captain Cameron will most likely want to avoid any gossip concernin' Edward and Mary. Any road, with most of the grain in this area yet to be milled and me the only one capable of doin' it, no one in Riverhaven or anywhere in a hundred miles is likely to stand for my imprisonment at this time of year."

"Think you're so clever, don't you?" Douglas's response reeked with sarcasm as Lady pranced and shied away from the cavorting vixen.

"Well, I'm fair bright and slippery as an eel. But the bad part of all this is that your demeanor tells me you didn't go before the lass on bended knee, declare your undyin' love, and get her promise to be your wife. I even had Lachlan...Edward, that is...ready to do the deed. Bloody hell, lad, aire you a complete fool? Could I have set it up for you any better? Edward would have married you right then and there, and what could her parents do afterwards?"

"I don't want to do anything underhanded. If I marry Morag, it will be with her family's consent and good wishes. I'll not have her torn asunder from them on my account. Family is important"—his words softened—"even if at times it doesn't seem that way."

"Aye, well, you daft bugger, you'll learn in time you've just cheated yourself out of one of the best things life has to offer. Without the love of my Louisa, I might have become a right wild pillock, not the refined gentleman I am today."

He put his heels to the red mare and rode past Douglas at a full gallop.

"Who's tending bar?" Douglas yelled after him as his thoughts came back to the mundane.

"Dunc MacDougal." His brother swung back to reply. "Said he never did such before but was willin' to give it a try."

Guid God!

****

Morag stood, with bowed head, in the kitchen of her parents' farmhouse, her trunk by her side, valise in hand, as her mother's admonitions rained over her.

"You brazen, ungrateful girl! Feigning sickness and ordering Mr. MacDougal to bring you back to the village when you were nearly a half day's journey underway! And hiding in the minister's house! Well, I shouldn't be all that surprised, I suppose. He and that wife of his…both of them rebels…Jacobites to the core. If Dunc MacDougal and Captain Caleb Cameron weren't their long-time comrades and still thick as thieves with them, I'd be preferring charges against that man and his wife! As it is, there would be no point. Oh, dear God, is everyone in this miserable outpost conspiring against me?"

"Now, now, Mrs. Green." Her husband sought once again to be the voice of reason. "You know our girl didn't want to go to Fredericton. She loves this farm and community. Sending her off to a strange place seemed more than a bit cruel."

"Cruel! Cruel! How can you call sending her away where she would be safe from that ruffian Douglas

Smith cruel?"

"I don't know that we've given the lad a fair trial, wife. He's been nothing but respectable since he arrived here. He has a job and a tidy bit of a homestead. Reverend Morgan speaks only the best of him."

"Of course our minister would. He's a Highlander just as this Douglas Smith is. Those people stick together…clannish is the right word for their support of each other."

"Mother, Father, please!" Morag could stay quiet and submissive no longer. "Let me assure you that you have nothing to fear from Mr. Smith. He…he has told me he is not interested in me."

"Has he now?" Her mother was not about to let the matter so easily rest. "And I suppose we're to take the word of an outlaw, a roué?"

"He isn't…" Morag started to protest, but remembering his last words to her stopped. He had admitted to being an outlaw who'd lived in a brothel. "Please, Mother—" Her tone dropped to one of sad submission. "I have a pounding headache. May I go to my room?"

"I suppose." Her mother's words fell to an exasperated tone as she dropped into a chair at the table. "All I can do now is pray that you've spoken the truth and your interest in Douglas Smith is at an end."

Morag climbed the stairs to her small room, her heart as heavy as the valise she carried.

Chapter Twenty-Three

Back at his job at the tavern, Douglas tried to immerse himself in his work, to concentrate on it and his plans for his small homestead. Work, work, hard work, that was the key to killing the ache and longing he was experiencing. He'd killed any affection Morag Green might have had for him with that ugly confession of his past.

At least he hadn't lost her to another man, not as he had lost Annie Burns…and she to his own brother, of all people. But, as he recalled that incident, he also remembered the pain of that defeat had been different. As a boy of fourteen, he'd been filled with hurt and anger, most of it directed toward his brother. Annie had simply been the bone of contention. Morag, on the other hand, had been the sole object of his passion.

He placed a pile of plates on a sideboard and began to wash them in a pail of warm water. He'd simply have to make fresh plans for his future, he decided as he scrubbed away grease. If he wanted a true home with a wife and children, he'd have to look elsewhere. Maybe one of the Gardiner lasses. Involuntarily he grimaced as images of simpering Tilly and boisterous Sarie wafted across his mind.

Definitely not either of them. Well, there had to be other eligible lasses somewhere not too far off.

"Douglas, lad, you're fair slopping water all over

the floor. Do you want me to slip and break my neck?" Frank Miller's reprimand brought him out of his meanderings.

"Sorry, sir."

"Leave it for now. There's a ship new docked at the wharf that's bringing me a shipment of whisky. Harness Nellie and Nick and go fetch it."

"Aye." Douglas dried his hands and headed for the stable.

****

At the wharf he stood at the team's heads and watched while sailors and dock workers secured the *Northwestern* to the pier. As the gangplank was lowered, a woman appeared at the rail, a startlingly familiar woman. Wrapped in a shabby gray cloak, she scanned the pier for a moment. Seeing him, her thin face lighted up and she raised her hand to wave vigorously.

"Douglas!" she cried. "Douglas!"

Guid God! It can't be.

Staggered by disbelief, he could barely believe what was happening when Daisy rushed down the plank and ran to throw her arms about his neck.

"Douglas, oh, Douglas, I've missed you so!" she cried.

The sound of an approaching wagon made him glance to his right.

Bloody hell!

A sick, despairing feeling engulfed him as he saw Morag seated beside her father as he drove their team onto the wharf.

She stared at him for a moment before turning her attention to the cargo being unloaded. Sitting up straight and stiff, she appeared disdainfully uncaring at what she saw. Her father swung to the ground and cast Douglas a disparaging glance before heading toward the piles of goods accumulating on the wharf.

"Get up on the wagon," he freed himself from the young woman's grip. "I have cargo to fetch."

He led her back beside the front wheel and hoisted her onto the seat. Something in his chest felt like a stone, dropping, dropping. He stifled the urge to rage at Daisy. It wasn't her fault. Like a faithful, rescued animal she'd followed him. And there were still those cases of whisky to collect. He guffawed inwardly. He might be a failure at courting, but he had lots of experience hoisting boxes of spirits.

****

"A pleasure to meet you, Miss Daisy." Frank Miller, seeming to mask his surprise at the appearance of the young woman Douglas brought back to the tavern, smiled at the girl.

"And I you, Mr. Miller." She bobbed a shy curtsy. "It's a fine establishment you have here."

"I'm right proud of it, lass, but it's no place for such as you. Douglas?" He turned to him. "I'd advise you to take Miss Daisy to Mrs. Morgan until you can find suitable accommodations for her."

"Oh, aye." Douglas's outlook brightened at the suggestion. "Aye, Mr. Miller, a right fine suggestion."

"Who is Mrs. Morgan?" Daisy looked up apprehensively at Douglas. "Does she operate a house such as Miss Lottie…?"

"No, no." Douglas was quick to cut her off. "Mrs. Morgan is the minister's wife. She's a fine woman. She'll decide what's best. Mr. Miller"—he addressed the tavern owner—"do you have any warm food for Daisy? I reckon she's near starved after weeks on board ship. She could eat while I unload the whisky."

"Of course I do." The big man pulled out a chair at a table. "Sit yourself down, Miss Daisy. I have a fine stew simmering on the hearth. And from the pallor of your complexion, I daresay a tankard of ale will not go amiss. Douglas, lad, might I see you in the kitchen for a moment?"

"Aye." As Daisy took the proffered seat, Douglas followed his employer.

"Douglas," he hissed once they were in a far corner of the adjoining room. "What is the story on this lass? Was she yours back in the Old Country?"

"No, no." Douglas heaved an exasperated sigh. "I found her beaten and near death in the snow one night," he continued, sotto voce. "I carried her back…to the place I was staying," he stumbled a bit. "My landlady gave her work in her kitchen and a place to live, safe and warm. Daisy became my friend…nothing more, I swear."

"But the poor lass became enamored of you…and small wonder." Frank Miller leaned against a counter and drew a deep breath. "She knighted you her hero and vowed to follow you to the ends of the earth."

"Argh!"

"Well, whatever." Frank Miller took a bowl from a cupboard and headed for the hearth. "I'll see the child well nourished while you put your back to bringing in that whisky. Then you'll take her to the manse."

"Aye, aye." Douglas headed out through a back door to fetch the team into a position for unloading the wagon's cargo.

As he hefted the heavy crates of whisky, he couldn't put the image of Morag sitting up stiff as a mainmast and staring straight ahead on the seat of her father's wagon. He could only imagine the contempt she must be feeling for him. Bloody hell! Might she be fancying Daisy was his former doxy, possibly even his wife? Certainly it must appear either such possibilities were likely.

As he carried in boxes and stacked them in the storeroom behind the kitchen, the activity brought back memories of doing a similar chore back in Scotland. Only those cases hadn't been legitimate purchases.

Maybe Daisy's arrival had been an omen, a sign that a man truly couldn't outrun his past. Some dark shadows were long enough to stretch across the Atlantic. Clive Jones slid into his mind as he strode outside to get the last box. He still didn't know who was the object of the man's revenge.

Back inside the tavern, he found Daisy finishing a bowl of stew, a steaming teacup beside it indicating Frank Miller had brewed her a beverage. Her expression, filled with joy as she looked up at his return, made his gut contract. He couldn't abandon this vulnerable young woman. Memories of what she'd told him of her former life after he'd taken her back to the brothel made that impossible.

"Daisy has agreed it will be best if you take her to the manse now." Frank Miller put his hands on his hips and gave her a kindly smile. "I'm sure Mrs. Morgan will welcome her."

"I wanted to stay here with you, Douglas," she said, eyes wide with what he could only describe as begging admiration. "But Mr. Miller has convinced me

I'd be much safer with the minister's wife."

"Aye, that you will be." He picked up the shabby valise he'd dropped by her chair. "The minister and his wife will take great care of you."

"But you'll come to see me, won't you, Douglas?" She stood, still gazing up at him with that worshipful expression he found difficult to meet.

"Of course. Now we'd best be going. I'm a working man, Daisy, and I must not be shirking my duties to Mr. Miller."

"No, you must not." She bobbed a curtsy to the tavern owner. "I thank you most sincerely for your kindness, Mr. Miller. And if you are ever in need of a scullery maid or someone to clean your premises…"

"Go along with you, lass." Frank Miller reddened at her gratitude. "This is no place for a fine young lady such as yourself."

Outside, as Douglas made to hoist her into the wagon, she halted abruptly and looked up at him.

"Douglas, you aren't angry that I've come, are you?" she asked, apprehension mirrored in her thin, pale face.

"Angry? Of course not." He lifted her to the seat and leaped up beside her. *Damn, but she's thin.* "But…" He continued as he took up the reins and turned the team down the road in the direction of the manse. "How?"

"I followed you the morning you left Miss Lottie's. I got to the quayside just as the ship on which you sailed was pulling away from shore. You were standing at the rail, but you didn't notice. I asked a dockworker where the vessel was bound, and he told me its first port of call would be a place called

Riverhaven in the province of New Brunswick. I determined to follow you."

"But how? You must have had little but the clothes on your back. And what if I hadn't been here?"

"I would have followed you onward…to the ends of the earth if necessary."

Her blind devotion touched him, made him swallow hard to suppress the emotion it evoked.

"You couldn't have done such, Daisy. It makes no sense." He tried to stifle his feelings with a gruff reply.

"I had a plan. I'm not so dull as some people think."

"You're not dull, Daisy. Never think such a thing. But, now tell me, what was your plan?"

"I went back to Miss Lottie's, packed the few clothes Miss Lottie had provided for me in an old valise I found in the attic, and headed back to the docks. I inquired for the next ship bound for this place called Riverhaven. It was weeks before I could find such a vessel that would take me…for what I had to offer."

"Bloody hell, Daisy…" Appalled, he looked down at her as the team plodded out of the village and into the tree-lined lane away from the village.

"I know what you're thinking, Douglas MacMillan, and I'm disgraced." For the first time since her arrival she spoke with spirit. "You know I'm not that kind of girl, never have been, never will be."

"I'm sorry, Daisy. It's just that I cannot imagine you having coin to pay for the voyage."

"But I do have a skill." She sat up proudly, chin thrust out. "After weeks of trying to find passage and working in the scullery of a local inn, I managed to sign on as cook on a ship bound for here."

"I've never heard of such a thing. A female cook on shipboard!"

"Their cook had fallen gravely ill, and they were scheduled to sail the next morn. They were desperate."

"Ah." He drew a deep breath, then started sharply. "I trust you were treated respectfully on the voyage?"

"I was indeed. The captain was a married man who'd brought his wife along. She was most fastidious in keeping me safe."

"Well, then, that is fine. But one thing you must promise me, Daize." He looked over at her. "You must never, never refer to me as Douglas MacMillan. Here, in this place, I'm known as Douglas Smith, and by such you must call me."

"If that is what you wish, Douglas, of course. But why? Are you afraid Dos MacLintock or his ruffians might find you?"

"Aye." It was convenient reason.

"Douglas…" She paused.

"Aye?"

"You're not married…or promised…or anything?" The words came out shyly.

"No." He glanced sideways at her. She'd been looking down at her work-reddened hands as she'd asked the question, but his response brought her attention back up at him, eyes bright.

"But there is someone." He returned his focus to the team. It wasn't fair to let her go on harboring hopes.

"Someone very special?"

"Aye."

"Someone very beautiful?"

"Aye."

"Do you love her, Douglas?"

"That makes no difference. She's not for me. Go along, Nick. Move your great hooves, Nellie."

****

At the manse, desperately hoping he'd find refuge for Daisy within, he rapped on the door. Shortly it was opened by the minister's wife.

"Douglas, how lovely to see you," she greeted him, then glanced at Daisy huddling by his side. "And you've brought a friend. Do come in."

She led the way to the drawing room and indicated they were to take chairs. Daisy, her gaze roaming about the room, at first refused, but after their hostess's "please" she sat down. Douglas, struggling to think of what was proper, abstained. "After you, ma'am."

With a smile, Mary took a seat opposite Daisy.

"Now, what can I do for you fine folks today?" She glanced from Douglas to the reticent young woman sitting with hands clasped tightly in her lap.

"I was wondering…that is, Mr. Miller was wondering…we were wondering…"

"Douglas, please do not hesitate with any request you may have. I'll be only too happy to oblige if it is within my power to do so."

"Well, it's like this." Relieved, Douglas took a seat facing the woman. "Daisy, here, is a friend from the Old Country. She's newly arrived and has no place to stay…the tavern not being a decent situation for a young lady, and I cannot take her on her own to my homestead. And I…we were wondering if you might have a space for her here."

There. He'd said it. He waited with bated breath for the woman's response.

It took but a minute.

"Of course Miss Daisy may stay here." She gave the young woman a warm smile. "Would you object to helping about the house, my dear? My husband frequently could use my assistance in the fields and elsewhere about the farm. We have a young daughter. If you'd not object to minding her from time to time…?"

"Oh, no, mistress. At home, my ma had a fair flock of them, and me being the oldest I often had to care for the wee ones. I like children." She glanced apprehensively at Douglas. This was the first she'd told of her past. He could guess the rest. A drunken father who beat both her and her mother…he'd seen the situation all too often.

"Well, then, excellent." Mary stood, and the pair of visitors hastened to join her on their feet. "Douglas, please bring in Miss Daisy's belongings. My dear…" She turned to the young woman. "I hope you won't mind. The only room available is small, with barely space for a bed and table."

"It will be lovely, mistress."

"Come, I'll show you the way. Douglas, it's at the top of the stairs. You may bring your friend's luggage there."

At the bottom of the steps leading to the second floor, Daisy paused in following her hostess.

"Thank you, Douglas," she whispered before he went out the door. "I know I'll be safe here."

"I'm glad you feel such." He let the words float back to her as he stepped outside.

As he reached to take her valise from the wagon, all he could see was Morag's stricken, then bitter expression as she'd watched Daisy embrace him on the wharf. He longed to be able to talk to her, to explain the situation, but he vowed to stay away from her…forever.

****

"Yes?" Daisy answered the knock at the manse door, wearing a clean gray dress and white apron.

Morag stared. Words deserted her. Here stood the woman she'd seen embracing Douglas on the pier.

"Who is it, Daisy?" Mary Morgan came to join the young woman at the door. "Oh, Morag, I'm so glad to see you. Come in."

Too stunned to refuse, Morag allowed the minister's wife to guide her into the drawing room.

"Join us, Daisy," she said as the girl held back. "I want you to meet Morag Green. You'll recall my telling you about her."

"Yes." Daisy's reply was little above a whisper as she stepped into the room.

"Please, both of you, sit down." Mary spoke with such authority both obeyed. "I believe there's been a great misunderstanding. Morag, in spite of how you saw Daisy greet Douglas on the dock, they are simply friends. Daisy has told me how Douglas rescued her from a terrible death in the streets of Edinburgh. Therefore, she feels a debt to him, a loyalty, if you will."

"It's true, mistress." Daisy raised her gaze from her clasped hands to look at Morag. "Mrs. Morgan has told me you and Douglas are promised to each other. If marrying you will make him happy, I wish you both well."

"There was never anything…romantic between you?" Morag could see no deceitfulness in Daisy's sincere blue eyes.

"No." She shook her head, again lowering her gaze

to her hands. "He treated me as a brother would…a caring, protecting brother. I followed him because…because I only felt safe when he was about."

"Douglas brought Daisy here because he could not think of a better place for her to feel secure," Mary said. "And she's been a godsend. She helps with the housework and Iona. It allows me time to help Edward about the farm and with church work. I'm hoping she'll be willing to stay with us for as long as she sees fit."

"Oh, yes, Mrs. Morgan." The young woman's pleasure and relief was reflected as she looked at the minister's wife. "I shall be only too pleased to work for you."

"Daisy is staying?" Iona burst into the room, a rag doll in hand. "Oh, Daisy, that makes me so happy!" She grasped the maidservant's hand and looked up at her, eyes bright, a broad smile on her face.

"Yes." Her mother smiled. "Daisy, I have only one request when it comes to my daughter. Don't allow her to seduce you into spoiling her."

"I shan't, Mrs. Morgan, I shan't."

"Miss Green." Becoming serious, Iona addressed Morag. "I wish you would marry Mr. Douglas. I know it would make him happy. I listened while he and Papa were talking when I was riding Lady. Papa thinks you should marry him, too."

"Riding Lady? Douglas's mare?" Mary stared at her daughter. "And just when did this happen, young lassie?"

"Last Sunday afternoon while you were at a meeting with the church ladies." She looked abashed. "Papa and I went out to visit Mr. Douglas at his homestead. He told me to say that I'd wanted to see

Lady, but I know that wasn't the real reason…although I did enjoy seeing Lady. She's so…"

"It certainly is nice to hear of your secret exploits with your papa," Mary feigned annoyance with her daughter. "And what, may I ask, happened then?"

"Well…" She made circles on the floor with the toe of her shoe, avoiding her mother's eyes. "Mr. Douglas put a bridle on Lady, Papa placed me on her back, and while Mr. Douglas led her, Papa walked beside me as I rode around the homestead."

"And you listened to their conversation? Or were you too involved in riding the mare?"

"I listened. No one told me not to. Papa was advising Mr. Douglas to marry you, Miss Green. He kept telling him"—she glanced furtively up at her mother—"that marrying my mama was the greatest joy of his life. He could wish no less for any man who truly loved a woman."

"Your papa shouldn't have taken you riding on a large mare such as Mr. Douglas's," Mary said, but the soft blush spreading up her cheeks told Morag she'd been pleased by her husband's words regarding their marriage. "And as for you listening in on your papa's conversation…"

"Please, Miss Green." The child released Daisy's hand and rushed to confront Morag. "Marry Mr. Douglas. He's a good, kind man. I'll come to visit you often. I'll bring you some of Mama's plum jam and…"

"Enough, Iona." Her mother ended the torrent of words. "Daisy, please take my daughter to the kitchen and allow her to help you make tea for Miss Green and myself."

"Yes, ma'am. Come along, Miss Iona."

The child started to follow the young woman from the room but paused at the doorway to look back at Morag.

"Please, Miss Green, do marry Mr. Douglas. I do so want him to be happy. And"—she added as she skipped away—"Papa will do the deed any time you like. He told Mr. Douglas as much."

"Out of the mouths of babes." After they'd gone, Mary turned to Morag with an amused smile. "I'm not sure where that quotation comes from, but at times there is truth in it. Morag, now you really must marry Douglas."

"I would…in a moment…you must realize that, Mary, but you know Douglas's impossible condition. He insists on having my parents' consent, and that will never be forthcoming. And he's never yet said he loves me. So you see, little Iona's wish is quite impossible."

Chapter Twenty-Four

"I want you to go to Angus Harris's store for a bag of salt." Frank Miller stepped into the stable where Douglas was busily cleaning stalls. "I'm about to run out, and I've a stew in the making."

"Aye, sir, right away." Douglas leaned the pitchfork against a wall and rubbed his hands on the seat of his breeches.

"And mind, don't dawdle," his employer called after him as Douglas headed out of the barn. "I'll have hungry customers at any moment, what with that new vessel fresh in from sea."

Douglas exited the stable and strode up the dusty street to the store. Hastily purchasing the salt, he didn't pause for his usual chat with Angus Harris, the proprietor, explaining his employer had immediate need of the product. Whistling, he slung the sack over his shoulder and headed back toward the tavern.

Douglas was at the door when he saw her. Standing beside her father's wagon on the wharf, Morag watched the ship newly docked lowering the gangplank. The farmer sat alone on the seat. A sudden urge all but overwhelmed Douglas to drop his purchase and attempt a meeting with her...even a few words. Without that shrew of a mother...

Common sense held him in check. What did it matter? He'd refuted her declaration of love, had revealed his sordid past, and signed that despicable agreement never to approach her again. All hopes he might have cherished toward her were gone. Still he couldn't resist pausing to stare at her, to admire her.

"Mr. Fletcher, Mrs. Fletcher, welcome home." Smiling, Morag called out to greet a couple coming down the gangplank. When they reached the wharf, she hastened to join them. She had just bobbed a curtsy when Douglas saw him.

Half hidden behind a pile of lumber, Clive Jones was leveling a musket toward the trio.

Distances told him he couldn't reach the gunner in time to prevent what the man intended, but he could get to Morag and her friends. Salt spewed over the tavern entrance as he threw aside the bag. Plunging across the wharf, he propelled himself into the group, taking them all to the ground. Cries from the two women, a yell from the man, and a searing pain in his side were his last memories.

Chapter Twenty-Five

Later, Morag would remember those moments only in fragmented images. Douglas collapsing in front of her, a crimson wetness spurting from his chest to cover the front of her gown, the nightmare confusion of people shouting, screaming, rioting about her.

"Morag." Her name was barely above a whisper as he looked up at her before his eyes closed.

"Douglas! No, no, no!"

"Come, come, lass." Her father was struggling to draw her from his body, but she refused to be pulled away.

"Lass, there's nothing you can do for him." Frank Miller was kneeling beside her, his broad rugged face contorted with agony. "Let them take him away."

"Come along, Miss Green." A man with stronger hands than her father's intervened, a man she recognized as the newly arrived Fletcher Atkin. His wife Isabella stood aside, her expression stricken, a hand clasped over her mouth, her countenance ghostly white.

When he succeeded in drawing Morag to her feet, she staggered and watched through a prism of horrified disbelief as several men lifted Douglas and carried him toward the tavern.

She slumped against the man holding her. *Douglas, Douglas.* His name revolved in her head as Fletcher

Atkin gathered her into his arms. Her next recollection was of his lifting her to the seat of her father's wagon.

"Papa…" In her despair, she resorted to her childhood name for her father as she looked at the man holding the reins. "Oh, dear God, Papa, tell me he's not dead! Tell me…!"

Without speaking, he held out his left arm to allow her to come into its comfort. Like the little girl she'd once been, she snuggled against him as she had years before when a beloved foal had died. He clucked to the team and headed them at a careful walk out of a village alive in a riot of anger and confusion.

****

A horse and rider flew past them. Morag didn't have time to recognize the man on its back, but she knew that red mare. Hope bounded into her heart. Brodie MacMillan was riding at full speed to fetch his wife. Douglas must be alive!

"Father, I have to go back!" she cried. Before he could stop the team, she'd jumped to the ground, narrowly avoiding being hit by a turning wheel. "He's alive. He must be, otherwise Mr. MacMillan wouldn't be riding at such breakneck speed toward his homestead. He's going to fetch his wife, the healer!"

"Child…"

"Father, I have to go to him! If not for him, you could be mourning me at this moment!"

Clutching up her skirts, she raced off back down the dusty trail toward the village.

****

She was nearly to Riverhaven when the sound of horses racing behind her made her turn. One white, the other red, they came racing toward her.

"Wait! Please!" Jumping out of their path, she raised her hands to stop the riders.

The pair reined to a dust-raising halt.

"Lass, we haven't time..." Brodie began, but his wife kicked her foot from the left stirrup and held down a hand. "Get aboard...quickly. There's no time to waste."

Morag grasped the hand, stuck her foot in the stirrup on her way to the mare's back, and settled with her arms clutched around Louisa.

"Hold tight," she advised.

"Yes." Morag barely had time to speak agreement before the woman sent the mare bounding forward again, her husband by her side.

****

"Mr. Miller, I'll need hot water...two buckets at least...and a pair of basins, and cloth torn into strips." Louisa MacMillan whipped out orders as she crossed the tavern and started up the stairs.

"Aye, missus, right away."

When Morag made to follow the woman, Brodie caught her by an arm.

"You stay below and help Frank, lass," he said gently. "I'll be helpin' my wife."

"But..."

"No buts about it." Brodie's tone brooked no refusal. "I cast my victuals and near went down on my knees the first time I helped my wife remove a musketball. Such a sight is not for you. Faintin' you'd do more harm than good while she works. Frank"—he turned to the landlord—"as soon as you do my wife's biddin', make Miss Morag a cup of strong, sweet tea...and add a bit of your best."

"Aye, Brodie." Frank Miller placed a gentle hand on Morag's arm. "Come, lass, we must get busy heating water for Mrs. MacMillan."

****

His shirt stained with blood, Brodie came down the stairs slowly, his face gaunt. Morag, seated in a chair, teacup in hand, jumped to her feet. She'd all but forgotten the stains on her own clothing in her concern for Douglas. She dared not ask.

"He's alive," Brodie said as he reached the bottom of the stairs. "Just barely." He leaned against the railing, and Morag could only guess at how difficult had been the time he'd spent assisting his wife. "Frank, we'll be askin' to borrow your team to move him to our homestead, that Louisa might continue to tend him."

"For sure and certain, Brodie, but won't the journey be too hard on the lad?"

"Louisa thinks it's the only solution." He shrugged. "She wants to tend him herself, night and day, for a time."

"Very well. I'll go and harness Nellie and Nick." He forced a wan grin. "No fear of them running away with him."

Brodie moved behind the bar and called after the tavern owner as he headed out to get his team, "I'll be helpin' myself to a drop of your best, Frank."

"Take as much as you need, and welcome to it," came the response.

Morag watched as he examined the array of bottles on the shelves, selected one, and poured part of its contents generously into a tankard.

"No use wastin' a glass when I need a deal more than one could hold." He strode to join Morag and sank into a chair opposite her.

"Does Mrs. MacMillan believe Douglas has a chance?" Her head was beginning to spin from the brandy-laced tea Frank Miller had given her, but she knew she must try to focus on the moment, on what was happening.

"She believes he has a fighting chance." Brodie took a drink and bared his teeth. "Saved your life, lass, he did. Even if that musketball wasn't meant for you, it most likely would have hit you if he hadn't gotten in the way."

"I know."

****

Morag watched as, under Louisa's supervision, several men Brodie had commandeered off the street helped him carry an unconscious Douglas down the stairs and out to the waiting wagon. His chest was swathed in heavy bandages, his countenance a terrifying gray color. She swallowed hard. He did not look like a man on the mend.

"You'll ride my wife's mare." Brodie startled her as a man led the red and white saddled animals beside the wagon. "Louisa must stay in the wagon with the lad."

"But I can't ride." Her protest came out in a gush.

"You can ride Snow." Brodie stood beside the animal, ready to help her aboard. "She's gentle as a lamb. Now, let me give you a leg up. There's no time to waste."

Almost before she realized what was happening, she was aboard the mare and struggling to gather up the reins Brodie handed to her. As she adjusted herself in the saddle, she saw her father approaching, riding

Brown. Astonished, she stared. She'd never seen him ride a horse, but now he was urging the dray to a shambling trot, which she knew was at the top of the gelding's speed.

"Daughter…" Sounding winded, he reined to a stop near the group at the wagon. "I've come to take you home. I would have been here sooner, but White pulled up lame and I had to get her back to the farm and unhitched before I could return." He paused to catch his breath. "The lad…is he still alive?"

"Yes, but just barely. I'm going to ride to the MacMillan homestead to help."

"You can't help more than Mrs. MacMillan can." Her father perused the woman in the back of the wagon beside Douglas. "You come along with me."

"Papa…"

"Go along with your father, lass." Brodie moved to help her from the white mare. "He's right. The lad has all he needs under my guid wife's care."

"Yes, do go home, Morag." Louisa MacMillan turned from her charge. "Douglas needs peace and quiet. The fewer people about, the better."

"Very well, if you think it's best." Morag allowed Brodie to assist her from the white horse and onto Brown's back behind her father.

Chapter Twenty-Six

"You come back here this instant!" Hazel Green shrieked as her daughter, mounted on Brown, rode past her mother standing on the kitchen doorstep. "I'll not have you going to that witch's house!"

"Mother…" She reined the gelding to a halt. "I've heard nothing of his condition for nearly two days. It is no more than my Christian duty to inquire about his health. Mr. Smith saved my life."

"Stumbled drunkenly into the path of a musketball, I've no doubt. Don't go making a hero of him!"

"He's no more a drunkard than Father." Head held high, Morag urged Brown into a shambling trot and rode off down the lane to the road.

"Is there no end to the shame you're willing to heap on this family in defending that Highland roué? Footpad, I've no doubt! Morag!"

Her name drifted away on the gust of the windy morning. She'd go to the MacMillan house and see to Douglas's condition. If she found him well and recovering, she'd gladly obey the commandment about honoring her father and mother and vow never to see him again.

****

At the MacMillan homestead, she saw Brodie emerging from the barn, pushing a wheelbarrow of manure. The thought crossed her mind that even romantic heroes sometimes had to do mundane tasks.

"Miss Morag." He abandoned his work and came toward her.

"Good morning, Mr. MacMillan." She looked down at him. "I've come…"

"Aye, I know why you've come, lass." He reached up hands soiled from barn work, and she accepted his assistance to the ground.

"How is he?" She could contain herself no longer.

"Fair to middlin', my guid wife assures me." He took Brown's reins and tied him to the veranda railing.

"And that means he will recover?" Hope blossomed within her.

"It's a bit too early to say, but she assures me signs are positive."

"May I…may I see him?"

"I reckon so." He held out an arm to indicate the way to the door of the log house.

Her heart pumping madly, she headed in that direction.

At the door, Brodie stepped sideways ahead of her to shove open the door.

"Louisa," he called softly as a great white wolf appeared in the entrance, "Miss Morag is here to visit your patient."

His wife, her hair plaited into a long braid over her shoulder, stood from where she'd been seated by a couch in the corner on which lay an immobile figure. "Come in, Miss Green," she said softly.

Morag hesitated, staring at the animal blocking her way.

"Jasper, move aside," Brodie ordered the creature. It obeyed but kept a wary eye on the newcomer.

Morag swallowed, drew in a deep breath, and complied. She moved across the room to join Louisa MacMillan and looked down at the blanched face of the unconscious man in the bed.

"He's sleeping," Louisa reassured her, her voice barely above a whisper. "I've given him a potion to help him rest."

"Is he in much pain?" Morag stared at Douglas, heart pounding frantically. He appeared near death.

"A fair amount. That is why I've chosen to render him beyond suffering it."

"Will he…?" Further words stuck in her throat.

"I'm optimistic, but at this stage, I cannot offer complete reassurance."

Dropping to her knees, Morag brushed fingers tenderly over his forehead and was startled to find it fiercely hot.

"He's feverish." She looked up at Louisa. "Is there nothing you can to do to lower it?"

"I've done all I can. Now it's up to him."

"Douglas?" Morag leaned close to whisper. "Douglas, I love you. I always will." She placed a kiss on his burning cheek and stood. "I must be going. I've already defied my mother in coming here. I know she will do all in her power to prevent my making another visit. Will you…send me news of his progress?"

"Of course." Louisa placed a placating hand on Morag's arm. "I'll send news with Mary Morgan. Surely your mother cannot object to a visit from the minister's wife, Highlander though she is."

"Thank you." Morag turned toward the door to find Brodie still standing just inside.

"Rest assured, lass," he said, his words soft with

Highland brogue, "my Louisa is the best healer in this country. She'll take fine care of the lad."

"Yes." After a final glance back at the man lying still in the bed, she left the log house. Brodie followed, untied Brown from where he'd tethered him, and lifted her onto his back.

"You've done a fine and brave thing, comin' here, lass." He squinted up at her. "I feel certain sure in my heart the lad knows you were here and that your visit will help him to heal no end."

She nodded, the lump in her throat precluding words.

As Morag rode back toward her home, tears trickled down her cheeks. After seeing him, no certainty of Douglas's recovery comforted her. When she headed down the lane to the Green farmhouse, she steeled herself for her mother's anger. She'd disobeyed severely, not only in going to inquire after Douglas, but by visiting him in what Hazel Green termed a witch's house.

A witch's house. Memories of the bright, clean cabin made Morag shake her head disdainfully. It certainly held no ambience of being such...unless you considered the selection of bottles of various liquids on a high shelf as suspect. The collection of herbs she'd glimpsed hanging from the ceiling she discounted. They were not unlike those her mother had drying in their kitchen.

Gail MacMillan

Chapter Twenty-Seven

Douglas returned to consciousness to discover he was lying in a bed...a bed that felt a thousand times better than any of the places he'd revived in over the years. As his mind cleared, he discovered the couch was in a corner of a room. Beyond that realization, he had no idea where he was. To further confound him, the place was shadowed in darkness, except for embers glowing on a hearth.

Slowly the mist began to clear from his mind. With a start, he recognized his circumstance as the interior of Brodie's cabin, the place he'd glimpsed briefly when he'd come to fetch Louisa MacMillan to care for Duncan Green. What was he doing there? He tried to move, but the effort sent pain searing up his side. He moaned.

"Rest." A man's voice spoke softly, thick with Highland accent. Turning his head slightly, he saw Brodie MacMillan getting up from a chair by the fire. He came to stand beside the bed. "You've had a rough time, but my wife believes you're on the mend."

"What...happened?" Douglas struggled to bring back memory.

"You were shot, savin' the life of Miss Morag...although the bastard who did it has confessed it was Atkin he was aimin' for."

"Morag...is she...well?"

214

"Right as rain, thanks to you. She came to visit."

"Visit? Morag here?"

"It was no more than her Christian duty."

A soft sense of pleasure coursed through him even as pain sickened his gut. She'd come, she'd come.

"Why?" Relieved of concern for Morag's health, he asked the question. "Why would Clive Jones want to kill this Atkin lad?"

"Seems as how Fletcher, back in his earlier years as a keen gambler, took the shooter's brother, an innocent young lad at the time, for a fair shipload of money. Terrified to tell his father of his loss, the boy shot himself. This fellow—Clive Jones, who is really Clive Weatherby—was away in the army in India at the time. That's why it took so long for this act of reprisal to take place. When he got home and learned the true circumstances of his brother's death, he swore revenge on Fletcher Atkin, only to discover his quarry gone from England. He managed to learn of his destination and followed him, only to once again learn his plans were foiled by Fletcher's absence. So, being patient in his desire for revenge, he waited for his return."

"Ah." Douglas closed his eyes as he digested the explanation. "So I didn't save Miss Morag's life. I just got in the way of a musketball intended for another."

"Were you hopin', laddie?" Brodie drew up his chair and sat down beside the bed. "Hopin' that if that was the case that old dragon of a mother might soften her ways toward you?"

"I didn't want anyone shot." He looked up at the man.

"No, no, of course you didn't." A sly grin curled Brodie's lips. "But I believe you did save the lass. In the moment it took Jones to aim, the lass had stepped between him and the Fletchers. Anyone who witnessed the event will agree. Now, maybe bein' a hero will give you a bit of a leg up in your courtship."

"Courtship? Hardly. I signed that cursed agreement…"

"Ah!" Brodie waved a denigrating hand. "A bit of paper. I've never let such foolishness stop me when the need arose. Come, now, lad. Fess up. What young buck with any pretension to bein' a man wouldn't be sufficiently charmed by such as Miss Morag and wouldn't bypass a few words inked under duress? She's a right beauty, for certain sure. I had a fancy for her once myself."

"You?" The word glowed with a combination of surprise and annoyance.

"Aye." Brodie leaned back in his chair and grinned smugly. "I'm not so old that I couldn't catch a lass's eye a few years back. But after I met Louisa, well, there could be no other for me. So…" He stood and headed for a sideboard. "So there's no need to get your back up. I no more care for other lasses than I wish to fly. Fancy water? A wee dram?"

"Water," Douglas replied, aware of his parched mouth. "Then a dram…for the pain. Lady…my mare?" Now that he knew Morag was safe, his thoughts turned to his mare. Had she been left untended in the tavern stable?

"Frank Miller has been seein' to her, never fear."

"Guid, verrae guid."

When Brodie returned to the bed with the mug of water, he allowed the man to put an arm about his shoulders to raise him sufficiently to drink.

"Easy, laddie. Too much will cramp you." Withdrawing the cup, Brodie straightened, placed it on the table, and went to the hearth to add a log.

"It's a miserable night," he said as sparks flew up for fresh fuel. "Before she put our son to bed and retired herself, my wife advised me not to let you catch a chill."

Douglas became aware of wind howling about the snug cabin and rain buffeting the windows. Ill as he was, he was glad to be inside. He knew the agony of lying sick or wounded at the mercy of the elements. As fever boiled up through his body and pain assaulted him, he also knew what he had to do.

"There is something I must tell you." He looked over at Brodie's broad shoulders as he stood looking down into the flames, one hand gripping the stone mantel above, a booted foot on the fender. "Something you must know…before I die."

"My wife doesn't believe such will be the case." Brodie released his grip, and turned back toward him. "She's a right fine healer, as you may know…"

"Listen!" The command was a strangled cry as he tried to pull himself upright. And failed.

"Verrae well, verrae well." Brodie pulled a chair close to the bed and sat down. He laid a restraining hand on Douglas's shoulder. "Rest easy. I'll listen. But speak quietly. Louisa and the bairn need their rest."

"Aye, aye." Douglas relinquished his struggle and drew a deep breath. It hurt and kept him quiet for a moment. Then he burst out, "I'm your brother. Your brother Douglas, who ran from home years ago. Your half brother, the one you called a bastard."

There. The hated word was out.

217

Silence except for the crackling of the freshly fed fire fell over the cabin.

Finally Brodie rubbed a hand over his forehead. "Brother?" he muttered finally. "You're Douglas, my father's son? No, it cannae be. The lad died years ago."

"No, he dunnae." His admission over, Douglas closed his eyes and sank deeper into the pillow. "Look at my right arm. The scar where Father's stallion kicked me…"

"Whit?" Douglas felt his brother's breath on his skin as he bent to examine the healed wound in the flickering firelight. "Sweet Jesus! When I first saw it, I wondered…but believed it couldn't be."

Silence punctuated only by Brodie's heavy breathing made Douglas force his eyes open.

"We were told you were dead, killed by redcoats." Brodie's words reflected his confusion as he looked up from staring at the scar. "Father made a marker for the family plot with your name on it."

"I escaped." He observed Brodie's reactions. "I went to Edinburgh. I…managed to survive there."

"But you were little more than a bairn…a lad of fourteen. How…?"

"Not a pretty story." His strength sliding away, Douglas had to be content with what he'd already revealed.

"Sweet Jesus!" Brodie repeated himself. Rubbing his hands through his hair, he stood and began to pace the room.

"I'll leave as soon as I can get on my feet…if I get on my feet." Douglas bit his lip as another surge of pain raced up his side. "I'm certain sure you don't want any more to do with me than you did fifteen years ago. All I ask is that if I die, bury me. I'd rather not be left to rot on the side of the road."

"Leave? Guid God, laddie, leave? Now that I've just found you again?" Brodie stopped pacing and sank once again into the chair by the bed. "You're my brother, my only living blood kin…besides my son…in this country. Why would I want you to leave?" He reached out a big, calloused hand and stroked dark curls back from Douglas's sweating forehead. His eyes brightened with tears.

"Our parting was…ugly." Weakness was overtaking Douglas, but his brother's reaction gave him solace. If he died now, these moments with his brother would allow him to go in peace. "Do you…recall what you called me on that day?"

"Aye, aye." Brodie looked into Douglas's face, his own contorted with emotion. "I called you a bastard. I've regretted it many a time since. You are my brother, our father's son as much as I am. The fact that he chose to have a dalliance with a tavern wench…"

"She was my mother." Douglas gained enough strength to break into his words.

"Aye, aye, that she was." Drawing a hand across his nose, Brodie looked at Douglas. "And no doubt a guid woman. Our father was at fault, drinkin' to excess, givin' my mother a world of misery…until he brought you home after your own mother had died in childbirth. I was only a wee bit of a lad, but I well remember the day he came into our cottage with you wrapped in a bit of blanket and introduced you as his son."

"There must have been a hell of a row." Douglas wet his lips, but the weak grin that followed made them crack, causing him to flinch.

"Aye, at first. Then you began to fuss. Mother looked down at you and something came over her face. Something soft and carin'. She took you from Father and went to sit in the rocker by the fire, hummin' softly.

" 'You've made a great mistake, Brian,' she said, once you slept. She didn't look up at the man she'd married a dozen years earlier. 'But it's not the wee bairn's fault. He is your son, and he'll be raised as such. Brodie,' she said without takin' her eyes off you. 'Run down to the field and see if you can draw milk from that old nanny goat. Your brother is hungry.' "

"And that was that?" Astonished by the tale, Douglas could only stare at Brodie.

"Well, no, not exactly. Mother and Father would have more than a few skirmishes over the years…they were a passionate pair…but they always patched things and kept us together as a family."

"She never treated me any differently from you. I never guessed she wasn't my birth mother until that day we fought over Annie Burns, and you…"

"I called you a bastard, said my mother wasn't yours, that yours was a tavern slut. Lad, I'm that sorry. I was young and hot after Annie. It just burst out…the secret our parents had made me promise never to reveal to you."

"What of our neighbors, servants…? No one ever spoke of it."

"Laddie, you remember our father…and our mother. They were a formidable influence in our part of the Highlands. No one dared suggest the son in whom they took such pride was not their own flesh and blood. Why, our da was a bear of a man. Can you imagine anyone daring to call his younger son a bastard?"

"But the girl…my birth mother…what of her?"

"She was just a young lass workin' at an inn. Our father had had a ragin' argument with our mother…I have no idea what about. They both had sharp tempers. He stormed out of the cottage one winter's night, flask in hand, vowing not to return until she begged his forgiveness. You knew our mother. That was not going to happen." Brodie paused, a corner of his mouth curling. "Any road"—he continued his tale—"Father was gone a good week. That was when you were conceived, I imagine. When he returned, he embodied contriteness…brought Mother a new gown and a bonnet and a great emerald ring. I don't know what else he did or said, but within a few days they were back together, as lovin' as a pair of doves. He was no' without charm…much like his sons." Brodie paused to wink at Douglas and the younger sibling managed a weak smile.

"I think he near forgot about his time with Eliza…until one day he was summoned to that very inn where he'd shared her bed." Brodie continued his tale. "When he returned, he brought you."

"It's good to know the truth." Reality slipping away, Douglas closed his eyes. Finally at peace with his brother, he could go.

The last he remembered was his brother's frantic cries.

"Douglas! Douglas! Bloody hell! Louisa, come quick!"

Chapter Twenty-Eight

"That woman again!" Hazel Green glanced out her kitchen window. "And riding astride. As a minister's wife, she should have at least some sense of decorum."

Morag, sitting at the table, dropped the teacup she'd been holding. Mary Morgan. Had Douglas died? Louisa MacMillan had promised to send word of his condition via the minister's wife.

"Now look what you've done!" Her mother rushed forward to sop up the tea with a rag. "You must come to yourself, my girl."

"Yes, Mother." Weakness consuming her, Morag could only sit frozen as she was and wait for the reason for Mary Morgan's visit.

"Good morning, ladies." The brightness of the minister's wife's countenance sent a surge of hope flooding through Morag as her mother opened the door to admit her. "It's a lovely morning, is it not?"

"If a person enjoys sun and southwest breezes." Hazel Green, as usual, was not ready to find good in anything.

"Yes, well, I do." Mary Morgan pulled off her leather gloves. "And I've brought good news. I've just spoken to Mrs. MacMillan, and it appears Mr. Smith is on his way to recovery."

"Thank God!" Morag jumped to her feet, a wave of relief dashing over her.

"Now, we mustn't be overly optimistic," Mary Morgan cautioned. "He's still got a goodly way to go before Louisa will declare him fit, but at least it's a step in the right direction."

"We must be grateful," Hazel Green responded properly, but her expression was far from cordial. "Some say he deliberately saved Morag's life. I have other thoughts on the matter. Nevertheless, I shall say a prayer for his recovery."

"That's most generous of you." Mary Morgan smiled. "I was wondering if Miss Green would care to accompany me to visit him at the MacMillan residence. I've a few edibles he might enjoy in a basket on my horse."

"Yes, of course!" Morag headed for her sunbonnet and shawl by the door.

"Of course not!" Her mother intercepted her. "I'll not have you visiting that man again!"

"But Mother, he saved my life!"

"Well, if he did, it was by accident. Nevertheless"—Hazel Green drew a deep breath and headed for the cupboard—"let it not be said I don't do my Christian duty." She put several freshly baked scones into a cloth and tied it into a bag. "You may take these to Mr. Smith." She held it out to Mary Morgan.

The minister's wife took the improvised sack. "That's most kind of you, Mrs. Green," she said. "And I will also mention Miss Green's heartfelt concern."

With a sly smile in Morag's direction, she turned and went back outside.

"Impertinent wench!" Hazel Green turned her attention to a pot of soup simmering on the hearth. "But what can one expect from a Highlander!"

Morag barely heard her mother's denunciation of the minister's wife. Her heart was fluttering too happily with her news. Douglas was recovering.

Chapter Twenty-Nine

The dreams, mostly nightmares, haunted him. Sometimes he was back in the Highlands, running, running through the heather. Darkness, everywhere darkness, hoofbeats behind him, a black void before him. He fell, falling, falling until he hit frigid water and battled to swim, to keep his head above the surface.

Suddenly, the situation changed and he was in a lush meadow filled with blossoming flowers and warm breezes and Morag. Morag in a diaphanous white gown was running toward him, arms outstretched, her beautiful face alight with joy. Before she could reach him, a huge abyss opened in front of her and she plunged out of sight. As he rushed forward in a frantic effort to save her, Hazel Green, her face bright with evil pleasure, waving her arms in his face, stopped him. How, he didn't know, only that his feet froze to the ground and he was powerless to move.

"Argh!" He started and lurched upward. A strong hand on his shoulder held him back. When he could focus, he saw it wasn't Hazel Green but his brother who held him in place.

"So you decided to come back to the land of the livin', did you, laddie?" His weathered face twitched into a grin, but his eyes were moist. "Guid, lad. Guid, lad." He ran a calloused hand over Douglas's forehead.

"What day…how long have I been…?" Douglas

struggled to form questions, but his brain seemed fogged and staggering.

"A while. You ran a great fever." Brodie turned to a basin of water, wrung excess water from a cloth in it, and began to bathe Douglas's forehead. "Rest easy, brother, rest easy."

The words soothed Douglas and he lay back, accepting Brodie's ministrations.

"I had strange dreams." He finally managed to put words into a sentence.

"Aye, Louisa said that might happen. She gave you a new, powerful drug to relieve the pain. Morphine, it's called."

"Hazel Green…she was chasing me."

"Dear God, that drug must be right dreadful if it made you dream of her." Douglas saw a full grin suffuse Brodie's face. "Maybe the pain would have been better."

"Aye, perhaps." Douglas found he could manage what he hoped was a return of his brother's cynical good humor. "But that drug did kill much of the suffering."

"Now." Brodie stood and headed into the bedroom. "There's someone I want you to meet."

He returned in a moment, pride glowing from his countenance and a rosy-cheeked child in his arms.

"Meet your nephew," he said. "Alexander MacMillan, this is your Uncle Douglas."

The child made a sound like a chuckle, a smile coming over his face.

"Your servant, Master Alexander." A warmth spread over Douglas as he managed to twist cracked lips into what he hoped was a semblance of an equally welcoming response.

"He'll be seein' his second birthday come Christmas." Brodie placed the youngster on the floor and stood back with pride as Alexander MacMillan paused only a moment before toddling toward Douglas, reaching out small hands.

With an effort that made him flinch, Douglas managed to turn sufficiently in his bed to accept them. So small and soft. He felt his breath catch in his throat. And his nephew, his family.

Alexander grinned before turning to his father, removing his hands from Douglas's and reaching up to his father. "Milk, Da," he cried.

"Aye, aye." Brodie scooped him up and headed for the door. "This young laddie hasn't a great many words yet, but he's learned how to demand food. We'll be back shortly, Douglas. Just a quick trip to the icehouse to get this lad sustenance. Louisa insists milk be kept chilled after it comes from our cow." He paused before going outside. "By the by, my guid wife is off seein' to a patient, so we men are on our own. I'm hopin' my efforts at cookin' won't kill the three of us."

After the door had closed behind them, Douglas heaved a great sigh…and flinched. It pulled at the wound under the bandages swathed about his chest, but the relief he was feeling minimized the hurt. Morag was safe, he'd made peace with his brother, and even Lady was being cared for.

He looked around the clean, tidy room, enjoying its ambience right down to the sunlight streaming in through the windows. The cabin gave him peace. He thought of the smiling face of Brodie's bairn, of all that his brother had, and how he longed for the same.

Mustn't be greedy or ungrateful. He was alive and he'd been reunited with his brother. When he was well enough, he'd return to his homestead and settle into the life of a bachelor. He knew he'd never be satisfied with any other woman than Morag, and having her as wife was impossible.

****

"Unc." Grinning, baby Alex toddled across the cabin. When he reached his uncle sitting in a chair by the hearth, he extended his arms. "Up," he demanded.

"Aye, aye." Chuckling, Douglas lifted the child into his arms and planted him on his knee. "You've got the brains of your mother and the brazenness of your da. The first"—he glanced over at Louisa bent over the hearth as she prepared their evening meal—"is all to the good. The second, well, now…" He grinned at his brother, who'd come in from working at the mill in time to catch the last remark.

"To be expected." Brodie took the teasing in good form. "After all, I was once known as Brazen Brodie." He pulled his sweat-damp shirt off over his head to reveal a broad chest glistening with perspiration.

"Brodie, outside." His wife turned to him. "Why do you think I leave fresh water and a clean shirt by the wash stand on the veranda?"

"Ah, verrae well, woman." He crossed the room to give her a spank on the bottom. "But it wasn't all that long ago you found me as such more than a bit interestin'."

"Go!" She pointed to the door. "You're a respectable married family man now, and you'll behave as one." Douglas, having lived with the couple and their son for several weeks, knew there was no seriousness in

Louisa's words.

"Aye, aye, respectable." He started for the door but spun around to sweep her into his arms and kiss her soundly on the lips.

"Ah," he said, drawing back to hold his wife out at arms' length, "laddie, let me tell you that when you love a woman, that never grows old."

Whistling, he turned and went out.

Chapter Thirty

As the days passed, Douglas regained his strength. He became able to help his brother with light barn work and assist Louisa in the vegetable garden. Little Alex toddled after him, giggling, arms held up to be hoisted into his embrace or, as his strength improved, onto his shoulders.

"He's right fond of you," Brodie said one evening after their supper, when Louisa came to take the child from Douglas. The little lad squealed in protest. "Hie, there, laddie," he spoke to the child. "None of your nonsense. Go along with your mother. It's past your bedtime, and your uncle needs to rest."

Pouting back over Louisa's shoulder as she carried him into the bedroom, Alex puckered his small face into a frown of resentment.

"Go along, little Alex," Douglas spoke in Gaelic. "I'll be here in the morning."

"Guid, guid." Brodie went to the cupboard to take down the whisky flask. "I must speak the tongue more often. I'm fair losin' the language, what with speakin' English for years back in the Highlands to fool the redcoats. And now here"—he waved a dismissive hand—"most of us have given up our mother tongue. I want my lad to know where his roots lie."

"But Mrs. MacMillan—Louisa"—Douglas quickly recalled her admonition against calling her Missus since he'd become known to her as her brother-in-law—"she's English."

"Aye, well, he gets enough of that talk without effort. Maybe someday, when things have changed, he'll be able to visit the Highlands and discover family…on his old man's side."

He poured a measure into each of two mugs and returned to hand one to Douglas before dropping into a chair opposite him. He took a drink, then leaned back with a sigh. "Gettin' old, Douglas, my lad," he sighed. "One time I could work all day and ride like a demon all night with nary an ache or a pain. Now, a day at the mill and homestead duties can leave me fair tuckered. The only solace"—he winked at Douglas—"is that Louisa is a dab hand at massagin' away some of the hurt." He reached out to give Douglas a nudge. "Someday, if you've luck, you'll have the fair Morag doin' a similar service for you."

"That's no' decent talk," Douglas snapped. "Miss Green is a lady."

"Aye, that she is, but ladies can surprise you sometimes." Brodie glanced toward the bedroom from which the soft sounds of Louisa singing the baby to sleep issued before leaning toward his brother. "Louisa is a lady, you know," he whispered.

"I know." Douglas couldn't understand his brother's secretive tone. "She's clever and…"

"No, no, you great pillock!" Brodie hissed. "She's a genuine lady, an aristocrat…back in England she would be Lady Louisa Spencer, daughter of Lord Maxwell Spencer. Mind"—he hastened on—"you're never to let Louisa know I told you. She's right sensitive about keepin' her heritage a secret."

"Guid God!"

"Hush! We've both agreed to leave our pasts behind us. I just thought you should know"—he leaned back in his chair—"that you have ties to the aristocracy. I imagine that would impress the wind out of the sails of that nasty Hazel Green."

Douglas chuckled.

"Whit?"

"You, a Highland outlaw, married to a member of…"

"Keep your voice down, for God's sake! I'll be sleepin' out here with you if she finds out I've told you about her."

"You are a character, brother, and no mistake." Douglas stifled his mirth. "Life around you can never be dull."

"Aye, that's true. Sometimes it gets a bit too lively. Now, I've a question I've been meanin' to ask you. How did you manage to find me after all these years?"

"That old lad who hangs around the tavern, Jonah Parsons, has a brother who is more than his equal in being an ale house vagrant in Edinburgh. Artie Parsons is his name. I heard of this old reprobate spouting off as to how his brother had become a boon companion of the famous outlaw Brazen Brodie in a place called Riverhaven in the province of New Brunswick. Everyone took him to be a great liar, telling tales for the price of a drink, but I wondered if there might be some truth in his stories, so after I got into a bit of a scrape and had to escape, I decided to have a chin wag with Mr. Parsons."

"Bloody hell! It appears it's right hard to get out of the shadow of a lad's past. Those Parson brothers have big mouths and no mistake. Any road, I'm happy as hell you found me."

"As am I, brother."

"Now, gettin' back to your problem. I've been thinkin'." Brodie leaned back in his chair. "There's more than one way to win a battle. I have a wee idea, something I've been ponderin' since the first time I clapped eyes on Miss Morag. Give me a day or so. By that time you should feel up to proposin' marriage, and I'll have it all arranged...with her parents' consent."

"Brodie, you know I signed an agreement to stay away from her..." Douglas tried to protest, but with a wave of his hand, his brother dismissed his words. He swallowed the last of his drink and stood.

"Stuff and nonsense. You'll be havin' a visitor tomorrow mornin' that will change your mind. Now, if I'm not mistaken, my guid wife has fallen silent. That means the bairn is asleep and she's most likely abed herself. High time I'm joinin' her." He stood and stretched. "Best cover your head with a pillow, young lad. I'm feelin' right romantic this evening."

What visitor? Who? And how could anyone change his mind about keeping his word?

****

Douglas was milking the cow Louisa and Brodie had purchased to provide milk for their son when he heard a rider in the barnyard. He paused and looked toward the door. A man's figure appeared in silhouette against the bright sunlight flooding inside. A big man, a man who paused for a moment to glance about before focusing on Douglas and starting toward him.

"Douglas, my lad." Reverend Edward Morgan stopped to put a hand on the cow's rump. "I see you're feeling better."

"Aye, that I am, Reverend." Douglas started to rise from the milking stool, but the clergyman stopped him with an upraised hand. "Don't let me interrupt you. I can state my business while you relieve this good beast of her burden."

"Very well." Douglas tried to return to his task but without concentration. What did the minister want?

"I have to get myself a decent riding animal." Edward Morgan overturned a bucket and, grimacing, sat down on it. "That dray, willing as he is, fair shakes my bones loose when I manage to convince him to canter…which is a chore in itself, I can tell you. Now to business. At the urging of my guid wife and the man who has informed me he is your brother, I've come to offer advice."

"Aye?" Douglas stopped making an attempt at milking and turned on the stool to face the minister.

"They believe, as do I, that you must profess your love for Miss Morag and ask her to marry you immediately."

"But I've vowed to stay away from her, I've…"

"Laddie, laddie, you must disregard your promise…this once. All it's destined to do is cause unhappiness for two fine people."

"But my word…"

"I know, I know. Your word should be your bond…in most cases…but not this one. I believe a higher power would overrule your promise to Duncan and Hazel Green. The guid God believes in the beauty and strength of love, true love. He also believes in following the positive path your heart holds open to you."

"I dunnae know." Douglas stood and drew his fingers through dark curls. "I want to believe you, but…

"I can say no more." Edward Morgan stood and drew a deep breath. "Each man must do as his soul dictates. Good day to you, laddie. I can only hope for the sake of both you and Miss Morag that you come to the right decision."

Chapter Thirty-One

Dawn was breaking over the trees the following morning as Douglas led a saddled Lady from his brother's barn. Brodie had brought the animal to his homestead from the stable in the village while Douglas had been recovering.

"No need to be payin' board for the beast when there's a perfectly guid stable right here," he'd informed Douglas on the day he told him he'd retrieved the mare. "And she'll be right handy when you're up to ridin' again."

Douglas bit down on his lower lip as he prepared to mount. He guessed it would hurt like hell, but it was something he had to do. A restless night poring over the reverend's words had brought him to a final decision.

He stuck his foot in the stirrup, sucked in a deep breath, and launched himself upward. He landed in the saddle with a grunt. A flash of nausea darted through his gut. Swallowing hard, he controlled it.

"Walk on," he instructed the mare as he gathered up the reins. "Right slow and careful, lass, if you please."

He paused, hidden in the trees near the gateway to the Green farm, to look over the situation. Shortly he saw Duncan Green come from the house and head for the barn. Impatience nearly overcame him, but he forced himself to wait.

Finally Duncan Green emerged from the barn, his harnessed team in tow. He attached them to a wagon, climbed to the seat, and headed down the lane to the road.

Douglas dismounted with an effort and stifled his mare's desire to call out to the team with a hand over her snout.

When Duncan Green had disappeared from sight, he returned his attention to the farmhouse. His vigilance was soon rewarded as Morag emerged, milk pail in hand, and headed for the barn.

Leaving Lady tied in the trees, he stalked his way around the perimeter of the cleared fields until he was at the rear of the barn. Easing open a door, he let himself inside. The ray of sunlight his entrance allowed made her turn on the milking stool. She gasped.

"Miss Green…Morag"—he wet dry lips and stepped forward—"I've come to…ask"—he blundered ahead, terrified his nerve would desert him—"you to do me the honor of becoming my wife. I love you…I always have and I always will."

There. It was out. His heart pounding, he waited.

She stood slowly, her gaze focused on his face.

Speak, woman, for God's sake, speak.

"I will understand if you refuse." He could not bear her silence. "Knowing what I've told you of my past…and which is the absolute truth…but I have changed my ways and, if you accept me, I promise to love, honor, and care for you with every breath in my body…and be a respectable member of this community as long as I live."

She started toward him, at first with slow steps, finally in a rush that took her into his arms.

"Yes, Douglas Smith, yes, of course I'll become your wife." Her words breathed against his shoulder gave him a wrench of joy such as he'd never before experienced.

"Morag…"

"Kiss me, Douglas…as you kissed me that day in the storm in your cabin." She looked up at him, her eyes bright with what he hoped to be the same happiness he was experiencing. Could a man want any more? He lowered his head to comply with her request, thinking this was now his Morag and he was hers.

"Douglas, let us be married today, at once!" Her enthusiasm, when she finally drew away from his lips, startled him.

"No, no, lass. Much as I wish such to be the case, it cannot happen…not for some time…not until I have built up my homestead, not until…your parents give their consent."

"Douglas, you know as well as I, it will never happen." She drew away from him, her face falling into an expression of disappointed dismay. "Mother will never…"

"Never is a very long time, sweet Morag. I will put all my efforts into changing her mind about me, about us. I will…"

"Do you think I don't know my mother? She's twice as stubborn as any mule. Furthermore, she hates Highlanders and always will. Douglas, let us go at once to Reverend Morgan, let us…"

"No, niver! We will have a public marriage, a legitimate marriage with proper celebrations. I won't run off ever again…not for any reason. Morag, I love you too much not to do what is right by you."

"Damn you!" For the first time since he'd known her, Morag Green cursed…for the first time, he suspected, in her life. "You and your quest to be respectable! Well, you can just go on seeking such a status…alone."

She swung away from him, snatched up her milk pail—causing the startled cow to lurch and bellow—and rushed out of the barn.

Douglas was left alone with the unsettled cow and a fluttering coop of chickens.

****

"So she turned you down." Brodie sat beside Douglas on a bench against the outside wall of his cabin. "Some wise old lad once said something like 'if at first you don't succeed, give it another try.' Ever heard that one?"

"No, and I don't give a damn about what some old bastard said a hundred years ago." Douglas took another quaff from the whisky bottle in his hand.

"There, now, laddie. I don't like you usin' that word…the one I never should have thrown at you all those years ago. Give me a swallow of that stuff. It appears to be some of Frank Miller's finest."

"I paid for it." The words snapped out as he handed the bottle to his brother.

"Did I suggest that you didn't?" Brodie took a swallow before continuing. "Damn, but you're in a foul mood. And it's a hell of your own makin', you realize. You're so determined to be regarded as an upright citizen who does everything just so, you're foulin' your chances at what could be the best thing in your life. So I guess it's up to me to set things right."

"And I suppose you consider yourself an expert on

such matters…having done it twice." Malice colored Douglas's response.

"Do I sense a tad of jealousy, lad?" Brodie took another drink and handed the bottle back to Douglas. "But, truth be told, I've never myself offered marriage to a woman."

"But you've been married twice…you…"

"Aye, aye, but in both cases it was the lass who asked."

"Bloody hell, you've got a high opinion of yourself."

"No, it just happened. Annie told me I'd best marry her if I wanted…"

"If you wanted more than a kiss and a cuddle."

"Aye, aye, that's right. And I did want to marry her, Douglas. I loved her." He stopped speaking and looked down at his boots. "When she died…and the bairn, it hurt so terrible bad, I took to outlawin' not just to get revenge but to kill the pain. It was like havin' a knife stuck in my chest…one I couldn't get out."

Silence except for the wind soughing through the tall pines around the cabin held both men for a time.

"I'm sorry." Douglas spoke finally, softly.

"Aye, well, ridin' with Highland Harry dulled the pain. I thought I'd never marry again, but then I came to this country and met Louisa, and I discovered my ability to love a woman hadn't come to an end. But, at first"—he stretched long legs out in front of him and turned to grin at Douglas—"I was a fool…like you. I thought my outlawin' days ruined me for such a wonder as Louisa. She had other ideas and, as you know, she's a strong-willed lass. She asked me to marry her, and I saw she would brook no refusal. So I agreed. She made a happy, contented man of me, laddie. I'm suspectin' your Morag will do the same for you…if you'll but give her a chance."

"I know she could." Douglas stood to gaze up into the branches over his head. "But I love and respect her too much not to offer a proper wedding with friends and neighbors in attendance…and her parents, even her mother, wishing us well."

"Bloody hell, but you're as obstinate as Hazel Green." Brodie got up and strode over to untie his red mare from where he'd left her fastened to a tree. "I'll definitely have to get involved." He swung into the saddle.

"Brodie, no!"

Douglas yelled after his brother, but he simply waved a hand in farewell as he headed down the lane to the road at an easy lope.

Chapter Thirty-Two

"I feel a right fool." Douglas shrugged his shoulders and twisted his neck as Brodie worked to adjust the neckcloth he'd carefully tied. "All dressed up on a week day. What will Morag think of me?"

"It's not Miss Morag I'm concerned about." Brodie gave the neckcloth a final pat and stood back to admire his handiwork. "It's that dragon of a mother, a woman who's a snob right down to her toes, that we have to impress." He grasped both lapels of his own dress coat and gave them a tug. "We have to show her the MacMillan lads can stand with the best of them when it comes to lookin' fine."

"But you're coming with me to ask for her daughter's hand—" Douglas wet dry lips. "Bloody hell, Brodie."

"Aye, if a man hasn't the gumption to stand up to his future mother-in-law on his own, other measures must be taken."

"Are you saying I'm a coward? Are you saying…?"

"No, no, of course not, laddie. Not in ordinary circumstances such as facing down a regiment of redcoats or throwin' a fine figure of a man out of a tavern." A wicked grin crossed Brodie's face. "But dealin' with the likes of Hazel Green is a whole different circumstance. And I must say"—he strutted across the cabin—"of these two fine-lookin' brothers, I'm the one gifted with gab."

"A wee quaff might just help." Douglas crossed the cabin and reached for a flask on a shelf.

"No, no, definitely not." Brodie was quick to stop him. "A lad serious about courtin' never shows up with the smell of whisky on his breath. Now, come along….before Louisa returns and declares this not the best of ideas. Bella"—he called into the bedroom where Harry Wallace's eldest stepdaughter was minding his child—"if my guid wife asks where I've gone, tell her I'm helpin' my brother with a wee bit of work. And mind, no need to explain to her that I'm dressed to the nines."

****

Together they rode down the road, past Douglas's homestead, and finally into the lane leading to the Greens' farm.

"I'm feeling right sick." Douglas swallowed hard.

"Ah, sweet Jesus, don't go pukin' now." Brodie cast him a belittling look. "That's the last thing you want to do."

They reached the dooryard and dismounted. Before they could approach the door, Hazel Green stormed out of the house. In her hand she held a broom.

"What do you two want?" she snapped, her face contorted into ugly lines of annoyance.

"Mrs. Green, may I say you're lookin' right bonny this fine mornin'?" Brodie started to move toward her.

"None of your fancy talk, Brodie MacMillan!" She waved the broom in his face. "State your business and get off this farm!"

"We've"—he indicated Douglas—"come to speak

to your husband…and your guid self…on a matter that concerns my brother here."

Bloody hell, Brodie! Have you taken leave of your senses, identifying me as your kin?

"Your brother?" Her voice rose to shocked squeak. "You mean this…this man is your blood relative?"

"Aye, and right proud I was to discover the fact. We were parted as lads in the Highlands, and it's only recently we've found each other again."

"Dear God, can this get any worse! My daughter involved with another MacMillan. Get off our property now, this very minute!" She shook the broom in their direction.

"Gentlemen." Both men turned to see Duncan Green limping toward them, pleasure brightening his expression. "What can I do for you?"

"We've come to speak to you and your guid wife on a matter of importance, Duncan." Brodie turned his most affable grin on the farmer. "A matter perhaps best discussed inside?" He indicated the farmhouse.

"I'll not be inviting the likes of you, Brodie MacMillan, into my home," Hazel Green cried, "not you, nor any member of your family!"

"Verrae well, if you choose to disdain decorum. My brother wishes to ask for the right to marry your daughter."

"Marry!" The word was another shriek from the woman's lips. "Marry! Are you both insane! Marry a Highlander who works in a tavern, who lives in a hovel…who tried to seduce her?"

"Mrs. Green, a minute." Her husband stepped forward in the role of peacemaker. "The lads are but inquiring…and very properly," he finished, looking over their finery.

"You can't make a gentleman out of a rogue and an outlaw!" Incensed, she waved the broom again. "Did you know this Douglas Smith is really Douglas MacMillan, this conniving creature's brother? Don't you dare welcome them onto our property."

"Mother, what is it?" Morag emerged from the house. Seeing the two men, she stopped short before dipping a quick curtsy in their direction. "Gentlemen," she said softly. Douglas was rewarded by seeing her usual shy blush brighten her lovely face. What right had he to think such an ethereal creature would marry him? The seeming ridiculousness of their quest gushed over him.

"Come on, Brodie, let's go," he muttered, gathering up Lady's reins and starting to mount.

"Hang on, laddie, hang on." His brother stayed him. "Mrs. Green, ma'am, I may have a bit of a reputation, but Douglas here is a steady, honest lad. Guid God, woman, he was the one who rode for my wife's help when Duncan here was injured, he was the one who organized the harvestin' of your grain, and he was the one who took a musketball to save your daughter. Could he have done more for you and your family?"

"The first two chores you mentioned he merely did to get close to Morag." The woman tossed her head disdainfully. "And as for saving Morag from a musketball, why, I'll wager he merely stumbled drunkenly into its path. After all, he does spend his days and nights in a tavern. Husband, see these roués on their way. If they're not gone within seconds, I'll be back with your musket!"

"Sweet Jesus!" Brody snarled as the woman turned and flounced back into the house. "The woman's a harridan and no mistake. Sorry, Duncan"—he turned to the husband who stood seemingly stymied staring after his wife—"but there's no reasonin' with her. Now, you…can Douglas have your consent, if not to marry your lass right off, to at least court her?"

"Brodie, you're putting me in a great quandary." Duncan lowered his head and shook it sadly. "I'm sure your brother has proper intentions in seeking to court my girl, but if I go against the wife…"

"And if you go against me, you'll be drivin' over a hundred miles to get your grain milled."

"Brodie, don't go making threats." Douglas stopped his brother as he saw his affable demeanor dissolving into outright anger. He turned to the farmer. "Mr. Green, thank you for hearing us out."

He understood the man's awkward position only too well. If Duncan Green defied his wife, his life would become a living hell. He swung into Lady's saddle. "Come along, Brodie. I have to get back to work."

"Bloody hell." Brodie's words were a disgusted mutter as he mounted. "Duncan," he spoke to the farmer again, "I can only hope your wife finds a man for Morag who will suit her requirements and"—he glanced at the young woman standing mutely on the top step—"who will process your wheat."

He swung his mount away and started down the dusty lane at a gallop. Douglas, after a final glance at Morag, followed.

Above the thunder of his mare's hooves, he heard her cry out his name.

Chapter Thirty-Three

"I think we'd best be invitin' Duncan for a wee dram." Once more in Brodie's cabin and both men changed into work clothing, Brodie took a flask down from a top shelf. "And addin' a few drops of this stuff." He picked up a bottle from among his wife's medicines.

"What is it?" Douglas was instantly suspicious.

"I dunnae know the name of it, but one night when I had a fair measure of pain after Vixen threw me, Louisa gave me a bit in a cup of whisky. It not only killed the pain, but it fair set my tongue waggin'. Although I don't remember all I said, I do know I told her tales of my life back in the Highlands, a few of them right raunchy…after I lost Annie. Thank the guid God, my wife is a broad-minded woman, not easily shocked, and prepared to accept me as I am."

"And your idea of slipping some it to Duncan Green would be…?"

"I've always wondered how a beauty like Mistress Morag could be the child of hatchet-faced Hazel and poor old Duncan." Brodie slipped both containers into pockets in his vest. "Their daughter was born shortly after they arrived in this country, I understand, and all seemed right and proper, but…"

"Brodie, are you saying Morag isn't their natural daughter?"

"I'm just speculatin'. Miss Morag has the looks of

a Highland beauty. Duncan and Hazel came from Yorkshire, right close to the Scottish border. What if a Highlander, some dark night, snuck down and made love to the oh-so-righteous Miss Hazel? What if…?"

"Brodie, what you're proposing sounds downright underhanded and unfair. I don't want any part of it."

"Oh, and it's not unfair for that miserable witch to tar all Highlanders with the same brush, to condemn a good man like yourself simply because of where he came from…or maybe because of what someone of our ilk did to her in the past? I'm not the first to question Morag's parentage, laddie. There's been speculation on the matter for some time around Riverhaven."

"But still…"

"Look here, brother, I know you've got guts. Otherwise you wouldn't have survived all those years on your own. Use them and answer me this. Will you make Miss Morag a guid husband? Will you care for her and provide for her and guard her with your life as long as you have breath?"

"Of course I will. You don't need to go asking such daft questions."

"Well, then, isn't providin' the lass with such a good man worth a bit of deception?" He gathered up three tankards from the shelves and headed for the door. "Come on. It won't do Duncan a bit of harm…the poor bugger needs a bit of relief from his darlin' wife. His expression told me he's nowhere near dead set against you as a son-in-law."

****

The three men sat on the grassy bank of the trout pond behind Douglas's cabin, each holding a tankard.

"This is one fine drink," Duncan Green smacked

his lips and drew a deep breath. "I've not had such in many a moon."

"I reckon as how Mrs. Green is opposed to liquor?" Brodie leaned forward to replenish the farmer's tankard, but Douglas noticed he'd stealthily switched the whisky flask for the one containing the painkiller.

Brodie drew the conversation to farming, speaking of Douglas's plans to begin such an undertaking. Warmed by the drink and one of his favorite subjects, Duncan Green began to speak freely and at length on the subject until Brodie subtly directed the conversation to other matters.

"Duncan, I reckon as how you wouldn't mind your girl marryin' a farmer, now would you? She's been brought up to the life, and I'm imaginin' she enjoys it."

"Oh, yes. Morag fair delights in the fields and the stock. She's a fine little cook and housekeeper as well. She'd suit some farmer as a wife right down to the ground."

"Then why not my brother here?" Brodie was his most affable, pleasant self. "He's got a house and a barn and a tidy bit of land, and shortly he'll be expandin'."

"Ah, now, Brodie, you know how the wife feels about Highlanders." Douglas observed Duncan Green relaxing under the influence of his brother's affability and the liquid he'd slipped into the man's drink.

"But Douglas is not Morag's father. You mustn't judge all Highlanders by what that lad did."

Douglas caught his breath as his brother deftly eased the information into the conversation.

"Perhaps not, but he broke Hazel's heart and run off…" His eyes becoming dreamlike, he stared up into the trees, apparently not aware of his faux pas.

"But you took his place." Brodie pushed for more information. "You married her and brought her here to this country where no one would ever know you weren't her child's papa. You've been a right good father to her, Duncan. No one could have done better."

"I tried. God knows I tried. When Hazel's father discovered she was with child, he paid me well to bring her out to this country where no one would know of her disgrace. That was why I was able to set up this farm, why we were able to live comfortable shortly after we arrived." He drew a deep breath. "But I sometimes think I made a large mistake. I'll never be free of that harping woman. Of course, at the time it seemed the wise thing to do. I was a soldier wounded in France. There's not much call for a man with a gimpy leg."

"No shame in it, Duncan. We've all made compromises, and we'll keep your secret to the grave…under certain conditions." Brodie patted him on the shoulder. "Me and my brother here gave up our home in the Highlands and will likely never be allowed to return. So"—he looked the farmer squarely in the eyes—"what do you say, my friend? Will you no' give your consent and blessin' for Douglas to marry your lass?" He pulled a paper from inside his vest. "All you have to do is sign this paper statin' such."

Douglas jerked backward. When in God's name had his brother written such a document?

"I wrote this up"—Brodie answered his question—"on the day I learned of your lass's rejection of my brother because he was fool enough to propose marriage only on the condition that she wait until he's a blessed lord of the manor. I'll be changin' his mind on that account once he receives your consent."

"You're a good lad." Duncan Green looked up at Douglas, his eyes slightly glazed, his speech slurring just a tad. "All right, I'll sign."

"And if your uppity wife tries to nay say, you must remind her both Douglas and I know her secret and will swear on the Bible to keep it only if she agrees to let my young brother wed your lass." Brodie leaned forward to replenish Duncan's drink, this time with actual whisky.

"That sounds a fair deal." Duncan paused to take a sip. "I've always wanted my girl to marry someone she cares for…and she's made it clear she cares for you, young fellow." He looked over at Douglas. "But take good care of her…else"—his eyes suddenly twinkled—"I'll send my wife to pay you a visit."

"I will, sir, I pledge to you I will."

"Bloody hell, who wouldn't, with such a threat hangin' over them?" Brodie muttered.

＊＊＊＊

Douglas sat in Brodie's cabin, watching his sister-in-law stirring up a batch of one of her concoctions at the table. His brother had gone back to work in the mill, little Alex napped in the bedroom, and the wolf dog Jasper slept peacefully by the door.

"You seem troubled." Louisa looked over at him. "Can I help?"

"I don't know." He heaved a deep breath. "I would value your opinion, yet…"

"Does it involve something my husband did?" A small sardonic smile curled her lips as she returned to her work. "If so, don't worry. Nothing he did or will do will astound me. I'm also very good at keeping a confidence."

"It's like this." He realized he could trust her and that he wanted the advice of someone wise and cool-headed.

When he'd finished the tale of how Brodie had extracted Duncan Green's permission to marry Morag, he leaned back in his chair and closed his eyes.

"I'm torn, Louisa," he said. "I want to marry Morag more than anything in this world, but I don't want it to be by coercion. I want it to be with honesty and fairness…and respectability."

"Of course you do." She paused in her task to give him her full attention. "There can be no respectability without honesty."

"Aire you saying my brother is lacking in both?" He opened his eyes and sat up straight, startled by the implication of her statement.

"No, no, not at all. Brodie simply has his own definition of honesty. He sees it as being true to himself. People around here have come to accept him as the truly good-hearted, affable man he really is and respect him as such."

"My mother must have injected calmer blood into the wild MacMillan spirit." He stood and headed for the door. "Thank you, Louisa."

Chapter Thirty-Four

"What do you want?" Hazel Green glared at Douglas when she opened her kitchen door in response to his knock. "Haven't you caused my family enough chaos already? Haven't you…"

"Mrs. Green, ma'am"—Douglas broke in on her tirade—"if you please, just hear me out. Then, if you still find me unacceptable, I'll go and not trouble you again." He knew he was risking all or nothing, but it had to be done.

She eyed him up and down suspiciously. He was dressed in his working clothes. Fine garments hadn't impressed her previously. He was counting on total honesty to save the day.

"Very well." She came out onto the doorstep. "Say your piece."

"Verrae well." No invitation to come inside. This wasn't going to be any easier than he'd expected. "Is your daughter about?"

"No, she's gone into the village with her father. But don't think you can take advantage of me."

"I wouldn't think of it."

"Well, then, state your business and be on your way."

"Mrs. Green, I love your daughter," he began. The confession was met with a glare. "If you grant me the great honor of allowing her to become my wife, I vow to care for her with every bit of body and soul and provide for her to the very best of my ability to the end of my days."

"Huh! Pretty words that mean nothing. And if you think that Highland accent of yours will influence me, you're quite mistaken."

"Perhaps you've heard pleasing words before...spoken in the same tone?" He took a great gamble.

"What? What are you saying?" The woman's narrow face flushed, then turned pale.

"I'm saying, ma'am, that perhaps once there was a Highlander in your life? A Highlander who didn't honor his pleasing words and promises...a Highlander who broke your heart?"

"You're mad!" she cried. "I'd have nothing to do with your kind, nothing, do you hear?"

"I can think of no other reason for your hatred of me and my kind." Douglas wet his lips and held his ground. "But it's no' fair, tarring all of my people with the same brush."

"And you're a shining example of the better class of those of your ilk?"

"I admit I have done things in my past of which I'm not proud, but that's over now. I plan to be a market farmer, supplying produce to the mill, lumber camps, and shipbuilding workers. Mr. Miller, my present employer, believes I can make a fine future doing such."

"How can I believe you, brother to that wild man Brodie MacMillan?"

"Brodie may sometimes take the law into his own hands, but as far as I can ascertain, he's only done such to help others. And, if it's my lineage that disturbs you so, Brodie is my half brother."

Guid God, have I gone mad, telling such facts to this woman?

"Half brother?" At least he'd gained her attention, at least she'd quieted with interest.

"Aye. We have the same father but different mothers. Our father never married my mother. Brodie's mother, our father's wife, took me in and raised me as her own. She made no issue of the fact that she wasn't my blood kin and our Highland neighbors were good enough to turn a blind eye to my antecedents. They saw no great shame in the circumstances of my birth. All that mattered was that we were a caring family with no lies existing to sully it."

His words had a miraculous effect on the woman before him. She put her hands over her face, a sob breaking from beneath them. He gave her time to recover. When she looked up at him, her face was contorted into lines of sorrow.

"You know, don't you?" she choked. "You know that Morag is not my husband's child?"

"I've heard rumors."

"I fell in love with a Highlander who came to work on my father's farm in Yorkshire." She used a corner of her apron to dry her eyes. "He was handsome and charming, and I loved him…oh, how I loved him. Then one day he was gone…gone to fight for Scotland…and I discovered I was with child. My father would not tolerate the disgrace, so he seized on Duncan to remedy the situation. Duncan had recently come home from fighting in France, where he'd been wounded, and taken up menial work on my father's estate. Papa paid him generously to marry me and take me off to America, where no one would ever know of my shame."

"But you were blessed with a beautiful daughter. Such could not be wrong."

"Blessed, you say?" She recovered sufficiently to glance up at him. "That dark shadow has followed me every day of my life. Don't you think that every time I look at her I'm reminded of him? Don't you think I fear she'll be a wild rogue like her father?"

"Don't you remember the love you shared with her father, even if briefly? Don't you find joy in the fact that Morag is a result of that love? Aren't you grateful for the caring and concern of Mr. Green, who has been faithful and kind all these years? I can see no dark shadows in your life, Mrs. Green."

She lowered her gaze to her hands, which had begun to twist a corner of her apron.

"Mrs. Green, life is what we make it. My early years, after I ran away from my parents' home as a young lad, were rough and frequently unlawful in order to survive. I hated it. I vowed that if I ever was given the chance, I'd make a good life for myself, that I'd have a family and treat them as my most cherished possessions. All I need to make that vision come true is Morag. Will you give us your blessing?"

"I…I don't know what to say." When she looked up at him, he was startled to see tears in her eyes.

"Mrs. Green, although I know you don't approve of her, my sister-in-law Louisa MacMillan is a wise woman. She said respectability is honesty…being honest first with yourself and then with others. Since coming to this country, I've been honest with myself. I didn't at first reveal my past, but neither did I make false claims about it. I know what I've been, but I also know what I'm becoming. Now I've shared it all with you in the hope that you will regard this soul baring as evidence of my good intentions not only toward your daughter but toward you and Mr. Green as well."

"Mr. Green told me how your brother connived to get him to sign some document…giving you permission to marry Morag on the condition you never revealed the truth about her birth." She met him squarely with her look.

"Aye, and for that I'm truly sorry. Here." He pulled the paper from inside his shirt and held it out to her. "Do with it as you will."

She hesitated only a moment before seizing it. He watched her eyes moving as she read its contents before she began to rip it to shreds.

"You'll not be needing such a document, Mr. Smith," she said. "You have my permission to marry my daughter…and my blessing."

The sounds of horses and a wagon entering the lane to the farmhouse made him turn. Morag was seated beside her father as the team lumbered toward them.

Unable to wait any longer, he ran to meet them. Getting between the big drays, he grasped each by a bridle and pulled them to a halt.

"What do you think you're doing?" Duncan Green yelled at him. "Have you taken leave of your senses, man?"

"Perhaps I have." He released the stopped horses and strode back to reach up to take Morag from the seat. "Morag, your mother has given us permission to marry…and her blessing."

"Douglas, surely not…" She stared at him.

"Surely, aye." He inserted his foot into a spoke of the wagon wheel and grasped her about the waist. When they were both on the ground, he drew her into a kiss, unmindful of her father's admonishing grunt.

When he at last released her lips, he could barely manage words. They came out in a mixture of a breath and a mutter, not at all what he'd planned, but his joy would allow for no further contemplation.

"Morag, I know I've asked previously, but then it wasn't possible, so I'm asking again. Will you marry me?"

"Douglas—" She stared up at him, her expression lighting up as she came to comprehend all that was happening. "Of course I will."

Her father, with another grunt but this time with a grin beginning to curl his lips, clucked to the team, sending them moving toward the barn.

Douglas and Morag were left alone in the dusty lane to revel in their happiness.

Chapter Thirty-Five

"Now, you'd best get a good night's sleep. I'm reckonin' you won't be getting' much on the morrow."

"What are you talking about?" They sat on the bench at Douglas's cabin as sun dappled the woods. "I want to ride over to see Morag. I want…"

"Haven't you ever heard the old wives' tale about it being bad luck to see the bride on her weddin' day…or even a couple of days aforehand?"

"Whit…?"

"Well, I knew we could fix things, so I've had my wife and her friend the minister's wife plan your weddin' for tomorrow. Lachlan, Reverend Edward Morgan as he calls himself now, had one fine long speech planned for your nuptials, but I convinced him to get straight to the point."

"Have you taken leave of your senses, man!" Douglas stared at his brother. "I've done no courting…and look at this place. Does it appear a fitting place to which to bring a bride?"

"The lass has accepted you, hasn't she?"

"Aye, well, yes, she has, but…"

"Well, then shut your trap. I'd suggest you get up early to take an allover wash in the trout pond yonder, and don't forget to give your teeth a good scrubbin' with salt. Not to worry about bein' late for the ceremony. I'm spendin' the night here with you. As

259

your witness, I want to make certain you show up bright-eyed and bushy-tailed for the ceremony." He stood and strode over to where he'd left Vixen tied to a tree and began to lead her to the stable. "I've brought my Sunday best. I won't have to go home to dress," he said, indicating a sack tied behind his saddle. "Now, I'm right tuckered. I may have had a few sips too many of that fine whisky. I'm goin' to have a bit of a nap."

****

That evening as Brodie and Douglas sat on the bench outside the cabin, the sound of a raucous crowd coming up the lane reached their hearing.

"Ah, the lads are here…and right on time." Grinning, Brodie stood to wave a greeting.

"Whit…?" Douglas also got to his feet as a group of local men, led by Frank Miller driving a wagon, erupted into the clearing. Some on horseback, some in the tavern owner's conveyance, they burst into the clearing amid shouts and yells.

"We've come to give you a proper sendoff on your last night of freedom, lad." His employer jumped to the ground to slap Douglas on the back. "Now, gentlemen…" He turned to the crowd. "I think you'll find ample to quench your thirst in the wagon. Tonight the drinks are on me."

****

Douglas woke to a blinding headache. Bloody hell, what had happened?

As his mind began to clear, he struggled to a sitting position on the edge of his bed to see Brodie asleep in the chair by the hearth, head thrown back, snoring.

Oh, God! His male friends and neighbors rallying to give him what they considered a proper sendoff toward his marriage day. The ale, the whisky… It came back to him in a blurry rush.

His stomach revolted, and he made a dash for outdoors. After his gut had quieted, he put his hands on his hips and threw back his head to stare up into the sunlight beginning to peek through the trees. Sweet Jesus! Brodie had declared this was to be his wedding day, and he knew from experience there was no stopping his brother's plans once they were in full swing.

The prospect of finally marrying the lass of his dreams was a glorious one, but not as he was now, struggling to recover from a night of outrageous drinking. He wet dry lips. Somehow he had to get himself decent. Turning too quickly, he stumbled and grimaced as his head pounded. He could think of only one possible cure, and he headed for the trout pond.

After a long soaking in the cold water, he sucked in a deep breath and headed for the shore. As he pulled on his breeches, his brother's chuckling voice made him look up.

"A tad the worse for wear, are you, laddie? Ah, well, that fresh water will help. Any road, I have a cure for what ails you, back at the cabin." Brodie stripped off his breeches and headed into the water. "But first, I can do with a bit of a dip myself. You get on up to the house and try to make yourself as good-lookin' as you can. I'll join you shortly."

****

"Feelin' better, aren't you?" Brodie straightened Douglas's neckcloth, then stood back to survey his handiwork.

"Aye, but that was one God-awful concoction you

fed me. It tasted like cow dung. What was it?"

"Just a little something my guid wife whipped up for me once when I overindulged. She did, however, warn me that if I ever came home in that condition again, she wouldn't promise me what she'd put in the drink. I brought along a jar of it in anticipation of how you might feel this fine summer's morn. How would you be knowin' what cow dung tastes like anyway?"

"Had my face rubbed in it once when I was a lad...after I'd tried to steal eggs from a farmer."

"Aw, bloody hell, laddie. I'm that sorry. You've led a hard life, and no mistakin'." Brodie's words reflected sincere regret. "But," he continued, his tone taking an upswing, "those days are behind you now... That is, unless you slip and fall in the droppings of one of the fine bovines you'll soon be ownin'. Now, let's go. I have our horses saddled. We mustn't keep the fair Morag waitin'. Or the brawny Reverend Edward Morgan. He might be a man of the cloth, but he can be one right pain in the arse when he's kept waitin'."

****

As they came in sight of the Green homestead, Douglas was so astonished he drew rein abruptly, causing Lady to shake her head in annoyance.

The dooryard was filled with people and wagons. Tables laid out near the house were filled with food and drink. And in the center stood Morag, wearing a soft blue gown, wildflowers entwined in her dark hair, a bouquet of moss roses in her hands. Stunned, he barely noticed Reverend Morgan standing to the left of her or her parents to her right.

"Move along, laddie." Brodie reached out a booted foot and nudged Lady back into motion. "A lass as lovely as that must not be kept waiting."

The celebration lasted well past the supper hour, with feasting and much toasting of the newly wedded couple. As darkness slid over the revelers, a bonfire was lighted, Brodie produced his fiddle, and Douglas and Morag were cheered to begin the dancing.

At first they moved awkwardly together to the strains of the waltz Brodie played, but soon, looking into each other's eyes, they relaxed and swayed about the grass as one. Cheers and clapping rose from the onlookers before they joined the couple in the dance.

Chapter Thirty-Five

Brodie tapped Douglas on the shoulder where he stood beside Morag, his arm about her waist, watching the dancers. Brodie's musical protégée, Geordie, one of Harry Wallace's sons, had taken over providing music for the festivities.

"Go along, laddie," he muttered into his brother's ear. "You and the lass have waited long enough, have given these guid folks enough of your time this night. Steal away quiet-like. I have your mare saddled and waitin' in the trees near the trail."

"Mrs. MacMillan?" Douglas looked down at the woman who'd become his wife brief hours previous and asked the question, fondness gentle in his tone. Although she'd married him, he was fraught with doubts about her willingness to leave her parents' farm and live with him in that small cabin.

"Yes, Douglas...my dear." She smiled up at him, blue eyes melting his heart and soul into one ecstatic mound of love and joy. "It's time we went home."

Taking her hand, he headed for where his brother had indicated Lady waited. When they reached the mare, Douglas hoisted her sideways onto the animal's back, then swung up behind her. Circling her with his arms, he took up the reins. Joyful anticipation flooded through him as she leaned back against him, giving him her trust and full acceptance.

As they rode toward his cabin, his happiness became tinged with apprehension. She'd seen his home, but now she'd actually be living in it, in conditions far removed from those of the comfortable farmhouse that had been her home.

Nothing he could do about it now. He had to resolve himself to what lay ahead and hope she could tolerate it until he could make her something better.

Resolved to put negative thoughts aside on this, the happiest day he could remember, he lowered his head to kiss her neck and was rewarded with a gasp of pleasure. It would work out, he knew it would.

When they arrived at the cabin, Douglas dismounted and reached up to bring his bride to the ground beside him. He couldn't resist. He had to kiss her again.

"I wish I had better to bring you to," he muttered against her hair. "But soon it will be better, and one day we'll have a farm as fine as your father's…maybe even finer."

"Douglas, my love, I've been here before, I've spent time in your cabin." She reached up to stroke his cheek. "I shall be perfectly happy here with you."

"Well, then, Mrs. MacMillan, let us retire to our humble abode." He took her hand and led her to the entrance.

"Good God!" The sight that greeted them as he shoved open the door stopped them both.

The crude, narrow bed had been transformed into a much wider one. Now it bore what appeared to be a feather mattress and a pair of pillows with snow-white covers. Linen sheets covered it as well as several finely crafted quilts.

The table in the center was covered with an ivory-colored cloth, a bouquet of wildflowers in the center. A variety of dishes, cups, and cutlery had been laid around it. By the fire sat the rocking chairs, and there were a pair of the ladderback variety at the table. The floor had been swept to pristine cleanliness, as had the hearth where kindling and logs lay ready for the flint and steel.

"Oh, my!" Morag's words were a gasp of astonishment as she advanced into the little room.

"Oh, my, indeed." Douglas remained just inside the door, staring at the transformation.

"Douglas, did you…?" She turned to him, eyes wide.

"Nay, lass, certainly not. I believe the community ladies must have been at work here. I did miss Mrs. Morgan and a few others for a time during the festivities…and young Sam, Harry Wallace's boy, who is a fine carpenter."

"It's so kind of them." Morag, her face glowing with delight, moved about the room, savoring the changes. She paused by the bed to look at a trunk by its side. "Look." Eagerly she raised the lid. "They've even seen fit to bring my clothing. Oh, Douglas, what could be more perfect!" She swung back to him, her delight warming every inch of his being.

"Nothing, my love, nothing." He moved across the room to take her into his arms. "This is our home and all I could ever want is right here."

****

He woke the next morning and eased out of that wonderfully comfortable bed. Morag still slept, her shining black curls spread out over her pillow. Pausing to look down at her, he wondered if his heart and soul could bear any more happiness. Married to the woman of his dreams, a snug cabin to call their own, and, as if that were not enough, reunited with his brother.

The perfection of his situation all but stifled him. He had to go outside, to breathe in the crisp clean air of the summer's morn, to gaze around his modest holding…that he was determined would grow quickly.

He pulled on his breeches, slipped a shirt over his head, and moved quietly out of the cabin. Once in the dooryard, he put his hands on his hips and sucked in a deep breath of cool morning air. Then he went to tend the horse, which he had hurriedly stabled the evening before, giving Morag a few moments of privacy.

A slight breeze sifted through the pines, making shadows move slowly and gracefully about the clearing.

Old sins, long shadows. The words came back to him. But these were new shadows, tender, welcoming shadows that offered a fresh start. A smile curled his lips. He turned and went back into the cabin. He wanted to share these perfect moments with Morag.

A word about the author…

Gail is the award-winning author of thirty-six published books. She is delighted to be an author with The Wild Rose Press, "where writers are encouraged, tutored and mentored in the best of ways," she says.

Contact her at:
macgail@nbnet.nb.ca
Twitter: tollerbeagle44
Facebook: Gail MacMillan

Thank you for purchasing
this publication of The Wild Rose Press, Inc.

For questions or more information
contact us at
info@thewildrosepress.com.

The Wild Rose Press, Inc.
www.thewildrosepress.com

www.ingramcontent.com/pod-product-compliance
Lightning Source LLC
Chambersburg PA
CBHW051538260626
47170CB00003B/999